ROBERT B. PARKER'S
LITTLE WHITE LIES

This Large Print Book carries the
Seal of Approval of N.A.V.H.

ROBERT B. PARKER'S LITTLE WHITE LIES

ACE ATKINS

THORNDIKE PRESS
A part of Gale, Cengage Learning

GALE
CENGAGE Learning·

Farmington Hills, Mich • San Francisco • New York • Waterville, Maine
Meriden, Conn • Mason, Ohio • Chicago

GALE
CENGAGE Learning®

LIBRARY OF CONGRESS CIP DATA ON FILE.
CATALOGUING IN PUBLICATION FOR THIS BOOK
IS AVAILABLE FROM THE LIBRARY OF CONGRESS

ISBN-13: 978-1-4104-9816-8 (hardcover)
ISBN-10: 1-4104-9816-6 (hardcover)

Published in 2017 by arrangement with G. P. Putnam's Sons, an imprint of Penguin Publishing Group, a division of Penguin Random House, LLC

Printed in the United States of America
1 2 3 4 5 6 7 21 20 19 18 17

In memory of Ron Borne,
True pal, lover of life,
and dedicated Sox fan
*Que le vin de l'amitié
ne jamais s'assèche*

Spenser's
BOSTON

to Susan's home and office,
Linnaean Street, Cambridge

Charles River Dam Bridge

CHARLES STREET

Charles River

ESPLANADE

Massachusetts
General Hospital

Longfellow Bridge

CAMBRIDGE STREET

ESPLANADE

STORROW DRIVE

State House

to State Police,
Boston Post Road

BEACON HILL
■ The Paramount

■ Hatch Shell

BEACON STREET

Boston Common

CHARLES STREET

The Taj Boston   Public Garden
(formerly the Ritz-Carlton)

MARLBOROUGH STREET

BERKELEY STREET

ARLINGTON STREET

■ Swan Boats

COMMONWEALTH AVENUE

Four Seasons Hotel
and Bristol Lounge

BOYLSTON STREET

■ Spenser's office

Jacob Wirth ■

Boston
Public Library   Copley
Square

Davio's ■

Old Boston Police
Headquarters

STUART STREET

TREMONT STREET

■ Grill 23

to Boston Police Headquarters,
Roxbury

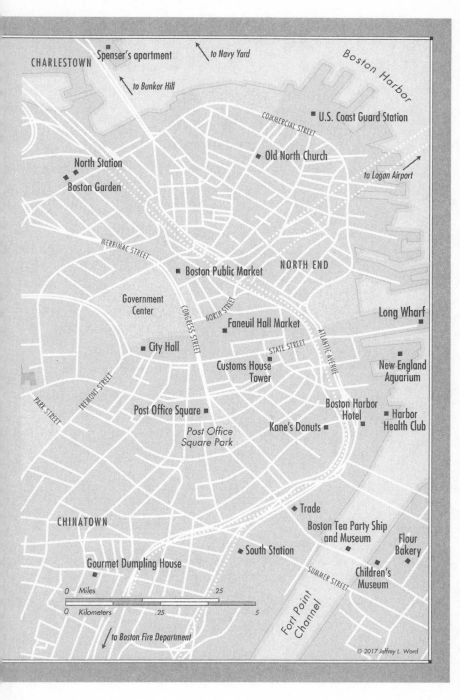

1

"Dr. Silverman thought you might help," Connie Kelly said. "She said you're the best at what you do."

"I do many things for Dr. Silverman," I said. "Although my chosen profession is the least important of them."

"So I take it you're more than friends?"

I nodded, adding water to the new coffee-maker sitting atop my file cabinet. I'd recently upgraded from Mr. Coffee to one of those machines that used pre-measured plastic cups. I placed my mug under the filter, clamped down the lid, and returned to my desk. Demonic hissing sounds echoed in my office. *Where have you gone, Joe DiMaggio?*

"God," Connie said. "I feel like the biggest idiot in Boston."

"I wouldn't worry about that."

"Why?"

"That's quite an elite club," I said. "The

line stretches all the way from Mass Ave down to Mattapoissett."

"I thought I loved him."

"Did he say he loved you?"

"Of course," she said. "That's how I found myself back in therapy. I haven't been to see Dr. Silverman for years. I thought I was cured."

"Dr. Silverman might say therapy isn't a cure," I said. "It's a process."

"She's a very intelligent woman."

I gave Connie a big smile, letting her know I echoed the sentiment. When the hissing and spitting ceased, I retrieved the mug and a carton of milk, a few packs of sugar, and a clean spoon. I set them on the desk near her and returned to my seat.

"I've worked a lot of unusual jobs," I said. "But I have to admit, helping with relationships isn't my specialty."

"I don't want help," Connie Kelly said. "I need to know who he really is."

"You mean deep down?"

"I know he's a phony, a liar, and a two-timing, backstabbing son of a bitch."

"Yikes."

She busily added sugar and milk to her coffee with shaking hands. Despite her mood, Connie Kelly was dressed in a white sleeveless silk top with a black pencil skirt adorned with chrysanthemums and a pair of black open-toe heels that highlighted her shapely calves. Her toes had been painted a festive red.

"As true as that might be . . ." I said.

"Wait," she said. "There's more."

Being a trained investigator and a master listener, I waited. Pleasant city sounds drifted up from Berkeley Street on a cool, almost fall-like breeze. I leaned back in my chair, resting my hands on my thighs, still dressed in a sweaty gray T-shirt and running shorts. I had intended to check my mail, not meet with a client. But she'd been there waiting before I opened the door.

"He has two hundred and sixty thousand dollars of my money," she said. "He swindled it from me and then disappeared."

I withheld from snapping my fingers and saying, "Now we're talking." Instead, I nodded with grave understanding. The promise of money made me quite attentive, especially after a slow summer and losing my apartment and all my worldly possessions in a recent fire.

"I don't even know if M. Brooks Welles is his real name."

"That name sounds familiar," I said. "Should I know him?"

"Are you a member of many social clubs?"

11

"Does the corner barstool at the Tennessee Tavern count?"

"Hardly," she said. "When we were together, he seldom passed on a charity event or dinner invitation. Come to think of it, I never saw him pick up a check. People loved being around a guy who got his face on TV."

"Actor?"

"Worse," she said. "Pundit."

She ran down the names of several cable news channels where Welles had appeared as an expert. I inquired about his area of expertise.

"He said he was in the CIA," she said. "He spoke on terrorism, military affairs, politics. Mainly how we'd failed to keep our country safe. He was a very popular speaker after the marathon bombings. He said the current administration and their liberal policies had failed us."

"How, when, and under what pretense did Mr. Welles take your money?"

Connie let out a long breath and reached for the coffee with both hands. She sipped and with great care returned the mug to the desk. "It's so naked and awful," she said. "It was two months ago. Real estate."

"Let me guess," I said. "A foolproof investment?"

"Land up near Walden Pond," she said.

"He said he'd hunted there as a boy and the place had given him great solace."

"The only thing I knew people to hunt around Walden Pond were rats."

"I didn't ask many questions," Connie said, shaking her head, her eyes growing moist. "I didn't ask him anything at all. I met very few of his friends and no family."

"Love is blind," I said.

I toasted her with my mug. She smiled for the first time since entering my office. "Bryn Mawr. English."

"You and Kate Hepburn." I reached for a yellow legal pad and my pen. "What is it that you'd like me to do?"

"I want you to run a background check on him."

I shrugged. "You could do that online. You don't need me."

"And," she said, "I want my goddamn money back and his ass hanging out to dry."

"Ah."

I wrote down a few notes, taking care with the details about his ass drying out. I put down the pen and drank some coffee. After running five miles, I was having fantasies about stopping off at Kane's for a couple of old-fashioneds to replenish my carbs.

"I'm four hundred dollars a day," I said. "Plus expenses."

She didn't flinch, and instead reached into her purse for a checkbook. The checks were sandwiched between handsome alligator covers. "I'd be glad to pay for a week in advance."

"I don't know how long it will take," I said. "And I can't promise any legal action or justice. Although I do know a very competent and very mean redheaded attorney."

"I understand."

"Just the facts, ma'am."

"The Bard and Joe Friday?"

"I am one literate son of a gun."

"I heard you often amuse yourself."

"Can't put anything by ol' Doc Silverman."

"Shall I tell you everything I know about M. Brooks Welles?"

I nodded.

"I don't know much, but I do think he might be dangerous," she said. "Very dangerous. I think back on things he told me and they make me shudder. He confided in me that he's killed many men."

I shrugged and thought about flexing my biceps or showing off the .357 Magnum I kept in my right-hand drawer. But doing so might seem gauche to a gal from Bryn Mawr, so I just listened.

"I asked for it," she said. "We met each other through an Internet dating site. He told me that after Vietnam, he joined the CIA and then went on to write books and produce movies. I saw him several times on television, so I trusted he was telling me the truth."

"Do you have a photo?"

She reached into her purse and pulled out a picture of a man in his sixties with silvery hair and a saltwater tan, wearing expensive duds. Starched white shirt wide open at the throat, navy blazer with brass buttons. Connie Kelly was seated beside him at some waterfront restaurant. They were laughing and looked very happy. I didn't wish to judge, but he looked a bit long in the tooth for her.

"I wanted a tall, successful, and interesting man. Someone who liked to travel and took time to enjoy sunsets."

"Piña coladas and getting caught in the rain?"

"I should have said honest but ran out of room on my profile," she said. "I guess I left the door wide open for this kind of thing. My husband left me two years ago for a flight attendant from Dallas. I am not what you'd call a stunner, but Brooks made me feel very beautiful. I do know I'm smart

15

and very good at what I do."

"What do you do?"

"I work as an administrator for Jump-start," she said. "Are you familiar with the organization?"

"Very," I said. "They do great work. Do you have children?"

She shook her head. She didn't touch the coffee again. But she ripped out the check and dropped it on my desk.

"Let me see what I can do."

She smiled again. "You're different than Dr. Silverman described you."

"Bigger? More stunning?"

"Quieter," she said. "More self-contained."

"I tried to put that on the business cards," I said. "But ran out of room."

2

I drove home to my new digs in the Charlestown Navy Yard and made breakfast. As I ate two poached eggs with a side of locally cured bacon from the Public Market, I pulled up YouTube clips of M. Brooks Welles doing his thing. It was liberating doing my job in a terry-cloth robe while munching on bacon. I wondered why I didn't begin every day like this. Skip the workouts, head right to the breakfast meats and sleuthing.

Pearl sat by my side as I worked. Her yellow eyes were dutiful and glowing. She wanted either to show me her love or me to share. I pinched off a piece of bacon and tossed it to the floor. On my computer, Welles was introduced as a former Navy SEAL, Vietnam vet, and CIA operative. Special consul to foreign affairs committees. He was sleek and confident. He spoke in a gravelly, knowing voice filled with authority and wore an American flag pin on his lapel. I resisted the urge to salute my MacBook.

He called the president at the time a clown and a fraud. He claimed he knew of dozens of Muslim paramilitary training camps within the United States. He said, based on his experience, that tougher immigration standards and screening processes needed to be put in place or we'd be visiting 9/11 all over again. He talked a lot about his time in the CIA, offering vague comments about his mission in South America making tough calls and doing the work in the shadows. Over the years, I had known men and women who'd done that kind of work. They seldom spoke of it. Even in vague terms.

Welles relished in it. More talk about working with Air America, battling the Communist threat, and now looking at a battlefront at home. As the interview continued, Welles was intercut with images of the marathon bombing. I had enough and closed the screen.

Pearl looked up at me. Ever vigilant, she knew I still had half a piece of bacon left. I tossed it to her and walked back to get dressed. Pearl trotted beside me, still not confident in the new place.

The old shipping warehouse had been built not long after the Civil War and had a nice view of the yards and the U.S.S. *Constitution,* with tall ceilings and a big plate-glass window, exposed brick walls, and floors fashioned from the decks of old ships. Rustic. Susan found it amusing I resided so close to Old Ironsides.

I slipped into a pair of jeans, a blue pocket T-shirt, and Nikes and went back to the laptop propped on the kitchen counter. I ran Welles's name through the Department of Motor Vehicles and a LexisNexis search. Nothing. Connie Kelly had passed on one of Welles's business cards for a company called EDGE. I ran the company through the Secretary of the Commonwealth database and found an address in Cambridge. *Tally-ho.* I slipped my .38 just below my right hip, reached for my Braves cap, and grabbed my car keys.

Pearl and I were off to Central Square. Her long brown ears blew in the wind as we drove along Memorial Drive against the Charles. Rowers rowed, joggers jogged, and bench sitters sat. It was mid-September and the air had turned crisp. The leaves had already started to turn red and gold, shining in Technicolor upon the still water.

The address led me to a narrow, wedge-shaped building where Western Avenue joined with River Street. There was a directory by a locked door with Lilliputian type. Undeterred, I slipped on a pair of cheaters and searched for any mention of Welles or EDGE. Nothing. Two real-estate firms, a lawyer, and a classic-car broker. I slipped the cheaters back into my shirt pocket and called the building's management company from my cell.

Twenty minutes later, a heavyset woman in a dark blue pantsuit crawled out of a small silver BMW. She had a cell phone screwed tightly into her ear and wore an abundance of gold jewelry. I knew her name was Joanne D'Ambrosio and she had an office in the North End. I told her I was a prospective renter.

"Alfred LaRue," I said. "Friends call me Lash."

"And what's your business, Mr. LaRue?"

"I vanquish foes."

She was half listening, looking at the number of someone who was calling. "We have three units available," she said. "How much square footage to you need? And how soon do you need it?"

She unlocked the front door and we walked down a narrow hallway. The carpet was beige, threadbare, and spotty as a

Dalmatian. The walls were scuffed with black marks and badly in need of paint. I ran my hands along some uneven spackling.

"The landlord looks to make improvements at the first of the year," she said. "The building had been in bankruptcy. That should all be worked out soon. Do you live in Cambridge?"

"No," I said. "But I keep a toothbrush here. I heard about this building from my old pal, Brooks Welles. He said it was quiet and reasonable."

If she recognized the name, it didn't register. She stood in the hall, checking messages on her phone.

"Is he still on the first floor?"

"I'm sorry," she said. "What's that again?"

"M. Brooks Welles," I said. "He runs a company called EDGE."

Her eyes narrowed. She lifted her chin and took a more solid glance my way. She was inspecting me.

"I thought I might pop in and say hello."

"How friendly are you?"

"Well," I said. "To be honest, I only just met him."

"He's no longer in this building," she said. "I shouldn't be telling you this, but Mr. Welles left with four months of unpaid rent."

"Say it ain't so."

"Oh, it's so," she said. "And he left all his garbage for me to clean up. He left me a goddamn Post-it note saying we could have his furniture. Gee, thanks. A Salvation Army desk and a chair with a broken arm. You met him? Did he ever tell you what he did for a living?"

"A little of this," I said, "a little of that."

"A four-flusher," she said. "That's what my father called people like him."

"Did he leave anything else in the office?"

"Like I said," she said. "Garbage."

"Any bills?" I said. "Files? Documents?"

"What did you say your name was?" she said, eyeing me. She crossed her arms and checked me out from ball cap to Nikes. I shrugged, reached into my pocket, and handed her my business card, the real one with the skull and crossbones to let people know I was serious. I offered her the full-wattage smile.

"Are you looking for a place to rent? Or are you full of it, too, Lash?"

"I could have used you a few months ago," I said. "I was burned out of my apartment."

Her eyes flickered around a bit, studying my face. She bit her lip, nodding.

"If you find the SOB, will you let me know?" she said. "That guy really stiffed me."

"Deal."

"Come on," she said. "Come on. This is where I keep the deadbeat's crap."

We walked to the end of the hall, where she opened up a small office. As promised, inside we found a cheap metal desk, a broken chair, and a few old milk crates filled with mail. Joanne D'Ambrosio stood back and watched as I dumped out the mail and sorted through the letters and envelopes. She returned to checking her phone.

"At first I thought he'd gotten sick or something," she said, tap-tapping away. "He wasn't here. He didn't answer the number I had. I kept his mail for about a month after I noticed it piling up. I was about to just toss it."

I separated the wheat from the chaff, made a neat pile on the desk, and wrapped what I found with a rubber band. Two electric bills and six credit card statements. Score.

"He said he was in the movie business," she said. "Said he was making a picture with Marky Mark. Some kind of spy action thing. Said he'd been a spy and they needed him as an adviser. That's not true. Is it?"

"Probably not," I said. "But you never know what a Wahlberg will do next."

"He flirted with me," she said, placing her

23

hands on her wide hips. "Said I was real funny. A real character. He asked me if I kept any headshots. So stupid. I sent him the photo I used on my flyers."

"Did you e-mail him?"

"Yes."

"Did he respond?"

She nodded.

"I'd like that address and any phone numbers."

"You know, it makes me feel dirty," she said. "I don't know why. I've known a lot of deadbeats. But usually I can tell. Makes me feel stupid that I bought into it."

"He's fooled others for a lot more."

She smiled and nodded. "Yeah?"

"Almost three hundred grand," I said. "That make you feel better?"

"Some," she said. "But I still want what I'm owed."

"Lot of that going around."

3

I walked over to the Mariposa Bakery on Mass Ave with Pearl and found a comfortable table by the window to look through Welles's mail. Pearl lapped up a bowl of water while I drank a cup of black coffee and made notes in a little black notebook. The first two envelopes showed Welles was six months late on his credit card payments and well over his limit. The bills were accompanied by a professional but unpleasant letter.

As I worked, two young women in yoga pants and thin tank tops over sports bras walked past my table. I looked up and smiled. They pretended not to notice the rakish middle-aged man and his charming dog. Restraint.

The third envelope contained a full bill from the last two months and a list of charges. Aha. The women moved to the counter and debated between maple and blueberry scones. They continued to ignore me.

I took out a pen and circled the charges that told me more about Welles or showed a pattern. Most of the charges had been made in the Greater Boston area, but at least ten had been made in Atlanta and Greenville, South Carolina. From the Boston numbers, I noted he was a fan of the Whole Foods on River Street, the Neiman Marcus at Copley Place, and the Four Seasons' bar. Couldn't be all bad if he liked the Four Seasons. I thought about organizing a stakeout at the bar with Hawk but then noted Welles had more recent, and frequent, visits to a spot in Eastie called Jimmy's LLC.

A quick search on my phone got me an address for Jimmy's Lounge, on the water by Logan.

It was nearly two o'clock, late for lunch and early for cocktail hour. However, drinking beer during the day was part of the job. Not to mention I was good at it. I wasn't sure if Jimmy's had the same open policy on dogs, but Pearl could nap in my cool backseat while I made inquiries.

A half-hour later, I sat at Jimmy's Lounge eating a soggy grilled chicken sandwich with a side of stale chips. The beer was Sam Adams Octoberfest and very cold. It almost made the sandwich tolerable.

"Sorry," the bartender said. "I don't know a guy named M. Whoosis Welles."

I showed him a photo I'd printed from one of his many TV appearances.

The bartender, a short, paunchy kid in a red T-shirt reading *Jimmy's, Where the Elite Meet,* shook his head. He studied it some more and scratched at his ear. "You want another beer?"

"Twist my arm."

Jimmy had really embraced the whole nautical theme at his bar. Lots of fishing nets filled with plastic crabs and starfish. A metal diving helmet and reprints of old diving charts lined the walls, along with beer babes in bikinis and grinning sports stars. I sipped on the draft and read back through the charges, cross-referencing the dates with days of the week. I whistled, "Yo Ho (A Pirate's Life for Me)."

"Who works Tuesdays and Thursdays?" I said.

"Phil."

"Would you mind calling Phil and asking him about Mr. Welles?"

He shrugged. "I don't want to get in the middle of some crap with his old lady. Are you in the repo biz?"

"Of a sort," I said.

"Phil comes in today at five," he said. "If you want to wait."

I drank some more beer, laid down a respectable tip, and drove over to a dog park by Logan. I made some phone calls and tossed a tennis ball around until Pearl grew tired. I kept some treats in the console of the Toyota Land Cruiser I was driving this year. It was a plain model from the late eighties with less than fifty thousand miles on it. Nice and roomy for dog and master. The four-wheel drive helped getting to the cabin I'd built some years ago in Maine.

At five, I was back at Jimmy's Lounge waiting for Phil, who walked into the bar at 6:20. He and the day shift talked for a bit and the earlier guy nodded with his chin toward me. I raised an Octoberfest in his direction; he looked away and headed back to the bar. He was a tall, lean guy with thick black-framed glasses, closely cropped dark hair, and a lot of tattoos. He didn't look my way as he busied himself with the liquor bottles, stooping down to check the levels on the taps. After a few minutes, he pointed to my beer and asked if I'd like a refill.

"No, thank you," I said. "Just waiting for my pal, M. Brooks Welles."

"You mean Mikey?"

"Sure," I said. "Ol' Mikey."

"Are you trying to jam him up?" Phil said.

"Wouldn't dream of it," I said. "He's an old friend."

"Hah."

"Do I look like a repo man?"

"No offense," he said. "But you look like a leg breaker."

I nodded in appreciation and took a slow sip of beer. I reached into my wallet and pulled out a fifty-dollar bill. Three for the beer and a little something extra for Phil's cooperation. The flash of green got his attention. He looked me in the eye and smiled.

"Need change?"

"Nope."

"He owes you money," Phil said. "Right?"

"Why do you say that?"

"He owes a lot of people money," he said. "Like I said, he's a nice guy. He has a ton of personality and all that. Looks like a freakin' old-time movie star. Tan. Silver hair. Makes friends with everybody. He told me that I needed to quit this job and go back to school. He said I had a real mind for business, the way I ran the bar. One night, he got me so damn into it, I was filling out forms online. He has a way of getting you excited about things. Maybe I trusted him because he was a vet."

"Army?"

He flashed a couple tattoos on his forearm. "You?"

"Long time ago," I said. "Different war."

He nodded. "Mikey came in here maybe three weeks ago, buying everyone drinks, saying he'd just landed some big military contract. And then he disappeared out the back door. I took all the freakin' blame. Jimmy about exploded. He wanted to fire me, but he's keeping me on until I pay him back."

"How much?" I said.

"Almost four hundred bucks."

"Jumping Jehoshaphat," I said. "That's a lot of overtime."

"Bet your ass."

"So," I said, glancing out the window. I spotted Pearl's snout sticking out the back window, sniffing at the salt air. "You don't really owe Mikey a thing. He owes you."

"Yeah."

"How can I find him, Phil?"

He rubbed his hand over his short hair. Phil looked tired, worn-out in his mid-twenties. He walked over to a coffeepot and poured out a cup. He picked up the crisp fifty and studied it. The tattoos on his arm looked like a map from *Road to Zanzibar*.

"Won't do you any good," he said. "He's

big buddies with Mr. Gredoni. I tried to run him down through Gredoni, and Gredoni told me that Welles was back overseas. Some kind of classified work. He promised me that Welles was good for the tab. He said he'd probably just drank too much that night."

"Mr. Gredoni pay you?"

"Nope."

"And where can I find Mr. Gredoni?"

"You don't quit, do you?"

"It's an ingrained character trait."

"John Gredoni?" he said, as if I should know the name.

I shrugged.

"Gredoni's Gun World?" he said. "Like the billboards by Fenway. He runs a big range on Route One in Lynn. It's a mile past the Golden Banana. There's a big neon gun outside. You can't miss it."

Most red-blooded men in the Greater Boston thought of the Golden Banana as a historic landmark. "And Mr. Welles and Gredoni are friends?"

"Big buddies," Phil said. "Gredoni said Welles once saved his life in Iraq. He called him the real deal. An absolute American patriot."

"What did you think?"

"I was with the Tenth Mountain Division," he said. "I did three tours. Something about the way he talked was off. He didn't talk like a military guy."

"What's Welles talk like?"

"Like someone who tries to talk the fucking talk," he said. "But never walked the fucking walk."

"Oh." I smiled. "One of those."

4

"So," Susan said. "Can you help Connie?"

"My pleasure," I said. "I just learned the trail of bread crumbs will lead me right past the Golden Banana."

"Will you be able to restrain yourself?"

"I have a weakness for donuts and naked women."

"But some naked women more than others."

"I do prefer educated Jewish women who can't cook."

"I can cook," Susan said. "I just prefer not to."

"Without us, half of Harvard Square would go broke."

She toasted me with her vodka gimlet as we sat next to each other at the bar at Harvest, a high step up from Jimmy's. Dim lighting, mod furnishings, delicious food. I had the Harvest burger. Susan had ordered a kale salad with pears. Pearl was back at

33

her house, sleeping off her hard day's work of detecting.

"Do you believe he's really out of the country?"

"I'll know more after meeting Mr. Gredoni tomorrow."

"I've seen his billboards," she said. "They are repulsive. The ones that say 'Bring on the big guns.' Women in bikini tops holding assault rifles. I never thought he could actually be a real person."

"Welles leaves quite a mess behind him," I said. "He owes a lot of people money. And this was just the first day. I'm waiting to hear back from several inquiries."

"What did Connie tell you?"

"That they met through a respectable Internet dating site," I said. "Apparently she bought into his stories because she'd seen him on TV. She said he was slow picking up the check but fast in the love department. I guess she'd really fallen for him."

"An understatement," she said. "I wish I could tell you more."

"Patient/shrink confidentiality?"

"There's a reason I get two hundred an hour."

"She told me Welles pried open that alligator-skin checkbook of hers and she made an investment into some kind of real-estate scam," I said. "Then he made like Elvis and left the building."

"Did she show you the actual agreement?" Susan said. She took a minute sip of the gimlet and toyed with a thin sliver of lime.

"Yep," I said. "I thought I'd run it by Vince Haller and see what he thinks."

Susan nodded. She set down the glass. It was still very cold, frosty at the edges.

"No details," I said. "But it did a real number on her?"

Susan nodded again. "She wasn't ready for a relationship," she said. "Her marriage ended badly. She has self-confidence issues and desperately seeks approval. Welles presented himself as the perfect man."

"For some, that's just second nature."

"Ha," she said. "So, can you deliver Mr. Perfecto?"

"Like I told Connie, I can't promise any legal action," I said. "But I can find him."

"And perhaps turn him upside down to shake out what he has left?"

"That's a crude, but accurate, summation of my services."

The bartender brought my burger and Susan's salad. We ate and I talked to the bartender a little bit about the Sox's disappointing season and my high hopes for the Pats. I dropped the name of a recent Pro-

Bowler named Kinjo Heywood. Heywood seemed a shoo-in for Canton. His once-kidnapped son was now an honor student.

"How's our baby getting acclimated to the Town?"

"She's found a place on the new couch," I said. "And she's claiming new places to mark her territory along the waterfront."

"You know, you didn't have to move out," Susan said. "We could have made it work."

"It'd be foolish to mess with success."

"Not to mention the pent-up lust caused by distance."

"Never gets any easier, Suze." I smiled.

She smiled devilishly and gripped my thigh under the bar. "Would you love me as much if I made it a cakewalk?"

"We tried living together once and it didn't work."

"I don't think you and I thrive on convention."

"But we know each other fully," I said. "No surprises. No secrets."

"We can even read each other's thoughts."

I nodded. "And what am I thinking now?"

Susan tilted her head and touched foreheads with mine. She closed her eyes in intense thought. "Hmm," she said. "You need a refill on your beer."

"Actually, I was hoping you'd move that

hand a couple inches higher."

Susan removed her hand and reached for the gimlet. "Here's mud in your eye."

5

Early the next morning, I met Hawk at the Harbor Health Club.

"Johnny Gredoni?" Hawk said. "Yeah, I know him."

"You like him?"

"Haw."

"You trust him?"

Hawk didn't answer. He finished his fiftieth rep of Russian twists on the decline bench and tossed the medicine ball at my chest. I caught it in midair and exchanged places with him. I began twisting in fine Soviet fashion and I could see Hawk counting each rep under his breath.

"Who is he?" I said. "Besides the emperor of Gun World?"

"Used to sell shit out of his trunk," Hawk said. "He'd sell to Winter Hill, boys in the North End, Joe Broz. Didn't matter. I'll say this, his guns were good and clean."

"What else?"

"He hired himself out," Hawk said. "Ran into him on some jobs overseas. Never a competitor. But I never wanted his ass on my team."

"Why?"

"Mouth bigger than his talents," Hawk said. "All into the high-tech gear. His execution was subpar."

I kept twisting until the fiftieth rep. I stopped twisting.

"Four more," Hawk said. "Don't cheat yourself, white boy."

I knocked out four more, unhooked my feet from the bench, and tossed him the ball. Hawk beamed a large smile. His black skin was hairless, flawless, and shining bright with sweat. He wore a sleeveless Adidas workout shirt with matching black shorts. He moved into our third and final set. I did not count his reps. I was a man of faith.

As I caught my breath, Henry Cimoli wandered up and stood as tall as possible next to my right shoulder. All white satin warm-ups and blinding white shoes, he didn't say a word until Hawk finished.

"Don't forget to wipe down the equipment. Do I need to remind you this is now a class joint?"

Hawk and I had been training at the

Harbor Health Club long before the Big Dig, posh hotels, and upscale restaurants had invaded the waterfront. Back then, I couldn't leave the gym without smelling like yesterday's cod and fishermen's cigarettes.

"Are we ever late on our dues?" I said.

"When have you two clowns ever paid dues?"

"Every day, babe," Hawk said. "Every day."

Henry shook his head and wandered off to where a dozen yuppies waited to learn the fistic arts from a Boston legend. Hawk and I moved onto the squat rack and loaded down the bar with four large plates. I completed twelve reps and racked the weight. Hawk didn't waste a second to follow.

"Grow or die," Hawk said.

After the weights, we ran to the Seaport for a four-mile loop. I then showered, shaved, and dressed, and soon Hawk and I were drinking coffee outside the Boston Harbor Hotel. Hawk blew the swirling steam off the top of the cup. He'd changed into a crisp white linen shirt with army-green linen pants, dark brown Oxfords, and gold Chanel sunglasses. Seagulls swooped down to inspect if we had baked goods.

Sadly, we were empty-handed except for the coffee.

"You want me to ride shotgun to Lynn?"

"I expect this to be a cordial visit," I said.

Hawk grinned. "And how does Johnny connect to your case?"

"Friend of a huckster who took nearly three hundred grand off a nice woman."

"Sounds like Johnny's kind of people."

"And who are Johnny's people?"

"Mercenaries, gun nuts, soldier-of-fortune wannabes, and career crooks."

"Can't wait to meet him."

"Tread lightly, bwana," Hawk said.

"What is this, *Killers of Kilimanjaro*?"

"You bigger than Robert Taylor."

"And you ain't Anne Aubrey."

"Far from it."

"How'd he go from the trunk show to the big leagues with signs outside Fenway?" I said.

"The old-fashioned way," Hawk said. "He cheated."

"Aha."

"Made millions from our current war on terror," Hawk said.

"Can I call him Daddy Warbucks?"

"Sure," Hawk said. "Why not?"

"He's the only solid lead I have on a man who seems to have no home, no working

41

business address or current driver's license," I said. "I hope to win him over."

Hawk raised his eyebrows.

"I can be very charming when I want to."

"You about as charming as a pit bull."

"The man I'm looking for was into some kind of land deal in Concord," I said. "He convinced my client to write him a check and then disappeared."

"Your client and him intimate?"

"More than that," I said. "She thought they were in love."

"Shall I quote Tina Turner?"

"Long as you don't quote Ike."

Hawk began to whistle "What's Love Got to Do with It." I shook my head and hoisted up the strap of my black gym bag. I switched the hot coffee into my left hand and offered my right.

Hawk shook my hand and nodded.

We parted ways and I headed up to Lynn.

6

Gredoni's Gun World was a modest-size prefab metal building hidden among used-car dealers, fast-food restaurants, and pawn shops along Route 1. The building was one story and ran long in the back, where pistol shots and automatic gunfire sounded on the range. The front of the shop resembled a high-end jewelry store, with shiny handguns and assault rifles displayed on black velvet. If Holly Golightly ever wanted revenge, this was the place for her.

An attractive young woman with long, bleached hair and large brown eyes met me at the counter. She wore a smallish black tank top with the Gun World logo: a blue planet with a continent in the shape of a .45. Clever. She laid her hands on the glass counter and smiled at me with straight white teeth. I noted a thin strap of a pink bra beneath the tank top and a pistol holster on her right hip. She had a deep, if unnatural, tan.

"How can I help you?"

"Is Mr. Gredoni in?"

"Is he expecting you?"

"No," I said. "But he'll want to see me."

"Name?"

"Spenser," I said. "With an *S.*"

"Is that your first or last name?"

"Just Spenser," I said. I smiled back at her. The micro tank top rode up high on her stomach, showing off pronounced hip bones. Incongruous with the .45.

She nodded, hit a button under the counter, and opened a door next to a large two-way mirror. The sounds of gunfire were muffled from the back range. *Ping, ping, ping.* A resounding *boom-boom-boom* from a shotgun.

As the symphony continued, I turned to admire the smorgasbord of weaponry. Most of the pistols were arranged by maker. The Glocks with the Glocks. The Smith & Wessons with their kind, et cetera. Shotguns were displayed in a long rack next to the assault rifles. Each gun tagged with a Day-Glo orange or yellow price tag. I checked out a few of the Winchester lever actions, with an eye toward replacing the one I'd lost in the fire.

The saleswoman reappeared, not as

friendly this time, and told me Mr. Gredoni would be with me in a moment.

"Do I get a free T-shirt with a purchase?" I said.

"It depends on what you purchase."

"I'm in the market for a Gatling gun."

Her smiled fluttered a bit. She cocked her head and studied me a bit. "We're having a sale this month. Twenty percent off AR-15s."

"If I need an AR-15, I'll call in an air strike."

"You can have them personalized," she said. "Many customers like to have their favorite sports team logo engraved on the lower receiver."

"Could you add a smiley face?" I said. "Maybe say, 'Have a nice day.' "

"Anything you want."

"Hot damn."

I smiled at her. She gave a half-smile, not sure of what to make of me, as a very short, thick-bodied man in military dress came out a side door. He looked to be in his mid-fifties, with jet-black hair and a mustache/goatee combo. His chest and belly tugged at a brown hunting shirt with double breast pockets and epaulets. His pants looked to be SWAT issue, black, with blousy cargo pockets. He wore a black hat that read

45

Remington and had half of a fat cigar plugged in the side of his mouth. He reminded me of a fat, miniature version of Rambo.

"Spenser?" he said, offering his hand. "I'm John Gredoni."

I shook his hand.

"How can I help you?"

"I understand you're pals with M. Brooks Welles."

The salesman smile faded. He plucked the cigar from his thin lips and stared at me. He didn't blink or nod. He just stared up at me and removed a stray bit of tobacco from his tongue. The woman in the tight-fitting shirt excused herself and left the room.

"I tried his office, but he'd relocated."

"What's your deal with Welles?"

"He's a difficult man to find."

"I haven't seen him."

"But you know him."

He shrugged.

"You do know him, or you're not sure?"

"I know I don't run my mouth about one of my best clients," he said, plugging the cigar back into his mouth. "Why are you looking for him?"

"I'm the leader of a Boy Scout troop," I said. "I wanted him to come and talk to the boys. You know, tell them what it's like to be a real American hero. Maybe give them pointers about wrestling it out with the Sandinistas."

"No," Gredoni said. "You're not. You're trying to make trouble. You got the look. Do you have any idea just who you're messing with?"

"Not really," I said. "Perhaps you can enlighten me."

"Mr. Welles is an important man," he said. "He's done important things. We have a lot of celebrity clients. Athletes. Politicians. Movie stars."

"Wow," I said. "How about Ben Affleck? I loved him in *Gigli*."

"They come here to learn about protection and find a place not to be hassled. I don't appreciate you coming here to make trouble."

"Have you seen Mikey lately?" I said.

"I'll tell him you were here."

"Don't you want to know why?"

Gredoni didn't answer. He just glowered at me, sucking on the cigar, the tip glowing red. I waved away the haze of smoke as he exhaled.

"I'm a private investigator," I said. "Mr. Welles stole three hundred grand from my client."

"Ha," he said. "You mean Connie Kelly?"

I nodded.

He shook his head with pity. "That broad is a fucking flake," he said.

"I disagree, but appreciate the alliteration."

"She's pissed because they had something hot and heavy and then he found out she was a head case."

"He took her money."

"No," Gredoni said. "She begged to be part of a big investment that didn't work out. She didn't have a problem with it as long as he was giving her the old baloney pony. When he broke things off, she started to stalk him. She doesn't understand that Mike has a lot of enemies. She sends guys like you around and pretty soon there will be a damn truckload of camel jockeys gunning for him."

"Wow," I said. "That important."

"Don't you watch the news?" Gredoni said. "Christ. He was a fucking Navy SEAL, top level at the CIA. He wasn't some paper pusher. He was out there for our government, doing deals, saving lives. He's still doing it. That's why he's gone back overseas."

"Where?"

"You know I can't tell you that."

"Because of the camel jockeys."

"Exactly."

"He might be the seventh son of Mata Hari, for all I know," I said. "But it doesn't change the fact that he owes Ms. Kelly a lot of money."

"Bullshit," he said. "He's an important man. Doing important things. Kelly is a jilted broad with a grudge."

"I don't think Welles is overseas," I said. "And I don't think he's a Navy SEAL. Or even as smart as a trained seal at the Franklin Park Zoo. I think he's a phony. And I'd be glad to look more into you, Welles, and those contracts you got with the Department of Defense."

"You threatening me?"

"Sure," I said. "Why the hell not?"

"You know this is the official gun range for the Lynn Police Department?"

"Congratulations."

"I got friends," Gredoni said. "A lot of them under that shiny dome on Beacon Hill. Go ahead and keep making trouble and you'll get your license pulled. But let me give you some advice. Mike Welles isn't someone I'd want against me. He's been in the armpits of this earth, fighting his way out. He's made banana-smoking third world leaders disappear in the wind. You think he'd be worried about a two-bit gumshoe

49

like you?"

I nodded and handed him a business card.

"Tell him to call anytime," I said. "We never sleep."

"Do yourself a favor, Spenser," he said. "Stay outta this one. It's a lovers' spat."

"What was the land for?"

"Jesus."

"If it's legit," I said, "there's no reason not to tell me."

"Old gun range," he said. "From back in World War Two. We were going to try and take it over for training. We paid for the land, but the liberal locos up in Concord gave the city council hell. You realize Welles trains a lot of top guys. I'm talking Delta Force, Spec Ops."

"Gee," I said. "What about Secret Squirrel?"

"Get the fuck out of here," he said. "I don't have time for this shit. But I sure as hell wouldn't want to be you."

"Are you sure?" I said. "You might like being taller."

Gredoni stuck the cigar back into the side of his mouth and simmered a bit. "Takes a real pair to walk into a place like this and be a smart-ass. What makes you so goddamn tough?"

"My strength is as the strength of ten," I

50

said. *"Because my heart is pure."*

I turned and left. Sir Galahad. Always stuns them on the way out.

7

Being a career cynic, I decided to drive out
to the property in question and see things
for myself. On the way, I picked up Pearl in
Cambridge and headed north on Route 2
to several miles above Walden Pond. There
was no reason I couldn't be a super sleuth
and a responsible dog owner at the same
time. Pearl seemed to appreciate the gesture,
jumping from the Land Cruiser when we
arrived, heading straight for a small trail
leading to the property. A *For Sale* sign and
one for the Strawberry Hill Gun Club had
been tacked up on a large tree. The land
was New England writ large, with stone outcroppings and dense forest of pine, birch,
and maple. Pearl romped through the dead
leaves and brush, circling wider and wider.

I followed the wood line along a gravel
road to a small lake and some type of log-
cabin lodge. A brisk wind cut through the
trees and I could smell wood smoke.

The lodge had been painted a dark brown and had a shingled roof. Smoke rose from a stone chimney that looked to have been constructed decades ago. The property seemed far from abandoned, with a half-dozen wood picnic tables and two stone fire pits. Signs warned guests about gun safety and to unload all weapons in the recreation area. I didn't expect trouble, but I kept my .38 loaded and firmly placed on my right hip.

Pearl circled the entire log house and came running back, tongue lolling out of her mouth. She seemed to say, "Look at this wonderful place I've found." If only I could scare up a covey of quail or some ducks. But I was sure there were laws against hunting ducks out of season with a .38 Chief's Special.

As we approached the lodge, a thin man with black-framed retro glasses and an unkempt black-and-white beard walked from the side of the building. He carried a section of garden hose coiled around his shoulder like a snake. He wasn't that old, but was rangy and wild-looking, with long-ish hair in the spirit of Jeremiah Johnson and Kurt Cobain.

"Hello," I said, brilliant with the small talk.

The man nodded back and set down the hose. Pearl met him with tail wagging and presented him with a hickory stick. I told him I'd come to check out the property. He said his name was Ray Angelo, manager of the Strawberry Hill Gun Club. We shook hands and talked about the change in the weather. And then the club.

"I thought the property had already been sold," I said.

"Who told you that?"

"John Gredoni."

"Jesus Christ."

"Not a fan."

"Thank God he didn't get hold of this place," he said. "He would have bulldozed all the trees and filled in the lake with cement. The land is owned by club members. They made the decision not to sell based on his plans. He wanted to turn this club into some kind of military base. Two gun ranges, obstacle course. Even a goddamn helipad."

"Ever meet a guy named M. Brooks Welles?"

Angelo shook his head. He wore a loose blue flannel shirt over an old Pats Super Bowl T-shirt with well-worn Levi's and work boots. He looked more like a Harvard professor than someone running a hunt

club. One of those purposely shabby characters seen on Harvard Square.

"This club was founded in the twenties,"
he said. "They did some training out here
during World War Two, but it's pretty much
been an oasis for people from the city. We
do skeet shooting, fishing, and have some
nature trails for schoolkids. The founders
would roll over in their graves if a guy like
Gredoni got hold of it."

"Why sell?"

"Taxes," he said. "Land's being developed
all around us. It's either sell or turn the land
over to state. Some kind of trust situation.
You have families here who've been paying
member dues for generations. It's more than
just a club. It's an investment."

"Was Gredoni out here much?"

"He did a meet-and-greet in the spring,"
Angelo said, stroking the bushy, unkempt
beard. "And then for a few months, he came
out here on a regular basis. Like he already
owned the place. He talked to me as if I
was one of his employees. Pushy little bastard."

"That he is."

"You're not interested in buying," he said,
stooping down to pet Pearl. "Are you?"

"No," I said. "I work for an investor who
got swindled. Ever meet a woman named

Connie Kelly?"

"Nope," he said. "But lots of folks came out here with Gredoni. He had three or four parties. They made a mess of the range with the assault weapons. A bunch of people came out and got drunk, some of them jumping out into the lake completely naked. We're a small, private club. Lots of families. It was embarrassing."

I handed over a card and told him more about my work. He smiled and asked me if I wanted to come inside. "I just made coffee."

"Any good?"

"Jamaican Blue Mountain."

"Take Me Home, Country Roads."

The building reminded me of summer ranch camps I knew as a kid back in Wyoming. The air smelled musty and old, but pleasant with the crackling fire. Ray handed me an old china mug with black coffee. I wanted to ask for a little sugar but didn't want to seem like a sissy to the outdoorsman.

We sat in a couple rocking chairs by the fire. The walls were adorned with black-and-white pictures of past generations of hunters and fishermen. A few old oil paintings of great canine hunters as well. A few flat-coated retrievers, several Labs, and some of

56

Pearl's German shorthaired pointers.

"I could tell Gredoni was full of shit from the start," he said. "I think he pretended to want to buy the property so he could throw a few parties. We didn't know for a few months that he had these military plans for the club. At first he said it would be business as usual. He even said I could stay on as manager. He didn't want anything to change."

"Who were his guests?"

"Investors," Ray said. "There was a lot of talk for some company called EDGE. It was a lot about military contract work. It wasn't until later that I figured out that he wanted Strawberry Hill to be the base of the operation."

"This seems more like Camp Granada than Camp Pendleton."

"Some of these guys," Ray said, "those he brought out? He introduced them to me as so and so, a Delta Force operator. Or so and so, former Marine Recon leader."

"Ever meet any ex–Navy SEALs, Vietnam vets, CIA super spies?"

"I'm sure I did," Ray said. "But it all seemed part of the show. Bringing all these Boston assholes into EDGE. Whatever that is."

"Hate those Boston assholes."

He smiled and drank some coffee. Pearl found a comfortable space by the fire. The inside of the cabin felt cool and old-fashioned, a harbinger of the fall and deep winter. I figured it was about time to switch from cold beers to straight bourbon.

"Dear God, don't tell me he's coming back."

"Gredoni told me he had trouble with the town council," I said. "That he had trouble getting approval for a gun range."

"How would he have trouble with approval if this already is a gun range?"

"Excellent point." I drank a little coffee. Pearl rolled over on her back, happy in her hunting-lodge element. "Are you suggesting Johnny Gredoni isn't trustworthy?"

"Ha," he said. "What do you think they were after?"

"Not sure."

"How much money did they steal?"

"Three hundred grand," I said. "Probably a lot more."

"And what is EDGE?"

I drank my coffee. It was a dark roast, fresh, and terrific. "I have absolutely no idea."

"I thought you were a top-notch Boston sleuth?"

"Just getting started," I said. "Give me time."

"Gredoni is toxic," he said. "Whatever he touches, he pollutes it."

"Been here long?"

"Ten years."

"Good job?"

"I was an English major at BU," he said. "Working on a novel."

I took another sip of the excellent coffee and enjoyed Pearl in repose. "Life is frittered away by details."

He grinned at me and stroked his beard. "Simplify. Simplify."

8

On the way back to Boston, I dropped Pearl at Susan's. Soon I was seated at the bar at Jacob Wirth's with an empty plate of schnitzel and was working on my second Samuel Smith's Oatmeal Stout. As I contemplated a third, Vince Haller edged in beside me and said, "You never call, you never write."

"I called now."

"I was beginning to think you and Fiore had some kind of exclusive deal."

"She only wants me for my body."

"Be careful with that stout, buddy," Haller said. "Or she'll be taking you off speed dial."

I'd known Haller most of my professional career. He seemed to keep a summer tan all year long that worked nicely with his silver hair and mustache. He was dressed for court today in a wool sharkskin suit, white button-down, and purple tie. Crisp and professional, befitting one of Boston's sharpest attorneys.

He ordered a vodka martini with extra olives.

"Okay," Vince said. "What do you have?"

"Perhaps I just wanted to reconnect with old friends," I said. "Reminisce about the good old days."

"When exactly was that?"

"Simpler times," I said. "When we gathered by the organ with Ma to sing 'In the Shade of the Old Apple Tree.' "

"Christ," Haller said. "How long have you been here drinking?"

I slid over a fat legal-size envelope and took a long sip. Haller shook it open and immediately started riffling through the pages as a duck to water. He shook loose a pair of glasses from his breast pocket and flipped through Connie Kelly's contract as the bartender shook his martini. For a moment, I believed Haller was working in time with the shaker. The bartender set down the drink, but he continued to read. Five minutes later, he stuffed the paper back into the envelope and picked up his frosty cocktail reward.

"And what do you need to know?"

"My client is Connie Kelly."

"I assumed."

"And I assumed she didn't get it read before she signed."

"Unless her lawyer got his degree from a Cracker Jack box."

"She wants her money back."

"I read the deal, but what exactly was she buying into?" he said. "Property for development for the EDGE Corporation doesn't tell me a hell of a lot."

"I was just out there," I said. "It's a rod-and-gun club in Concord. Connie's ex-boyfriend had her cough up three hundred grand to buy into this foolproof scheme."

"And the boyfriend's name?"

"M. Brooks Welles," I said. "But his pals call him Mikey."

Haller looked like he'd just choked on one of the extra olives. He coughed a bit, composed himself, and took a second sip of the martini for reassurance. "Mr. Welles is indemnified in the contract."

"I saw that."

"And did you see the hold-harmless clause?"

"What exactly is that?"

"That means whatever kind of crap happens, the signee cannot hold Welles responsible," he said. "One step more beyond indemnification."

"Shit."

"Legally speaking," Haller said. "Yes."

"So the contract is with EDGE Corporation only?"

"Yep," he said. "You got it."

"And she can't sue Welles?"

"Nope."

"And would it be a problem if EDGE Corp is in chapter eleven?"

"Are they?"

"I'm afraid so," I said. "I pulled the status yesterday."

"Do you have doubts that this was ever a legitimate business plan?" Haller said.

"I do."

"Did Mr. M. Brooks Welles represent himself in a false fashion?"

"I'm still working on that," I said. "But in short, yes."

"Damn," Haller said. "This martini hits the spot. If this case gets any worse, may I recommend a double?"

"Focus," I said. "How do we get Welles into court and get Ms. Kelly her money back?"

"You would need an attorney to make Swiss cheese of this contract, track down EDGE Corp's assets, and prove Mr. Welles to be an absolute and complete liar. And hopefully a known felon."

"Piece of cake," I said. "Right?"

"Nobody wins in these kind of things," Haller said. "That money is long gone. And where is Mr. Welles?"

"Doing his best Claude Rains impression."

"What exactly did your client think she was investing in?"

"Some kind of high-end gun club," I said. "Welles is partners with, among others, John Gredoni."

"Gredoni's Gun World," Haller said. "Have you seen his commercials with the girls in camo bikinis firing shotguns? Truly inspired."

"Elegant."

"You want my advice?" Haller said.

"That's why I'm here."

"This is a sticky, sticky tar baby," he said. "You'll get so deep and twisted into this thing, you may never find your way out. You need to level with your client, that if she gets Welles into court it will be expensive, potentially embarrassing, and she's pretty much guaranteed never to see a nickel. She may spend half as much as she's already lost."

"How much do you make an hour?" I said.

Haller told me. I whistled. "Maybe you should pick up the check."

"Oh, no," he said. "You invited me, Spenser. And how about some tickets at Gillette this season? I read in the papers you were tight with Kinjo Heywood."

"I taught him my patented pass rushing techniques."

Haller nodded and finished the martini. He tossed the last olive into his mouth, chewed, and swallowed. "Out of curiosity, who the hell is this M. Brooks Welles, anyway?"

"Decorated Vietnam veteran, Harvard grad, former CIA operative," I said. "He likes rich, elegant women, drinks at the Four Seasons, and high-priced assault rifles."

"How much of that is true?"

"The last bit."

"But you won't quit," Haller said. "Even if your client wants you to."

"Probably not."

"And why is that?"

"I don't like liars."

"That simple?"

I nodded.

"Will your client be upset about her legal options?"

"More embarrassed," I said. "This guy humiliated her. She seems to be a kind woman without a lot of self-confidence."

"You need to tell her the odds."

I texted Connie Kelly to meet and signaled the bartender for another round. Might as well soften the blow.

9

Connie Kelly worked on Tremont Street, a block over from the Common. I met her by the T station and we walked together toward the Charles and the Public Garden. Kids were playing tag football and the last few games of baseball. Summer had come to a close and soon the Common would be covered up with leaves and then mounds of snow. Ice skaters would be out on Frog Pond and the trees would be strung with tiny white lights.

"Did you find him?" she said. No hello, no small talk. Right to the point.

"No," I said. "But I know a lot more than when I started."

"Who is he?"

"Well," I said. "I could find no driver's license, deeds, or military record. He vacated his office in Cambridge four months behind on rent. Oh, and he owes Jimmy's Lounge in Eastie four hundred bucks."

"That's it?" she said. "Jesus. When you called me, I thought you really had something. What about the CIA? And Harvard Law?"

"No records at Harvard under that name," I said. "But the CIA is the bastion of con men. They never confirm or deny employment for any agent."

"Crap," she said. "I guess it doesn't really matter who he is or what he's done. I just want my money back and to go on with my life."

I nodded. We walked some more. I figured if we kept walking, I might stir up the courage to tell her that she was legally screwed. A pack of teenagers blindly strolled down a path by the Civil War monument, hunting invisible creatures on their iPhones. When I was a teenager, I preferred to cruise drive-ins with convertibles for girls. To each his own.

"Did Welles ever introduce you to a little fireplug by the name of Gredoni?"

"John Gredoni," she said. "Sure. Of course. We had dinner with him a few times. He was buying into the Concord land, too. I'd seen him on TV. He's a respected businessman."

"If bikinis and bullets make you respectable," I said, "I'm halfway there."

"He's not honest, either?"

"I seriously doubt it."

"Did they set me up?"

"I'm betting there were others."

"You find him," Connie said. "And I've already spoken to an attorney who will haul his lying ass into court if the police keep sitting on their hands."

"That's where it gets a little tricky."

"How so?"

"I showed your contract to an attorney friend," I said. "A very high-priced, very good attorney. You should see his suits. Very nice. Sharkskin."

Connie stopped walking. She put her hands on her hips and stared up at me. She had on a navy shirt dress, cinched at the waist with a wide brown leather belt, and pair of strappy heels. Her blond hair was blunt-cut and well styled. She did have a very plain face, but one that radiated with thought and intelligence. If I had been an international man of mystery, she would have been just my bag.

"I didn't ask you to do any legal work for me," she said. "I just wanted you to find him and help me locate my goddamn money."

I held up a hand. "It's all part of the same equation."

A second pack of teens, two of them with blue hair, nearly ran over us with devices in their hand. They were muttering something about finding a creature called Charmeleon. I had absolutely no idea what they were talking about. After they passed, Connie looked up at me. Her mouth twitched a bit, as she waited for me to tell her what to do.

"Your contract specifically protected Welles," I said. "You can sue EDGE Corp, whatever the hell that is, or was, but Welles is free and clear."

"Son of a bitch."

"Yep."

"I didn't even look at the document," she said. "I was going to take it to an attorney, but Brooks made me feel ashamed of it. He made it seem as if it were a trust issue. We had dinner at the Top of the Hub, where he presented me with flowers and a Montblanc pen."

"I'm sorry."

"He probably stole the pen," she said. "Like I said, I'm the biggest idiot in Boston. Acting like a girl in junior high with a crush on the high school stud."

"He conned you," I said. "He's probably conned a lot of people. If you can give me more time, I can find out who and when. But you have to know, whatever I do probably won't help get your money back."

"What if I sue his company?"

"It's in bankruptcy."

"Great," Connie said. She about started to laugh. "Just great. This thing just gets better and better. How many more ways could I get screwed?"

We walked another five feet and she stumbled a bit, losing a heel. I picked it up and helped her to a park bench, where we both took a seat. I removed my ball cap and crunched the bill a little bit, like a pitcher reconfiguring the situation. Three balls. No strikes. And the bases loaded. C'mon, Spenser.

I almost shared the analogy before Connie began to cry. I placed my cap back on my head and put an arm around her. She buried her head into my shoulder as a young couple passed, looking at me as if I was the source of the problem.

"I don't want you to quit," she said. "I want you to find him. I want you to help me confront him. You can do that? Can't you?"

"Yes, ma'am."

"Good," she said. "I want to have the satisfaction of taking a blowtorch to his bullshit."

"I don't believe Welles is in Afghanistan."

70

"No."

"Do you?"

"I'm not so sure he could find it on a map," she said, and wiped her face on her dress sleeve. I patted her shoulder and removed my arm. I stretched my legs, watching two squirrels tumbling around for a couple pieces of popcorn.

"I'm betting there are more like you," I said. "I think Welles and Gredoni created EDGE just to pull in investors and then crashed it. I think they are working hand in hand with some people on the fringes who still don't know they've been conned."

"If you find enough of them?"

"Maybe we can light torches and chase them back to the castle."

"Where's the castle?"

"I don't know that, either."

"Is Gredoni a fraud?"

"He has his shortcomings."

Connie laughed. "I would have never believed in Brooks if I hadn't recognized him from TV. Didn't they at least check him out? These are international news stations. People believe in them. Trust what they say about politics and international relations."

"Walter Cronkite signed off long ago," I said.

"Is there anyone out there who'd know

71

how a liar like him got booked?"

"I do know a woman who moves in those very circles."

"And even if he doesn't have a driver's license," she said, "maybe someone can recognize his pictures. Surely he's been arrested before."

"I know many people who move in those circles, too," I said. "Ever think of being a private eye? The hours are terrible, but the pay is lousy."

"The anger has switched something on," Connie said. "I haven't slept in weeks. I have chest pains. I think of all different kinds of ways I can corner him and ask him why he did this. Why did he want to ruin my life? Why me?"

"Because you crossed his path," I said. "And you had a few hundred grand to spare."

"Not really," Connie said. "I took out a loan on some family property."

I felt the blood flow to my face. I stood, reached for her hand, and helped her up. She smiled up at me, a golden light flooding the Common, making even the kids with blue hair seem like something from a Norman Rockwell painting. Bits of dust kicked up from the ball field shone in an orange haze as we headed back toward Tremont. I didn't want winter. I wanted a very long Indian summer.

As we parted, she leaned up on her toes, kissed me on my cheek, and told me it was nice to finally meet an authentically good man. I nearly blushed, had I been the blushing type, and looked for a horse to ride away on.

Where was Trigger when you needed him?

10

I met Captain Brian Lundquist of the Massachusetts State Police at six a.m. the next morning. He'd chosen the Agawam Diner in Rowley, as it wasn't far from where he lived with his wife and two kids. I liked the food there and happily agreed. A waitress refilled our cups and walked away with our orders.

"Ever have the pies here?" Lundquist said.

"Frequently," I said. "But never for breakfast."

"You only live once."

"I'm doing my best to prolong that experience."

Lundquist smiled with his big teeth and big apple cheeks. He was local but always reminded me of a big galoot right off an Iowa farm. I'd met him a few years back on a heroin-trafficking case in Wheaton. Since Healy's retirement, he'd become my main contact with the Staties. A good man and a

74

straight shooter.

"Ran the name you gave me and passed the photo around," Lundquist said. "I didn't know your guy was a celebrity. A lot of cops knew him from the news. He's a retired spy? Some kind of war hero?"

"That's yet to be determined."

"Oh, yeah?"

"Ever know a war hero without a driver's license or nothing in the system?"

"I couldn't find anything, either," Lundquist said. "Ran M. Brooks Welles. A few hits in the Northeast. But the age and description didn't jibe with who I found in the NCIC."

"What's that tell you?"

"Either he's full of more shit than a Thanksgiving turkey or he's the real deal."

"How so?"

"Maybe he had his entire record cleaned," Lundquist said. "Living completely off the grid. A man without a past. Or too much of one."

"Is that even possible?" I said.

"You have to know people," Lundquist said. "But it can be done."

Lundquist had on a threadbare deep brown corduroy jacket over a blue button-down. No tie and khaki pants. When he walked in, it looked like he'd had on the same government-issue cordovan loafers since we'd met. His acne-scarred cheeks gleamed red with a fresh shave.

"How's Healy doing?"

"He says he's happy," Lundquist said. "But he checks in every other week. I've had lunch with him more this year than when we were colleagues. He said you talked him into doing some woodworking. You really do that? Or was that a joke?"

"Ask Susan," I said. "I'm quite skilled with my hands."

"Spare me the details."

The waitress brought me hash and eggs and raisin French toast for Lundquist. He didn't waste any time before forking right into the mass and taking a big bite.

"Why are you looking for this guy, Welles?"

I told him.

"Three hundred grand?" he said. "Shit. He must be pretty damn good in bed if she didn't read the contract."

"Any way to run his name with some Feds?"

"No better than you," he said. "But I do have a better relationship with the locals."

"True," I said. "What a shame the SAC had to leave in disgrace."

"Yeah," Lundquist said. "A real shame."

"My client knows she may never get her

76

money back," I said. "But she wants him held accountable. Would you guys ever look at this as a fraud case?"

"Maybe," Lundquist said. "Tell me more."

"If I can prove M. Brooks Welles is an alias and he sought out my client for the purposes of separating her from her money through nefarious means."

"Since when is sex nefarious?"

"Depends if you keep your socks on."

Lundquist didn't respond. He kept eating. I drank some coffee and broke into the hash. We ate for a few minutes before I got back to the business at hand.

"What if I can find others who got conned?" I said.

Lundquist shrugged. He seemed to have more interest in taking down the French toast than in taking down any con men. He chewed a bit and drank some coffee. He stabbed another forkful of French toast but held the fork as he thought about it.

"Who's this other guy you mentioned on the phone," Lundquist said. "The gun guy. The partner?"

"Johnny Gredoni."

Lundquist ate some more French toast and chewed and chewed. He looked at me and swallowed. He tilted his head to the side and said, "As in Gredoni's Gun World?"

"As in the billboard, 'Double-Barreled for Her Pleasure.' "

"Crap."

"I hear a bell ringing."

Lundquist pushed away his plate. He checked his watch and slurped down some more coffee. "You sure Gredoni is working with this guy?"

"Heard it from the man himself," I said. "I'm trying to track down his name on corporate records for something called EDGE."

Lundquist shook his head and blew out a long breath. "That man moves a lot of inventory."

"Where?"

Lundquist tilted his head from side to side in a noncommittal gesture. "Something our friends at the ATF have been trying to find out for a while."

"I heard he became a rich man through DOD contracts."

"That doesn't quite cover it."

"You guys working on something?"

Lundquist swallowed, his face brightening, and smiled. "You know I can't comment on something like that," he said. "What do you take me for? A rookie patrolman?"

"Never," I said.

"I could never say that John F. Gredoni was the focus of an ongoing joint task force with ATF, State, and Boston Police. I mean, come on, man. That could get me fired."

"Glad you didn't say it."

"Will you bring me what you learn about his buddy?"

"You bet."

"I'll try to find out what kind of horseshit Welles was peddling in Concord and what can be done about it."

I nodded and ate some hash. I broke apart the egg yolk and dotted it with the edge of my toast. The sun was coming up across the parking lot, illuminating the diner with a clean, bright light. Construction workers, electric linemen, a couple more cops sat down in booths and at the long bar. The morning was starting to pulse.

"Ever think about retiring, Spenser?"

"And do what?" I said.

"Exactly."

Lundquist smiled. He soon finished, stood up, and left me with the check.

11

Pearl had to be the luckiest German short-haired pointer in the Commonwealth of Massachusetts. When Susan met with patients, Pearl was often with me. When I worked nights, she stayed with Susan. I never knew a dog who was better exercised, fed, and appreciated than Pearl the Wonder Dog. I hoped that in my next life, I'd come back as the trusty sidekick of a stouthearted detective. At the moment, Pearl lounged on a short leather couch that was intended for clients. I made coffee and returned calls while Pearl snoozed. A true team effort.

At eleven, my phone rang and I picked up.

"To what do I owe this honor?" a woman said.

"I was calling to see if there's any hope for me," I said.

"Sorry to disappoint you," Rachel Wallace said. "But I've now been in a loving, committed relationship for the last five years. With a woman. As you well know."

"Can't blame me for trying."

"Would you please shut the hell up and tell me how you've been?" she said. "How is Susan? How is Hawk? How is the damn dog?"

"I only have a visual on the damn dog," I said. "Her name is Pearl, by the way. She's offended you forgot."

Pearl snorted and turned her back to me.

"Oh, screw the damn dog," Rachel said. "Are you in New York? Or calling because you need something?"

"I'm hoping you might help connect me with some people who don't need my charisma and physical beauty in person."

"God help them."

"Are you still doing your rounds on the cable shows?"

"Someone has to keep those morons and hypocrites straight," she said. "One cable news channel in particular may be worse than Tokyo Rose. Only without the good music."

"Or the sultry voice."

"Oh, it has the sultry voice," Rachel said. "Cute little blond bunnies talking about the destruction of American principles over your morning coffee. It makes geriatric men

81

weak in the knees and facilitates angina. Don't you keep the TV on in the kitchen while you cook?"

"I have a new kitchen," I said. "No TV."

"Did you and Susan finally move in together?"

"Not exactly," I said. "My apartment was destroyed in a fire."

"Oh my God, I'm so sorry."

"Don't be," I said. "No one was hurt. But as it's being rebuilt, I'm not exactly a favorite with the tenant board."

"Why? You didn't start it."

"No," I said. "But I may have pissed off a few guys who did."

I told her about the waterfront condo in the Navy Yard, the latest bits of gossip about me and Susan. A recent trip to Paris. Another planned trip, to London. I told her about Hawk now seeing the ex-wife of a famous NFL player but never talking about it. I told her that despite a little work on my right knee, I was overall healthy, happy, and of sound mind and body. The Boston Beat goes on.

"Wonderful news," she said. "But enough small talk. What's the favor?"

"Actually, it's more of a question," I said, leaning back into my office chair. "How does one get booked as a talking head on

82

the cable news circuit?"

"You?" she said. "On TV?"

"Not me," I said. "I'm just trying to understand the process."

"I assume this is not talking about gender equality or LGBTQ issues."

"No," I said. "More about machismo, guns, and fighting terrorism."

"Not exactly my specialty," she said. "Although terrorism comes in many forms."

"You have published works," I said. "By known and respected houses. That's hard to fake. Like Evander Holyfield, you are the Real Deal."

"I don't know who you are talking about," she said. "But I would hope so."

"What if I were to say I was an international super-spy and a combat veteran of a covert war," I said. "Who's to know?"

"That's a very good question," she said. "I often doubt the credentials of the foils they pair me with."

"Who books you onto these shows?"

"A booker."

"Aha."

"It's an agent of sorts who gets you on the Rolodex of producers," she said. "When there's breaking news or a hot-button issue, you are on speed dial."

"Do they still make Rolodexes?"

"Probably not," she said.

"Excuse the indelicate question, but does it pay well?"

Pearl looked at me from the sofa, sniffed at the air, and turned full onto her back, all four legs pointing into the air. She had looked at me as if to ask me to lower my voice. She gave a resonant grunt from down deep in her belly.

"It doesn't pay at all."

"Come again?"

"You don't get paid," she said. "Oh, you may get a few hundred dollars if there is travel. But usually they want people in major cities, close to the studios. I do it mainly just because I like to sell a couple books and piss off the heteronormative patriarchy."

"Present company excluded."

"Present company especially included," she said. "Why the interest?"

I relayed the story about Connie Kelly, the match made in hell, the phony land deal, and dubious résumé of one M. Brooks Welles.

"He sounds like a supreme creep."

"I haven't had the pleasure yet," I said. "He's a little difficult to find."

"I can make some inquiries," Rachel said.

"Do you know which cable shows and when?"

I ran down the list of dates, topics, and hosts on the cable channels. Rachel knew two of the producers personally and would call on my behalf.

"Are you still drinking good bourbon?" I said.

"Is the pope Argentinian?"

"I shall have a bottle delivered forthright."

"Not necessary," Rachel said. "But appreciated."

"Will Blanton's do?"

"Nicely," Rachel said.

She hung up. Pearl snored. I looked out the window for a long while, wondering where everyone was going in such a rush.

12

Henry Cimoli wore a pair of punching mitts, calling out combos, taking the jabs, and crossing over my head with a wide but sharp sweep. I'd already gone through six rounds of jumping rope, heavy bag, speed bag, and now the mitts. Twice he reminded me I was moving like his sister. And his sister had been dead for ten years. Henry had the charm of the ages.

"You're not favoring the knee anymore," Henry said.

"Nope," I said. "Good as new."

"Can they do something about the head?" he said. "Maybe a replacement?"

"Oh, beauty," I said. *"Passing beauty. Sweetest sweet."*

"And maybe your brain while you're at it," Henry said. "By now, it's gotta look like scrambled eggs in there. One, one. One, three, two, two. Good. Good."

The buzzer sounded and I helped myself

to my water bottle. The front and back of my shirt were soaked. Henry told me to finish out things with two rounds on the heavy bag and a cooldown on the treadmill. He patted my shoulder as he walked away, the highest form of praise.

I finished things up, took a shower, and bought a turkey sandwich at a food truck on the Greenway. Thirty minutes later, my hair still damp, I was on the twelfth floor of the Suffolk County Courthouse, asking a woman in records about any recent filings against M. Brooks Welles, John Gredoni, or a company called EDGE. She reminded me that most records were available online.

I told her I'd already searched and perhaps a new filing may have been made this week. Or perhaps I'd been searching in an improper manner. I doubted the latter, but it never hurt to play to the ego of the keeper of records. Several times I'd found files through the main office while striking out online. Like working out, the first rule of success was just showing up.

The woman, whose name was Doyle Valley, clicked hard through the keys and then disappeared from her desk. I stood there at the counter, whistling " 'S Wonderful" to myself. Just as I'd reached how she'd made my life so glamorous, Doyle appeared with

87

a computer printout. " 'S marvelous," I said.

"This was just filed two days ago," she said. "It should have been online."

"Tenacity," I said. "The key to being a good investigator."

"You're a pretty good whistler, too," she said. "I'm surprised one of the judges didn't come in here and tell you to shut the hell up."

"It's good to see you, Doyle."

She smiled. "Next time, don't forget the muffins from Flour."

"Done."

I took the printouts and headed back to Government Center. I sat down on the steps and flipped through a filing from a guy named Nick Kostas of Lynn against John Gredoni and EDGE Corp. Apparently Kostas had been one of the chosen few to invest in Ye Olde Concord Gun Club. Kostas's attorney used a lot of words like *fraudulent* and *misleading.* With all the blood flowing after the workout and fuel from the turkey sandwich, I surmised that Kostas probably wasn't a fan of Gredoni's and perhaps had some light to shine on the whole subject. According to the suit, Mr. Kostas was now a hundred grand lighter. Welles was not named in the suit.

I pulled a small notebook out of my

pocket and wrote out the new addresses for EDGE Corp, the home address for Gredoni, the name of Kostas's attorney, the amount of swindle, and the home address for Kostas. I quickly found a phone number, got his wife, and then got another number to their rock-hauling business in Lynn. I called that number, left a message with a secretary, and walked over to a vendor for a cup of coffee.

I returned with sore legs back to my seat on the steps. I spent the next fifteen minutes watching women of all ages, sizes, and colors walk past me. I liked the way most women walked. I liked the way they dressed. And talked and smelled. I was pretty damn sure I was a fan of women in general. Did this make me a sexist or a feminist? Or somewhere in between.

I drank some coffee and felt better about myself. I stretched my legs. It was an overcast day in Boston with a hint of rain. A cold wind came off the water, and for the first time in a long while, I wished I'd brought my jacket.

I thought about how Susan never seemed to care about my appreciation of other women. I knew I hadn't given her a reason to worry. Not in a long, long while. For Connie Kelly to have invested financially

89

and so personally in a con artist must have hurt like a son of a bitch. Whoever Welles turned out to be, he must have been a shrewd operator. In the few times I'd met with Connie, I found her to be a highly intelligent and professional woman. A view Susan shared with me.

I drank some more coffee. It began to sprinkle on Government Center. The rain felt like cool mist. I folded the filing in a square and placed it within my jean pocket. Connie Kelly, Nick Kostas, John Gredoni, EDGE Corp. The amount I knew about the ghost man M. Brooks Welles could fit within a thimble.

Could Lundquist have been right? Could Welles actually have a connection to the CIA? That still wouldn't make him a great boyfriend or the kind of guy who wouldn't stiff a bartender. Maybe he was a real-life Jason Bourne . . . but only if it turned out Jason Bourne's biggest skill was being an asshole.

I called Nick Kostas back. The secretary said he was still out. I didn't believe her, and for a lack of anything better to do, drove up to Salem.

13

I found Nick Kostas eating a meatball grinder on the hood of his white pickup truck. The pickup truck had four wheels on the back axle and looked as if it could haul the Statue of Liberty from New York to Miami Beach. Kostas was substantial-looking, too, an older Greek guy with a lot of gray hair and calves as large as my thighs. I told him what he needed to know. At first he'd tried to walk away when I mentioned John Gredoni.

"You want me to throw up my lunch?" Kostas said, wiping some red sauce off his chin. "I've been talking to my priest about all that crap. Trying to let it go and move on. Gredoni really fooled us on that deal. He acted like we could double our money in a year. What do they say about conning an honest man?"

"That you can't?"

"It was greed," Kostas said. "I took a risk.

I got screwed. Wasn't the first time. Wasn't the last. Are you working for a lawyer or something? 'Cause I already got a good one. If Gredoni doesn't pay up, I'll be in the gun business soon."

A four-foot stone wall squared Kostas's business. Mountains of field gravel and sand rose behind him. Large sections of marble, granite, and pavestone sat on pallets around a white trailer office. A dump truck rumbled through the front gate, loaded up with sand and gravel, and sped away. Kostas wore a wide gold chain around his thick neck. The chain swayed forward as he worked on the last bit of the grinder, trying not to splatter his shirt.

"Did you know he filed a restraining order against me?" Kostas said, wadding up the napkins and sandwich paper. "What am I going to do? Throw rocks at him? Ha. Mr. Big Fucking Guns is scared of Nicky Kostas from Salem. I never owned a gun in my freaking life."

"Ever meet a guy named M. Brooks Welles?"

Kostas shook his head, placed a fist to his mouth, and belched. "There it goes," he said. "The indigestion again. First you talk Gredoni, and now his flying monkey, Secret Agent Man."

"How'd you meet Welles?"

"Because they were joined at the freakin' hip," Kostas said. He moved away from his truck and toward the trailer. I followed. He yelled at a couple guys moving some pave-stones to be careful and then headed up the steps into the trailer. Inside, he turned to me. "Every meeting we had about the land thing, Welles was there. You know who he is? Right?"

"Not exactly."

"Don't you watch television?"

"Mainly PBS," I said. "I'm a sucker for *Downton Abbey.* I like the costumes. The manners."

Kostas snorted. "Yeah? Well, Welles is always on the news. He's freakin' famous. He was writing a book about his adventures. He told us out at the gun club that he'd be bringing the best of the best to Boston. He said all this terrorism shit was only going to get worse."

"Making the range a wise investment?"

"Yeah," Kostas said. "Sure. Hey. You want a Coke? Or some water?"

I shook my head. Kostas sat down at a small desk and flipped through a stack of pink message slips. "This," he said, "is why I had my head up my ass and not paying at-tention to getting screwed. Have you met

Gredoni? You see how he is?"

"Yep," I said. "I've had the displeasure."

"He's a cocky little bastard," Kostas said. "But he can really turn on the charm when he wants. You should've gone out to one of his wild-game cookouts. They had an open bar, a rock band, and all the bird, fish, and shit you could eat."

"How many investors?"

"We were told it was a limited thing," he said. "Twenty. But now? I'm not so sure. It was all great until, you know, it wasn't. I went to his place out in Lynn and he threatened to have me arrested. That's when he got the restraining order. Said I'd threatened his life."

"Did you?"

"I said if he didn't come up with my dough I'd knock his fucking head off," Kostas said. "But you know. I was just talking. I get excited sometimes. What the hell."

"Did he threaten you?"

He shook his head. "He told me to talk to Welles. Said Welles handled the money and he was an investor like everyone else."

"Wait a second," I said. "Did he allude that Welles cheated him, too?"

"He didn't allude shit," Kostas said, staring hard at a slip and then back at me. "He told me he'd been screwed like everyone else. He said, and I will quote direct to you, that fucking Welles had left him with a burning pile of dog shit before he jetted off to parts unknown."

"You believe him?"

"No, Ace," he said. "That's why I freakin' sued him."

"How many times did you meet Welles?"

"No more than two or three times."

"What's he like?"

"Are you sure you don't want a Coke?"

"No, thank you," I said. "Caffeine makes me jumpy."

He stood up, walked to a mini-fridge, and got himself a can of Coke. He sat back down heavy in the chair. Despite his care, some of the grinder had spilled on his T-shirt. "He looks like a Washington guy. He was always dressed to the nines. Never saw him without a suit and tie. Gray hair, mustache. Gold government-looking glasses. Kind of closemouthed. But man, when he talked, you listened."

"How so?"

"I don't know," Kostas said. "I don't know how to put this. He was always so, you know, fucking sure of himself. No doubt important people would come to train in Concord. He threw out a lot of Revolutionary War history and bullshit. Said he'd majored in history at Harvard. Never said CIA, only said 'the Company.' Told us he was an insider to the way the modern world would be shaking out. Made us feel like if we didn't invest we were bad Americans or something. I believe in this country. My dad immigrated here from Athens. I see this guy on TV. And I'm thinking, you know, if this guy worked for our government and did the shit he's talking about, then I should trust him."

"And Gredoni said he took all the money."

"Yep," Kostas said. He punched the tab on the Coke and drained it quick. "I'll tell you another thing. Fucking two-gun Gredoni is scared shitless of the guy."

"How so?"

"He told me," Kostas said. "He told me that I needed to write this thing off and look the other way. He told me that Welles was black ops. One of those fucking guys. He said Welles did shit off the books and I didn't want to cross him."

"What did you say?"

"I told him I didn't give a crap and he needed to make this thing right."

"How did he respond?"

"He said he was in over his head," Kostas said. "He said he'd done some business with this Welles guy in Iraq and thought he could

96

trust him. But he said it turned out that this Welles guy was one bad seed."

"I think he's a fake."

"I'll say this for Gredoni," Kostas said. "His fear was real. He didn't even like to mention the guy's name. But I hold Gredoni responsible for bringing a snake like this into a business deal. I knew Gredoni for a long time. We both had fishing boats at the club in Revere. We fished. Drank a lot of beer. I figured he was all right. He was always straight-up. But boy, was I wrong, and my wife won't let me forget it. That's why my stomach has been giving me problems."

"Can you put me in touch with some of the other investors?"

"You really think you can do something about this?"

"If it looks like a duck and talks like a duck," I said. "You better look under the feathers."

"What the hell does that mean?"

"I have no idea," I said. "I'm making this up as I go along."

Kostas gave me a few names for the growing list. I thanked him and headed back to Lynn to take a second run at Gredoni. When at first you don't succeed, keep bugging the hell out of people and see what shakes out.

14

I was halfway to Lynn when Connie Kelly called me.

"He called."

"Welles?"

"Yes," she said. "He told me he was sorry. He said he never intended for things to go like this. Everything was left in a mess because of Johnny Gredoni while he had to go overseas."

"To fight the war on terror."

Connie didn't laugh. She was silent for a moment while I navigated the traffic on Route 1. I turned down WBUR to hear a little better. I could hear a nervous sigh.

"What did you say?"

"I told him I'd hired someone to find him," she said. "But he already knew. He knew your name."

"I've handed out a lot of business cards."

"He was upset," she said. "He said I was making a mess of things and had every intention of straightening things out."

"Good for him," I said. Traffic began to move. The man in front of me didn't. I honked my horn and passed him.

"He wants to have dinner."

"Tonight?"

"Oh, God," she said. "I didn't know what to say. Or to do. I tried to call Dr. Silverman but only got her answering service."

"She's in session all day."

"I know," she said. "I know. I'm just such a mess. He said he'd take me to dinner and explain everything. He blamed everything on Gredoni. He said it was all tied to some international business that Gredoni didn't understand. He said he was a local yokel without any knowledge of the people he'd crossed."

"What people?"

"I don't know."

"Are you meeting him?"

Connie didn't answer. She breathed heavily into the phone. My progress to Lynn had slowed. Someone behind me honked his horn and passed with his middle finger raised. I didn't respond, keeping my dignity.

"Are you meeting him?" I said.

In a soft, small voice she said, "He said he still loves me. I'm so damn screwed up."

"Where?"

"Let me give him a chance," she said. "Maybe he'll explain. Maybe I've just been paranoid. I'll call you tomorrow and explain. I just wanted you to know and maybe put a hold on things to see if I plan to follow up."

"He's conning you."

"You haven't even found out where he lives," she said. "How can you be so sure?"

She had me. I kept on driving. I was enjoying the older car. It had a V8 and a nice bit of pickup. In the fall, Susan and I planned to take a trip to my cabin, leave the city behind and get back to nature. The back hatch was long enough to lie down with sleeping bags and neck. Do people still neck if the kids don't say it anymore? If one tree falls in the forest and no one hears it . . .

"I have to go."

"Where?" I said. My voice had more edge to it than I meant. I remembered the crying woman in the Common who'd taken out a loan for Welles's scheme.

"You might make trouble," she said. "I need to talk to him about us. I need to face him on my own terms."

"Okay," I said. "But I'd like to at least say hello. That way if you decided to follow up, I'll know a bit more about him."

"Will you threaten him?"

"Not if he plays nice."

"Will you make light of him?"

"Probably."

"Fair enough."

"You've already taken this thing pretty far," I said. "And you're not the only one now. There are at least a dozen people he cheated. Don't you want to help them?"

"I don't know," she said. "I'm somewhat conflicted about this whole thing."

She started to cry. I figured maybe I'd rather meet Welles than spend another precious moment with Johnny Gredoni at Gun World. It started to rain a bit, the skies darkening, a long line of taillights headed back into Boston. I turned on the wipers.

"The Blue Ox."

"Come again?"

"It's a restaurant in downtown Lynn," she said. "Do you know it?"

"I haven't been there," I said. "But a guy I know said they make terrific old-fashioneds. He once had six."

"Oh, God," Connie said. "What have I done?"

102

15

It had been a long while since I'd been to downtown Lynn, Lynn, City of Sin. The old mill town had the charm of both a hipster paradise and London during the war. Coffee shops, yoga studios, and hot new restaurants shared space with windowless buildings and vacant shoe factories. It didn't take much to find a parking place, but getting a seat at the Blue Ox wasn't easy. It was packed.

I arrived early, found a spot at the bar, and, good to my word, ordered an old-fashioned. My buddy was right. It was excellent. I drank slow, spaced with a couple ice waters, and ordered the lobster tacos. Again, the Ox didn't disappoint. I could see most of the tables from where I sat and hoped I'd have a good vantage point for the meet.

One more old-fashioned and an ice water later, Connie Kelly arrived. I watched her being seated and after a few minutes, caught her eye. She nodded in my direction. I nodded back. As a communication expert, I figured we might communicate in Morse code. Assuming she could hear me knocking my glass against the bar. And assuming she knew Morse code.

She ordered a drink. She crossed her legs. Connie fussed with her hair, took in deep breaths, and downed a couple glasses of white wine. She wore a very short red floral dress and black tights with black suede booties. A purple cardigan hung loose off her shoulders. She had never told me, but I figured she was somewhere in her late thirties, early forties.

I sipped on my cocktail. An extra-large ice cube rattled the glass with a slice of orange and two Luxardo cherries. Good cherries could make or break a cocktail. Sometimes the amount I knew about cocktails astounded me.

After a bit more of preening and sipping, Connie turned her head and stood. A silver-headed man in a tailored navy suit, a crisp white shirt, and a dark tie strolled into the room. He offered a toothy smile, thanked the hostess, and turned to Connie. He opened his arms. She turned into him, sideways, and he kissed her on the cheek. I wanted to spit out the cherry.

I could not see much or hear a whisper of their conversation. I finished the tacos but refrained from another drink. A good hour passed. The Blue Ox bustled with energy and good food coming fast and hot from the kitchen. I talked with the bartender about cocktails, beer, and movies. We decided that our favorite opening scene was in *Butch Cassidy and the Sundance Kid,* when Sundance refused to leave the card game unless he was asked to stay. The young bartender knew all the good lines. I liked him.

Connie and Welles ordered dinner. It looked like she had a salad. At one point, she laughed and then covered her mouth. To any other patron at the Blue Ox, they were having a wonderful romantic dinner. A summer/autumn romance. *Take my hand. I'm a stranger in paradise.*

I grew impatient as dessert arrived. I had my feet planted firmly on the floor, waiting for a plate to drop on Welles's head. No such luck. I tried to catch Connie's eye. She averted my gaze. As I settled up with the bartender, ready to make my own introductions, she stared at me. *Put me in, Coach.* She nodded. It was time.

I walked over to the table. Connie bowed

her head and studied the napkin in her lap. I asked a table next to us if I could borrow their chair. I turned the chair around and sat with my arms resting on the back. They had yet to touch their desserts. Two pieces of cheesecake with fresh blueberries.

"You're Spenser," Welles said. He beamed with enthusiasm.

I nodded.

He offered his hand. I studied it. I smiled. I did not break my attention toward him until he retracted his hand.

"Lots to discuss, Mikey," I said.

Connie continued to play with the napkin. Welles shrugged, leaned back in his seat, and neatly crossed his legs at the ankles. His dress shoes gleamed in the low light.

"Ask away," he said. "I have no secrets. Not from you. Or from Connie. I've been away. It's very complicated."

"Speak slowly," I said. "I'll try and process it."

He shrugged. The tight tailoring made the shrug harder and less convincing. He continued to smile, reaching over to fork off an edge of cheesecake. "Like some?" he said. "I think Connie's lost her appetite."

"Ms. Kelly would like her money returned."

He chewed, forked off a second bite. I was

106

no longer smiling. I studied him with great interest. He showed no signs of nervousness or contempt. He looked as if he was just simply enjoying the cheesecake.

"Connie will have the return of her investment with EDGE," he said. "And so much more. But if you'll excuse us, we're having a dinner about repairing our relationship. I don't think you need to be privy to those details."

"Spoken like a true Harvard man."

He grinned, dotting the edge of his lip with a napkin. "Class of '71."

"Nope."

"Excuse me?"

"You never attended Harvard," I said. "You never fought the Vietcong. And you never worked for the CIA."

"And how exactly did you come to this accusation?"

"For starters," I said, "Harvard has no record of you. There is no sign of you in U.S. military records."

"I don't think a guy like you will find out my history on the Internet." Welles gave a smug little laugh.

"And what's a guy like me?"

"Very local," he said, smiling. "Very Boston. I work without borders. The things I did during Vietnam were never made public.

Nor will they ever be."

"And Harvard?"

"You, or someone, is simply mistaken," he said. "That was a long time ago. Files get misplaced. What's all this about, anyway? Connie, did you invite this man here? Or have you been followed? If you've been followed, I'll make sure he's escorted out."

"Better call in the Army, Navy, Air Force, and Marines," I said. "Because you make one move, you'll be flying through that plate-glass window."

Welles laughed. I still didn't like his laugh. Or his misplaced confidence. He took a sip of wine and just stared at me for a while. Connie Kelly seemed like a child to me, shaking her head from side to side, saying, "No, no, no."

I didn't know if she meant no to me. Or no to him.

Welles broke away from the staring contest, looking over my shoulder, and through the discussed plate-glass window. His smile faded. He turned behind him to look at the bar and a hallway stretching past the bathrooms. He swallowed and pushed the plate away.

"As much as I'd like to have you join us for brandy," Welles said, "I, as they say, have bigger fish to fry."

My laughter came up so fast, I nearly snorted. I wasn't a snorting man. Connie's eyes grew big and turned to me.

"Two very unsavory characters have followed me here," he said. "They want to do me some harm, I'm afraid. Good night, sir."

"They'll have to wait in line."

"This is more than some personal matter, Spenser," he said. "These men have guns. And they know how to use them. They want to kill me. There's a contract on my life. The reason I've been out of touch, Connie. This is such a goddamn mess."

I did not turn a millimeter to follow his gaze. I continued to study him. "At the bar is my friend, Harvey," I said. "He's a six-foot-tall rabbit with a penchant for martinis. Maybe he can help?"

He leaned in, teeth clamped. "This is not a joke," he said. "No matter what you think of me, we need to make sure Connie is safe."

I shook my head. He stood up abruptly and turned toward the bathrooms and emergency exit. One way to leave the check. I followed him out of the restaurant and through the fire exit.

16

The fire exit emptied into a long alley crowded with garbage cans, dumpsters, and loading docks. I ran after Welles, who did his best in dress shoes. I, on the other hand, was fleet of foot and properly dressed for the challenge in a pair of Nikes. It took me about five seconds to catch up with him and snatch him by the jacket, just as a large SUV came barreling toward us. I couldn't see much beyond the grille and the headlights, but the vehicle was moving fast, knocking down trash cans and kicking up sparks as it rubbed railings from the docks. Welles just kind of hung there, frozen in the bright light, until I grasped him both by the collar and belt and tossed him behind a dumpster and followed suit.

The SUV passed. I caught my breath.

The SUV braked hard. Two men crawled out and walked into the alley. It was very dark, only a couple streetlights shining. The men were dressed in dark clothes and wore ski masks. If Welles had put on this show to get my attention, he'd done well. I pulled my .38 and peered out from the edge of the dumpster. Someone began to shoot, bullets from automatic weapons pinging off the metal and ricocheting down the alley.

"I told you," Welles said, almost excited. "I fucking told you. They're here. They want to kill me."

"Who?"

He didn't answer. He seemed out of shape, or very scared, breathing hard. The men walked in tandem down the alley, the sharp outline of their guns distinctive in shadow. One of them hoisted a gun to his shoulder and started firing at the dumpster where we hid. I answered back with two shots from my .38. It sounded a little like a Chihuahua snapping at a pit bull. The return fire was a long stream of bullets.

One thudded dully into a disintegrating piece of plywood placed in an empty doorway. As the gunfire resumed, I kicked out the wood, finding glass behind it, and then kicked through the glass. I took off my leather jacket, wrapped my forearm, and hollowed out a section large enough to crawl through. Welles didn't need to be told what to do, and he jumped through the opening first and scurried into the vacant building.

I fired off another two shots, slowing the men but not stopping them. I dove into the doorway, finding broken glass and splinters on a wet floor in a pitch-black room. I called for Welles. He didn't answer. I heard footsteps splashing in puddles. Farther into the vacant building, a bit of light leaked behind more plywood and I could just make out Welles's shadow as he kicked at an opening, grunting and kicking more. Behind me, more glass broke and the room strobed from the muzzle flashes of gunfire. I lay flat to the floor, aiming my .38 toward the light, and fired my final two shots. I reached into my pocket and pulled out more bullets and reloaded. If properly motivated, I could be incredibly fast.

A huge cracking and breaking sound came from the front of the building and light flooded halfway onto the floor. The room was junked with empty buckets, pallets of lumber, and fallen sawhorses. I saw Welles for a second and then he disappeared.

More automatic fire from behind me. My heart jackhammered. My mouth was dry and my breathing uncontrolled. I took in a deep breath. I didn't worry about Welles, I just watched the small square of light behind me. I aimed the gun carefully until I saw the muzzle and then a man's masked face and eyes behind it. I squeezed off a shot. I heard a grunt and a brief spray of gunfire before the second man pulled him back into the alley.

I got to my feet and ran for Welles's exit. I again wrapped my left hand with the jacket and held the gun in the right. I made my way through the glass and broken wood out onto Oxford Street. The street was bright and shiny, the blue neon from the Blue Ox glowing along the sidewalk. Connie Kelly came out of the front door, openmouthed and shaking her head.

I heard police sirens and then an engine starting in the gravel lot across the street. A dark sedan backed out and raced forward. I ran after it, getting close enough to Welles to see him at the wheel as I knocked on the glass with my gun. He didn't even say as much as good-bye, passing me as if I were a paparazzo, hitting the accelerator, knocking me free and rolling to the gravel. I tried to make out the license plate as I watched a black GMC SUV speed around the next block and race after Welles.

I couldn't make out their plate. Maybe because they didn't have one.

I jogged back toward Connie. The bartender and restaurant manager joined us out on the street. Both were on cell phones, calling the cops.

"What the hell just happened?" the bartender said.

"What people will do for a free meal," I said. "The nerve."

Connie was trembling. I shook the glass and splinters from my leather jacket and placed it over her shoulders. Chivalrous. I walked her back into the restaurant. We watched from our table as more than half of the Lynn Police Department showed up. I identified myself and gave them an abbreviated version of what I'd seen. I did not volunteer that I had fired my weapon. I told them I'd been tailing M. Brooks Welles and had followed him into an alley. Where it seemed a couple men were waiting to ambush him.

Did I know Welles? No.

Did I know where to find him? No.

Did I know why anyone would want to kill him? Besides being an arrogant ass? Um, no.

The cops went in to talk to Connie. I drank some coffee the bartender brought me and made small talk with some of the patrolmen. After two hours of talk and a brief trip to Lynn PD, where detectives interviewed us for a second time, we were free. It was nearly two before I followed Connie back to her condo in the South End to make sure it was Welles-free and returned to the Navy Yard.

I took off my jeans and shirt and laid them across a chair. I made a bourbon on ice with a dash of bitters and watched the dark water outside, the colorful lights shining from the ships along the docks. After a while, I lay in bed and fell fast asleep.

17

The next morning, the needle was again lost in the haystack. I ran down a few names Kostas had given me. All had similar stories, none had leads to where to find Welles now. I tried to trace the phone Welles had used to call Connie. It came back disconnected with a registration to a pay-as-you-go plan from Kmart. I then tried to run the license plate from the Chevy Malibu that left me tumbling in the dust. The car had been rented from a national car company at the Logan airport yesterday. Citing privacy concerns, the corporate office refused to give out any details of the customer. *Good for them,* I thought, hanging up the phone in my office. I helped myself to a second donut from the Kane's sack and drank some more of the coffee I'd made. I worked on slowly enjoying the sugar donut with a sip of coffee. I'd already finished the morning paper, gone through a round of phone calls, and paid a couple bills.

I reached over for the phone and called Connie Kelly's cell. I told her I didn't think she'd be hearing from him for a while.

"You don't really think he orchestrated such an elaborate plan to get out of paying for dinner?"

"I do."

"You're kidding."

"Would you put it past him?"

"I'm confused."

"What exactly did he tell you last night?"

"The first thing he said was that his life was in danger," she said. "He said he loved me but didn't want to put me in harm's way."

I nearly gagged on the donut.

"I don't know exactly what," she said, "but he's into something very bad."

"Well, the bullets were real," I said. "And Welles's fear was real. I'm sure he has built quite a list of dissatisfied customers."

"Or he was telling the truth," she said. "He said he'd been overseas. When I pressed him, he said he'd been working with a group in Africa."

"We Are the World."

"I'm scared to death," she said. "He's scared, too. He swore to me he'd get my money back as soon as he could get to it."

"What's stopping him?"

"He wouldn't tell me. Last night was more about emotional reassurance."

"Oh," I said. "That."

"He really does love me, Spenser," she said. "You don't know how good that was to hear. I'd about made myself sick wondering if he really loved me."

"Not just for now," I said. "But forever and a day?"

"It's no joke," she said. "I'm not some lovesick moron."

"Of course."

"You can be glib all you want," she said. "But you work for me. Maybe I want you to help him. What about that? Let me worry about our arrangement."

"That's not why you hired me."

"My money isn't good?"

"No," I said. "It's good for the job you offered. Not to babysit a con man."

"Someone tried to kill him."

"Just as the check arrived," I said.

She promised to call if she heard from Welles, and hung up. I finished my sugar donut and read the comics while deciding my next course of action. Sadly, neither Arlo nor Janis had any sleuthing advice. I just learned that women believed men cared only about sex and thought about it con-

118

stantly. I shrugged, put down the comics, and picked up my cup. No arguments there.

So far, Welles had left fewer crumbs to follow than those on top of my desk.

Beyond the usual databases I subscribed to, I had also tried to learn more about Welles's registration with the dating website. They would tell me next to nothing, although they had offered me a month free. I had Connie Kelly call and the company promptly removed Welles's profile from the site. No help there.

With little else to follow and with my client getting cold feet fast, I drove out to the car rental office at Logan. I walked inside, feigned an indignant style that Sam Spade would have loved, and told the man at the counter I'd been in an accident. My car was a mess.

"The guy who hit me wouldn't stick around for the cops," I said. "He told me he'd rented the car from you guys and that you'd pay for everything."

"Do you know if he declined coverage?"

"I don't know nothing, buddy," I said. "Besides what he told me. But I got a messed-up truck and I'll be out of work for a few days. I was going to call a lawyer, but figured I'd see what gives. You know?"

"What was the customer's name?"

"M. Brooks Welles," I said. "Or Mike Welles. He didn't know how you had him in the system. Can you believe this guy? Can you believe it? Leaves me in the middle of traffic to figure it all out. Acting like he's some kind of big shot."

"I'm sorry," the man said. "When did he rent the car?"

"Yesterday."

"Sorry," he said. "I don't have anyone named Welles. Are you sure it was this location? We have thirty-two locations across Boston."

"Can you check those, too?"

He tip-tapped at his keyboard. As he continued to type, it was getting harder and harder to hold the grimace. I felt like my face might melt. After a while, he shook his head and gave me a definite no. No Welles, Mikey, Brooks, or M. Brooks.

I then presented him with the license plate numbers. He took the scrap of paper to his keyboard and continued to look. "Huh," he said. "Yes, that's one of our cars. A new Chevy Malibu?"

"That's right."

"But it wasn't rented by Mr. Welles."

"Oh."

"Are you sure it wasn't a Mr. Gredoni?"

"John."

120

"Yes," he said. "The vehicle was rented in his name yesterday using his credit card."

"Did he have full coverage?"

He looked it up. "Yes," he said. "He did."

"That's great," I said. "Just terrific. I'll just follow up with my insurance company. Boy, do I feel so much better. Were you here when the car was rented?"

"No."

"Is anyone here now who rented this car?"

He looked at the screen and then back at me. Pride in his job had turned to a look of distrust. I smiled big and reached out and shook his hand, thanking him again. A real customer for life.

I got back to my car and thumped at the wheel. Either Johnny Two Guns was a better friend than he was letting on, or Welles had lifted his personal information and gotten a credit card set up in Gredoni's name. I drove north on Route 1.

It wasn't much, but it was a solid reason for a return to Gun World. I was betting Johnny had missed me.

18

A skinny guy in a khaki shooter's shirt and a droopy reddish mustache worked the showroom of Gredoni's Gun World. I didn't recognize him and he didn't seem to recognize me. I asked for Johnny and the guy told me he was busy giving a shooting lesson at the range. I showed him my firearm permit, paid twenty bucks, and he buzzed me into the back.

I found Gredoni in a wide concrete cavern with a husky kid in a Bruins jersey and a crooked ball cap. I wasn't a fan of crooked ball caps but resisted the urge to straighten it. He was holding a Glock 40. The kid looked off-balance, arms outstretched, and giggling like a boy touching a woman for the first time.

"Okay. Okay. Get a grip with both hands," Gredoni said. "Take a deep breath and a good sight."

The kid giggled even more.

"But don't do it too much," I said. "Or you'll go blind."

Gredoni turned, gave me the hard look, and returned to the lesson. "Make sure your hand is tight at the bottom," he said. "Or it will hop up. Keep her tight and it will jump less. Take a little bend in your knees."

The range ran about thirty yards behind the shop, with white paper targets down at the end. The targets were on a motorized runner that Gredoni had moved about fifteen yards out. The target looked to be the outline of a Middle Eastern man with a bushy black heard. Strategic circles around his midsection.

"My hands are sweating," the kid said.

"That's all part of it."

The kid took a wider stance, his baggy jeans drooping off his butt, and squeezed off a shot. The kid flinched. "Holy shit," he said. "That was awesome."

"Wow," I said. "Right in the fez. Assassinating Sydney Greenstreet?"

"Spenser," Gredoni said. "Shit. What the hell do you want?"

"I'm a paying customer," I said. "A little R-and-R. You know, shooting not only lowers stress but improves coordination."

"Bullshit."

"Okay," I said. "I came to bust your balls."

123

He eyed me, snorted, and turned back to the pudgy kid. "Put a little kink in your arm and a little lean forward," Gredoni said. "Bend the legs. Especially with a big gun."

Gredoni stepped back and watched as the kid raised the weapon in his hands, squeezing off several rounds one after another. The kid turned around, laughing and waving the barrel wildly. Gredoni snatched it from his hand, checked the load, and told him he had one in the chamber. "Jesus," he said.

"Before we both get shot," I said. "How about a quick word?"

"If you came to shoot," he said. "Shoot. If you came to talk, I don't have anything to say."

"Just how long are you going to cover for Welles?" I said. "I spoke to some of your investors. I know what you had planned for Strawberry Hill and why it didn't work out."

Gredoni shook his head, picked up a pair of earmuffs, and started to move them up to his ears.

"Did you know he's using your name now?" I said. "And your credit card?"

"Bullshit."

"Used it yesterday at Logan," I said. "He rented a Chevy Malibu. Never really thought of Welles as a Chevy guy. I thought he'd rent an Aston Martin with machine guns and an ejector seat."

"You sure?"

"Yep," I said. "Good call on the collision. Last time I saw Welles, two shooters in a black SUV were chasing him out of downtown Lynn."

"Crap."

"Yep."

Gredoni's apt pupil walked over to a table and ran his hand over an M4 and two black tactical shotguns. He looked up at both of us, grinned, and gave a big thumbs-up. I wondered if Gredoni rented out the range for birthdays and bar mitzvahs.

"Someone's after him," I said. "And I'm betting you're number two with a bullet. So how about we start back at the beginning. Who is Welles?"

Gredoni swallowed and nodded. He walked from the range back into the shop and told the guy with the mustache to take over. He pressed a button, unlocking the front door, and we both walked out together to the front parking lot. As soon as we were outside, he lit a cigarette.

"Concord didn't fall apart from permitting," I said. "Did Welles run off with the money?"

"Shit fell apart," he said.

"Why?"

"We were juggling separate business plans," I said. "We're working on it. Okay? It's complicated."

"Why?" I said. Ah, the art of repetition.

Gredoni leaned against the wall to the gun range. A mural of the American flag and a soaring eagle clutching the Constitution in its talons had been painted on the cinder block. The shooting continued inside, sounding as if the kid had put down the Glock for the M4.

"He's using you," I said. "The same way he used everyone. If you don't help me catch him, the investors will turn on you."

Gredoni didn't answer. He seemed to take a lot of comfort in the cigarette, drawing the smoke deep and then letting it out slow. "You see these guys after Welles?"

I nodded.

"How many?"

"Two."

"What they look like?"

"Don't know."

"Whatta you mean you don't know?" he said. "Aren't you the private eye?"

"I was too busy diving behind a dumpster," I said. "Besides, they had on ski masks."

"Guns?"

"Assault rifles," I said. "I didn't ask for

the make and serial number. They dressed and moved like military guys."

He nodded as if that made a lot of sense.

"You help me," I said. "And I help you."

"These guys?" Gredoni said. "These ass-holes Welles pissed off, they aren't the forgiving type. And I'd back off this. You're way outclassed here."

"Don't kid yourself," I said. "I'm a pretty classy guy."

"Shooters," he said. "Guns for hire. Soldier-of-fortune types. He brought them on board, had them do some training to attract investors. Now we're tits-up, and they still haven't gotten paid. They really want their money."

"Oops."

"We trained the Lynn police," he said. "Freakin' Boston police. SWAT. We taught a class down in Quincy at an old airfield. With his connections, he'd fly these guys in like sports stars. They all had nicknames like Hammerhead, Crow, Blackjack. I mean, shit. Real hardasses. If I were you, I'd get out now."

"I need to know more than nicknames to help Welles," I said. "And get my client's money back."

"So far, they've left me the hell alone," he said. "I'd like to keep it that way."

"Your buddy Welles might end up floating facedown in the harbor."

Gredoni looked at me, tossed the cigarette down, and crushed it with the heel of his boot. The boots did little to help his deficiency in height. "He'll fix everything," he said. "He's a smart guy. He's got big ideas, big plans. Tell your client, the Kelly broad, she'll get her money back."

"Please excuse my pessimism."

"Give us two days."

"You talked to Welles?"

He didn't say anything. He just glared at me.

"Those guys weren't just trying to scare him."

"Two days," he said. "He's figuring it all out. Everybody will be happy. Something really big is going to happen. Welles will make it work. It's what he does."

"And if it doesn't?"

"Then I guess we're all screwed," Gredoni said. "And it won't freakin' matter."

"What's the deal?"

Gredoni just stared at me with dead eyes. I waited.

Without another word, Gredoni shook his head and walked back into Gun World.

19

Later that afternoon, I tried my best not to contemplate the toxic charisma of M. Brooks Welles as I crushed dried lavender with a stone pestle. Pearl sat on my kitchen rug as I worked. I had set Joe Williams's "A Man Ain't Supposed to Cry" on the turntable. Joe sang "I've Only Myself to Blame" as I added a couple teaspoons of the lavender to a bowl filled with sprigs of thyme, honey, olive oil, lemon juice, and grated lemon zest. I mixed them together and then added the marinade to a large Ziploc bag filled with two breasts from a free-range chicken. The chicken had lived so humanely it had apparently died with a clear conscience.

I set the chicken in the refrigerator and started to prep an appetizer of thin slices of potato topped with chopped pear and sprinkles of Roquefort. I had a bottle of Côtes du Rhône on the counter and a bottle of Macon chilling. Covering both bases. My condo was open and inviting, with a few strategic lamps giving off a pleasant glow. I had left my gun and cap hanging on the coatrack by the door. The harbor outside was turning dark with rain pelting the window.

I sang to Pearl, *"I have given you my true love, but you love a new love."*

Pearl stared at me and cocked her head from side to side. I started to slice the potatoes as I heard a jangle of keys and Susan walked through the door and into the living room and kitchen. "What's that smell?"

"Roquefort."

"I loathe Roquefort."

"Even if sprinkled with pears on slivers of potato?"

"Possibly even more."

"Trust," I said. "Trust is key."

"Speaking of trust," Susan said, "have you heard something about a reconciliation with Connie and her con man?"

"She told me she's confused," I said.

"That's an understatement."

"He must really be good," I said. "He has Johnny Gredoni screwed up, too. The man stole his credit card and his identity and Johnny didn't blink. He told me that Welles works in strange and mysterious ways."

"Did he really say that?"

"Sort of," I said. "He said to give Welles two days and all will be made right."

"Do you believe him?"

"Of course," I said. "That's why I spent the afternoon cooking. Everything will go perfectly."

"Ha," Susan said. "And what have you been working on?"

"Poulet au citron et lavande."

"So what you're saying is that you're trying to impress me with fancy chicken."

"Can't fool you."

"And Joe Williams?"

"It's been a long day," I said. "And a man ain't supposed to cry."

"Too many lies?"

"And too many people wanting to believe them."

"Sounds like we had a very similar workday," Susan said, kicking off her black pumps and finding a spot at the kitchen island. She watched as I prepped the salad. I washed the greens in a colander and set them on a paper towel to dry. I began to cut up a green pepper and a purple onion.

"What will you do if Connie wants you to drop it?" she said. "And goes back with Welles?"

"Probably the same as you."

"Nothing," she said.

"Maybe more than nothing," I said. "I signed on to help Connie. Not help Welles. Or whoever he might be."

I uncorked the Macon and poured her a nice serving in a stemless glass. I was drinking rye. Neat. The rain tapping on the windows gained intensity while Susan turned to stare out at the waterfront.

We sat on my new sofa, listening to Joe Williams. After a while, I switched out the record for Count Basie. Upon completion of side A, I set the potato slices and the chicken in the oven. I poured Susan some more wine and helped myself to a bit more rye. The rain fell pleasantly along the docks and out into the ocean. From the second floor, the Charlestown Bridge and the lights of the North End bloomed in interesting patterns. Or perhaps it was the rye.

"The chicken might take a while."

Susan gave a wicked grin. "That's about like saying your car ran out of gas."

"Did I mention that my chicken is free-range?"

"That," she said, "and then some. But I know where it roosts."

She set her bare feet in my lap and I turned off the lamp on a side table. The

132

record finished and we were left with silence and then the sound of rain tapping hard against the window.

"Do you mind if we just sit here and relax?"

"Not at all."

"I can take care of your chicken after dinner."

I made a crowing sound. Susan ignored me.

"It's nice here," she said.

I nodded. Pearl walked up, snuffling at my hands, and then inserted herself between us. She jogged her snout up and down, insisting on getting a good head scratching.

"You don't owe Connie a thing," Susan said. "Just because she's my client."

"I'm a nosy guy," I said. "I'm very curious about all this. And I hate liars."

"You don't say."

I extracted myself from lavishing Pearl with attention and moved over to check on dinner and change out the record. Since the fire, my vinyl collection had grown to an impressive spot on my shelf beside my books and a few wooden sculptures I'd carved. One of them remained after the fire, a blackened horse, a bit cooked but otherwise intact.

As I peered from the window across the

waterfront and down the road where I'd parked the car, I noticed a black SUV not unlike the one that had chased Welles. I walked over to my bedroom and picked up a pair of binoculars, trying to see if anyone was inside.

I could see the shadowed faces of two men. One of the men looked back at me with similar field glasses.

I waved.

The SUV started, lights came on, and it wheeled onto the access road and away in the rain.

"What is it?" Susan said.

"Not sure," I said. "Ask me in the morning."

20

Three days later Brian Lundquist called me at my office and told me he was at the Starbucks across the street. Although I was a dedicated Dunkin' man, I crossed Boylston and met him at a little table looking across Berkeley at the old Museum of Natural History. It was now a high-end furniture store that sold five-thousand-dollar sofas and sheets with a million-thread count.

I grabbed whatever they called a medium cup and sat down across from Lundquist. It was late afternoon, gold and sunny, and the coffee shop was nearly vacant.

"How's the con man?" he said.

"Winsome," I said. "Charming."

"Getting any closer to what he's up to?"

"It seems he's so personable and likable, no one can fault him," I said. "My client waffles daily on whether to drop my services."

"Like I said, must be good in the sack."

"Or a complete sociopath," I said.

"Or that."

Lundquist reached for a couple fake sugars and added them to his coffee. I'd rather drink rat poison. He stirred the coffee and said, "When were you going to tell me about what happened in Lynn?"

"When I figure out exactly what happened," I said. "One moment I was offered cheesecake and the next a black SUV is trying to run down my con man."

"Welles."

"M. Brooks," I said. "Or Mike. Mikey. Or just ol' Brooks."

"Any closer to finding out who he is?"

"Nope," I said. "But Johnny Gredoni promises Welles is very real and will deliver on what he says."

"I heard those guys in Lynn nearly got you."

I smiled and showed a slight width between my thumb and forefinger. "Missed it by that much."

"Did they want to scare him or kill him?"

"If I hadn't been there, he'd have been roadkill," I said. "They had a GMC SUV. A Yukon with no license plate."

"What'd Welles say about what happened?"

"Not much," I said. "In the confusion, he

took off and disappeared again. I traced his car to a rental. The rental was in Gredoni's name, although Gredoni says he didn't know about it."

"So," Lundquist said, looking very happy with himself. "Basically you've been chasing your tail."

"You know, Healy was much nicer," I said. "He offered encouragement."

"Bullshit," Lundquist said. "I worked with Healy half my life."

"So do you have something to share with the group?" I said. "Or just jonesing for a Malawi cold press with notes of citrus and chocolate?"

"When did coffee stop being coffee?"

"When someone figured out guys like us would pay five bucks a cup."

"It's ninety-nine cents to fill my travel mug at the Shell station."

"Ambiance," I said. "We pay for ambiance."

"Oh, yeah," he said. "I forgot. Well, your friend Welles seems to have been born into thin air a few years ago. I found nothing on him prior to that. He showed up in Boston, becoming quick buddies with a lot of folks in law enforcement. He made a lot of friends fast. I just spoke to the chief in Foxboro. He freakin' loves the guy. Their

137

website has pictures of their training. Welles is IDed as ex-CIA. Navy SEAL. Vietnam vet."

"Any cops check him out?" I said. "Or just take his word like everyone else?"

"Word came from Gredoni," Lundquist said. "He knows a lot of cops. A lot of departments do business with him. He's been around a long time. And despite being an absolute prick, sells pretty good merchandise at good prices."

"I heard he used to deal with some unsavory characters, too."

"Oh, yeah," Lundquist said. "We know all about that. He worked with Broz until that organization turned to crap. Some folks in the North End and Providence. He did some straw buys for folks who weren't allowed to buy weapons, but we could never make a case on him."

"And now," I said, "what about that ATF task force that you never mentioned?"

Lundquist gave a crooked smile and sipped his coffee. He looked over his shoulder at the barista and then back to me. "That's still going on," he said. "Something really big is about to happen. We're not supposed to talk about it, but it's what the ATF has been waiting for."

"Gredoni told me a similar story," I said.

"He said Welles was going to work it out. Get everyone paid."

"Once we arrest this jackass," Lundquist said, "I can print him and find out who he really is."

"Why not just do that now?"

"And spoil the operation?" Lundquist said, shaking his head. "I don't think so. Just wait."

"For this theoretical roundup that may or may not happen."

"Exactly."

"Yeehaw."

"We don't know where or when," he said. "Some of my colleagues were hoping you might have heard something."

I shook my head. My coffee was still too hot to drink. I took off the lid and blew across the black surface. "Gredoni said the men who tried to harm Welles were former employees," I said. "He said they were guns for hire who put on these tactical dog-and-pony shows for the locals."

Lundquist nodded.

"I've been checking into these guys," I said. "But coming up with more aliases and questionable résumés. They get off on all this secrecy."

"I thought you just wanted a refund for a jilted woman?"

"It seems Mr. Welles has misplaced the cash," I said. "Some of these guns for hire might know where to look."

"I can press some of the cops I know for names," he said. "But you don't want to be anywhere near this shit show when it blows. We'll be shutting it down hard and fast. This is a lot bigger than just Boston. It's a lot bigger than just Gredoni and this asshole Welles, too. We're talking about crossing state lines. Cargo containers filled with enough ammo to take over some third-world country."

I raised my eyebrows. "Yikes."

"Fucking right 'Yikes,' " he said. "No one wants to screw this thing up. I just was hoping you'd heard something. Or knew something."

"I know Welles is fake," I said. "I know some of his employees were probably fake, too. I know some of them want Welles dead or disabled. I know that Johnny Gredoni wants me to back off until my client gets her money. Other than that, it's pretty dark."

"Yeah," he said. "Us, too. Wiretaps aren't what they used to be."

"Can I interest you in an orange scone with your Malawi blend?"

"I'll stick to stale donuts and the gas-station crap," he said. "It's more honest."

I saluted him with my coffee and Lund-quist turned to leave. I bought a blueberry scone and walked back to my office.

21

Feet up on my desk, scone crumbs scattered on my shirt, I finally got a call back from Rachel Wallace. "It always amazes me when the person I'm calling actually answers the phone," she said.

"My personal assistant is on vacation."

"Since when did you get an assistant?"

"I thought about it," I said. "But my office is one room. I get an assistant and then I'd have to get a bigger office. I upgrade and then I have to get a partner. I get a partner and then comes the vengeance when the partner is killed."

"Spenser and Archer."

"Strangely unfamiliar."

"I'm no Effie," she said, "but I did track down a few details about your globe-trotting boogieman. For a while, during the Arab Spring, he was extremely popular. More than fifty bookings. He had his dance card punched a lot."

"So to speak," I said.

"And then it seems he went off the radar," Rachel said. "I had a friend at CNN find out just who had booked him and what credentials he'd produced. But that producer was gone."

"And then you tracked down the producer for me?"

"You did offer a bottle of Blanton's."

"Only if you share it," I said. "We could sit around and pretend to be Sartre and Simone de Beauvoir."

"That would involve sex."

"Sometimes with multiple partners," I said. "And a lot of existential discussion between the sheets. In that spirit, what have you learned?"

"Besides one is not born, but rather becomes, a woman?"

"Yes," I said. "Besides that."

"There apparently is a man in Florida, a real former Navy SEAL, who spends a great deal of his day outing fakes," she said. "It's become his life's mission. He called the producer and reported Welles for not only not being a SEAL, but also never being a seaman who ever buffered a balustrade."

"I found no naval record, either," I said. "But Welles promises to be so top secret that even the Navy doesn't know."

"To quote the SEAL debunker," Rachel said, "Welles is completely full of shit. And a disgrace to everyone who served in Vietnam. Do you wish to talk with him? He was very nice and very direct and helpful about how SEAL records were public and easily accessed. He says he outs about thirty fakes a day."

"No," I said. "I only wondered how Welles was ever put on television."

"These people would put a tap-dancing llama on the news to boost ratings," she said. "They don't care. According to the producer, Welles appeared distinguished with the silver hair and all. And he looked good in a suit."

"That's all it takes?"

"And absolutely supreme confidence in your subject matter and what you wish to defend."

"Hence the word *confidence* in con man."

"Precisely."

"When was his last appearance?" I said.

"Four months ago."

"That coincides with the failed land deal in Concord and skipping town with my client's money."

"His house of cards is tumbling."

"It certainly seems that way," I said. "Thank you for looking. Maybe when this

144

is over, I can deliver the bottle in person."

"You know you still have a little credit for that thing you did for me that one time."

"I only had to walk through most of Boston in a snowstorm," I said. "No biggie."

"Hold on," Rachel said. "Hold on. There's one last thing."

"Don't tell me," I said. "Welles once climbed Mount Everest."

"Let me get this straight," she said. "Your man has been outed by his lover, his business partner, and half of Boston."

"Pretty much."

"Where does a disgraced con man go to find refuge and solace?"

"The YMCA?"

"Or the publishing industry."

I set my feet on the ground and rolled the chair up close to the desk. I reached for my legal pad and a pen. "Give it to me straight, Effie."

"Late last year, your Mr. M. Brooks Welles signed a six-figure deal with a major publishing house."

"I take it the book will be illustrated with lots of rainbows and gumdrops of Never Never Land."

"No," she said. "It was billed as a hard-hitting account of Welles's time in the Vietnam jungle, the mountains of El Salvador, and on the front lines fighting terrorists in the Middle East."

"You're joking."

"I never joke about my work, 007."

"What's it called?"

"American Patriot."

"Of course it is."

"Many things irk me about this," Rachel said. "Mainly that my last book advance was for considerably less."

"How much less?"

"Considerably."

"Who's the editor?"

She told me. I didn't know a lot of New York City editors. We ran in different circles.

"Do you know him?"

"I do."

"And?"

"Let me put it this way," she said. "He just gave a multimillion-dollar advance to a first-time author, a blogger who's promised to have written *Gone Girl* meets Harry Potter."

"Poor Harry," I said. "I guess this guy isn't much of a fact-checker."

"There are no fact-checkers in the publishing business."

"I thought you had people running through every word you write."

146

"For magazine pieces, they will rake you over the coals," she said. "No one checks a word in book publishing besides basic copy-editing."

"That's insane."

"This editor in question considers himself the modern Maxwell Perkins," she said. "But Marlin Perkins would do a better job."

"And more appropriate," I said. "Would he speak to me if I came to New York?"

"Probably not," she said.

"I can be persistent."

"I know," she said. "But I would bet he already knows considerably less about Welles than you do."

"True."

"Everybody's pulling a con in this world," she said. "Aren't they?"

"It will drive a man to drink."

"A woman, too."

I stood, thanked her, and hung up. After meeting with Lundquist and following up with calls, I'd nearly forgotten lunch. I called Hawk and told him to meet me for a late lunch at Trade.

"What's the price, babe?"

"I need you to introduce me to some of your friends."

"Stepping out on Susan?" he said, laughing.

"*Gunga Din* stuff," I said. "Guys who get you work overseas."

"Oh, that."

"Indeed."

"Lunch," he said. "Then I'll introduce you to an old friend."

22

I always liked Army/Navy stores. When I was a kid, not long after we'd moved from Wyoming, it's where my uncles would pick up used winter coats, old boots, camping gear. They also reminded me of my short stint in the Army. GI Surplus in Roxbury had been around since I'd been in Boston. They advertised with a bright red decommissioned missile out by Blue Hill Avenue. The owner of the store was an older black guy everyone called Sergeant. I didn't know if it was meant as in York or Shriver. I didn't ask.

Hawk gave the introduction. Sergeant had a bald head ringed with gray hair and a gray beard. He kept an office way back behind the mountains of pants, boots, T-shirts, and cases of guns and knives. He sold flags for every country you could imagine. He sold ammo. He sold cigarette lighters that looked like hand grenades. And according to Hawk, he also traded a lot in men who'd travel for the right price. When we found him, he was seated at a small table, painting little tin soldiers.

"I heard of you," Sergeant said.

I nodded.

"Hawk said I could trust you."

I nodded again.

"Don't know much about this white dude, Welles," he said. "He's not one of my people."

"He had a company called EDGE," I said. "He trained cops in Lynn and BPD SWAT. He claimed he was a Navy SEAL and instructed on shooting and tactics. I heard he brought in some real pros to fill out the bill."

Sergeant shook his head. He set one of the tin soldiers under a large magnifying glass and bright lamp. The finished soldiers looked to all be redcoats. "Can't help you, man."

"This guy started the company with Johnny Gredoni."

"Two-Gun Gredoni?"

"Damn," I said. "I thought I'd coined that phrase."

Hawk shook his head, finding a nearby bin full of old *Life* magazines from the 1960s. He pulled out an issue with Sophia

Loren on the cover. From a quick glance, she seemed to be wearing some kind of see-through negligee. Behind his dark glasses, Hawk gave a wide grin.

"You don't need to be messing around with that son of a bitch," Sergeant said.

"Why?"

"Can't trust him," he said. "He's a god-damn cheat."

"How's that?"

"Got two prices," Sergeant said. "Two shops."

I looked to Hawk. He was engrossed in Sophia and her nightie. He licked his finger and turned the page.

"How'd that work?" I said.

"He's got the store up in Lynn," he said. "But he sells most of his shit off the books. Out the back door. Cuts all us honest gun folks off at the knees."

"Who is his supplier?"

"If I knew that, I'd have a fancy-ass shop on Newbury Street."

"That's hard to imagine," I said. "You'd have to compete with Diane von Fursten-berg."

Sergeant shrugged, picked a fresh soldier, and examined it under the magnifier. Hawk put down the magazine and strolled for-ward. Hawk had a way of moving that made

151

cats seem clumsy. He had on a pair of black jeans, a black silk shirt, and black cowboy boots.

"You get us a line on these EDGE people?" Hawk said. "Find out some names. Who they are. What they do when they ain't stateside."

"Sure," Sergeant said, now adding a bit more red to the red coat. "What's in it for me?"

"How long I know you, Sarge?"

"Long time."

"I do what I say?" he said. "Made you a lot of money."

Sergeant took off his half glasses and set them aside. He turned off the light on the magnifying glass, folded his arms, and studied Hawk. It looked more like he was appraising him. After a long moment, he nodded.

"Sure," Sergeant said. "But you ain't the one asking. Are you? He is."

"Same thing," Hawk said. "You deal with him. You deal with me. You understand?"

"I get some people in trouble it's my black ass," he said. "You understand that?"

"Spenser ain't the law," he said. "He one of us."

"You ain't never brought him in here before."

"He ain't never asked."

I smiled and tried to look modest. Sergeant began to arrange his figures on the table before him, the precise lines of a British regiment, stacking them in neat order to be mowed down by the colonials hiding behind trees and rocks.

"You friends with Quirk?" Sergeant said.

I nodded.

"I don't like that son of a bitch," he said. "He been hassling me his whole life. He tried to shut me down since I came to town."

"Spenser is Spenser," Hawk said. "He look like a cop?"

"Yeah," Sergeant said. "He do."

"Don't rush to judgment," I said. "Those aren't donut crumbs on my shirt. I actually had a scone."

"Damn, man," Sergeant said. "You trying to ruin me, Hawk. You bring a man like that in here? After all we been through."

"I promise you," Hawk said. "Me and Spenser been through much more."

Sergeant stared right at me for a long while. He did not blink but finally nodded. Hawk turned and headed out of the store. I offered my hand. Sergeant ignored it and went back to working on the British Army. I followed Hawk back outside.

153

"That's it?" I said.

"That's it," he said. "If those men are in the life, he'll get you names."

"Gee," I said. "He must've really taken to me."

"Haw," Hawk said. "Sergeant don't like nothing but the green, babe."

23

Two days later, as Susan and I enjoyed our traditional lazy Sunday, someone knocked on my front door. I left Susan in bed reading a book by Karen Abbott about women spies of the Civil War. She had cold coffee at her side and a warm Pearl snuggled nearby. I set aside the sports section of *The Globe,* put on my robe, and answered.

Frank Belson and Captain Glass stood on my stoop. A visit from Belson rarely implied good news.

"Can we come in?" Captain Glass said. She was a tall, lean woman with short black hair and a chiseled, sharply drawn face. Today she sported something from her endless supply of navy blue suits and white silk tops. She had on sensible black shoes and smelled vaguely of cigarettes. Or perhaps it was Belson's cigars.

"I wondered when I might see you again, Captain," I said. "Apologies on the arson

155

case aren't necessary. But if you have an accommodation . . ."

"Spenser," Belson said. "Open the damn door. This ain't a social call."

"It almost never is," I said, opening the door. "Coffee? I'm making a fresh pot."

Pearl wandered into the room and started to bark. Belson got down on one knee and offered an open hand. Pearl snuffled it and started to wag her tail. She walked a wide circle around Glass, sniffing and exploring, while Glass tried to ignore her.

I washed out the coffeepot and filled it with cold water. Belson stood at the tall counter of the open kitchen. He looked freshly shaved, although his jaw still shone with a blue-black beard outline.

"Johnny Gredoni's dead," he said. "Someone spotted a leg sticking out of a dumpster in Chinatown."

"Are you sure it wasn't a large pot sticker?"

"Pretty sure," Belson said. "It had on a combat boot."

"Natural causes?" I said.

"Sure," Belson said. "If you call being shot in the back of the head natural."

"Damn it, Frank," Glass said. "What are you doing? You don't need to discuss any details with him."

"Spenser would've asked anyway," he said. "And I would've told him. Oh, you didn't shoot him, did you?"

"When did it happen?"

"Sometime last night," he said.

"I guess not," I said. "I was at home."

"Do you have a witness?" Glass said. She had her hands on her hips and an unpleasant look on her face. Her blue suit was without a wrinkle. Quirk's replacement, after he'd been kicked up to assistant super, possessed many of his traits.

"Pearl," I said. "We were watching a William Powell marathon on TCM. She's a big fan of Asta."

"And who the hell is Pearl?" Glass said.

I nodded to Pearl. "Her."

"A dog," Glass said. "Come on. Get dressed. You're coming with us."

Susan opened the bedroom door and walked out in my big gray sweatpants and a T-shirt that read *Bang Group.* Her hair was twisted up on top of her head. She joined us in the kitchen area. I finished adding the scoops of coffee and pressed *brew.*

"I'm not Quirk," Glass said. "I don't give special favors."

"We haven't been introduced," Susan said. "I'm Susan Silverman."

Glass introduced herself, emphasis on

157

Captain, her eyes never leaving me. I couldn't blame her, knowing I looked absolutely stunning in my blue terry-cloth robe.

"Were you with Mr. Spenser last night?"

"Yes," Susan said. "At least twice. What's all this about?"

"Johnny Gredoni is dead," I said. "Glass here never trusts me and wants me to drive down to headquarters with them until I confess I'd always admired the Boston Strangler and I'm nuttier than Woody Woodpecker."

"He's not going anywhere," Susan said. "Not today."

Glass, hands still on hips, grinned a bit. "It's not up to you, Susan," she said. "I'm working a homicide."

"Today is our day off," she said. "Some people actually have social lives outside work."

Captain Glass scowled. Belson looked away, smiled, and started to whistle a bit.

"I was here," I said. "Ask what you want to ask."

"Why did you go up to Lynn and threaten John Gredoni last week at his place of work?"

"That never happened."

"We just left Gun World," Glass said.

158

"They said they have you on surveillance video."

"I was there," I said. "But I didn't threaten him. He was too short to threaten. It would have made me feel bad about myself."

"Why were you there?" Glass said.

"I am a private investigator," I said. "I was investigating."

"What?" Glass said.

"That's confidential," I said. "Do you take milk or sugar? Or both."

"I'll take a goddamn answer."

"Is she always so charming, Frank?" Susan said. "Or is it part of her investigative technique?"

"I don't know," Belson said. "We've only just started working together."

"Oh," Glass said. "And what would you know about investigative technique?"

"I'm a licensed therapist," Susan said. "I deal a lot with anger management. Pent-up aggression."

"And besides being my number-one groupie," I said, "she's a Harvard Ph.D."

No one spoke for a while. The coffee beeped and I poured out four cups. Pearl walked behind me while I worked. The air was thin, most of it being sucked far out of the room, leaving a little chilliness in the large open space.

"As I can see I'm outnumbered," Glass said, "how about we calm down, step back, and sit down. A man is dead and Spenser was seen having a heated argument with him. We can't wait until Monday for answers."

Susan nodded. She picked up her coffee, Pearl at her side. They headed back to the bedroom and she gently closed the door.

"I don't think Dr. Silverman likes you, Captain," Belson said, adding some sugar to his coffee. Glass glared back, picked up a cup, and followed me to the sofa.

"I can't tell you who I'm working for or much about the case," I said. "But I'll admit I wasn't a fan of John Gredoni and can't pretend I'm shaken by his passing."

"Would your client want to kill Gredoni?" Glass said.

"No," I said. "She barely knows him."

"What's her name and connection to Gredoni?" Glass said.

I crossed my legs and shook my head. "I was working a missing-person case," I said. "My missing person was connected to Gredoni."

"Goddamn it," Glass said.

"You get any angrier and you might spill your coffee," I said.

Belson scratched at his cheek and re-crossed his legs. He took a sip of coffee, looked out the window onto the black water, and back to me. "What did Gredoni tell you about the guy who was missing?"

"That he didn't know where to find him."

"What was the connection?" Belson said.

"She already asked that."

"Yeah," Belson said. "But now I'm asking it."

"They were business partners," I said. "Listen, I'm tired and haven't had much coffee. Before you two arrived, I had planned to make breakfast for Susan. To get on with my day, you might want to check with Lynn PD about an attempt on the life of a man named M. Brooks Welles. You may also want to speak with Captain Brian Lundquist with the state police."

"I know Lundquist," Glass said.

"He knows more about Gredoni than I do," I said. "He may clue you in to who exactly might have wanted him dead. As a simple PI, I'm not privy to such details in law enforcement."

Belson smiled. "See, Captain," he said. "Spenser can be as reasonable as any normal person."

"He seems like an asshole to me."

Belson shrugged. "A man of many talents."

161

24

I'd called ahead, but Connie still seemed surprised when she opened the door to her apartment in the South End. She'd been exercising, wearing black Adidas shorts and a black sports bra. Her skin was moist with sweat, and she wiped her face with a towel as she let me in. She walked into a foyer where the furniture had been cleared on a large Oriental rug and a flat-screen TV played an instructional yoga video.

I sat down in a wooden chair by the window and across from the television. An Asian man with a bald head had just launched into a crane pose. It looked to be highly uncomfortable and possibly painful. Susan could probably do it without breaking a sweat.

Connie turned off the TV and offered me hot green tea. I declined. She offered me a beer and I accepted. It was Sunday, after all.

"Have you heard from Welles?" I said.

She shook her head and sat near me in a plushy blue chair.

"John Gredoni is dead."

"Oh my God," she said, saying the most common thing people say when people die. Rarely do you hear *Good riddance* or *Thank God.* Both being appropriate for John Gredoni.

"Someone shot him."

"The men after Brooks?"

"Probably," I said. "But Gredoni had a lot of enemies."

She nodded. Her skin was very tan and her upper arms were as muscular as a professional athlete's. She was barefoot and wore her blond hair up in a high bun. Without makeup and professional clothes, she looked much younger than I knew her to be. How she ended up with a silver-haired gent like Welles made little sense.

"Why didn't you mention Gredoni when you first came to me?"

Connie shrugged. "I didn't think he was important," she said. "When we were together, Brooks introduced me to a lot of people. It was hard to keep track of all of them. Gredoni didn't seem any more important than the others."

"Did you know he was Welles's business

partner in the land deal?"

"I knew he was involved," she said. "But I didn't know to what extent. Brooks didn't discuss such matters with me."

"Did you attend any of these wilderness shindigs up in Concord?" I said. "For the other potential investors?"

"The cookouts?" she said. "One or two. They weren't very big. Almost like big dinner parties. Why are you asking me all these questions? Do you think I know something about Brooks and this man's death? I barely even met this Gredoni person. He was absolutely repulsive."

"I can't argue with you," I said. "Are you sure Welles hasn't been in touch since the other night?"

She tilted her head, inhaled, and gave me a very stern look. "I think I would've known."

"Oh, what a tangled web he weaves."

"Yes, I was deceived," she said. "I was made a fool. Now I only want my money back."

"But you still love him?"

"I agreed to meet him for dinner," she said. "I wanted to be civil. I wanted him to squirm and explain himself to me. I did not forgive him and go running crying into his arms, if that's what you're asking."

Connie left for a moment and returned from the kitchen with a glass of water.

"I may have a soft heart or be a soft touch, but goddamn it, I know I was duped. I feel bad that Brooks is in danger. But no, I'm not still in love with him."

"Okay," I said. "I apologize. I get a little paranoid when people start shooting at me."

"It seems they were shooting at Brooks."

"Hard to tell the difference in the dark."

"Do you have something new?" she said. "Or did you just come over to inform me about Mr. Gredoni's demise?"

"I came to tell you that if Welles happens to call, you need to stay far, far away from him," I said. "What exactly did he say, anyway?"

"We've been over this," she said. "He was unrepentant. Everything I asked had a pat answer. Everything was going to work out in time. He spoke down to me as if I were a little girl. When I'd ask about my money, he would talk about his love for me."

"What else?"

"He wanted me to fire you," she said. "Brooks said you would only make trouble for him. He told me some men were trying to kill him and involving you could only draw them in closer."

"For once, he may have been telling the truth."

Connie took a long, deep breath. It was raining out along Brookline Street. A man emerged from a brownstone carrying a bright yellow umbrella and headed down the steps.

"What did you say?"

"I said I'd fire you if he brought me my money."

"And?"

"He said he'd have my money by the end of the week."

"Check is in the mail?"

"Something like that," she said. "He only promised he was on the verge of a major deal."

"Any hints?"

"Not a one," she said.

"And the rest?"

"Boring love talk," Connie said. "Would you think less of me if I told you I let him run his mouth? I wanted to hear his excuses and promises and all his meaningless flirtations. Maybe for the first time, I was behind the mask. It was all acting and calculations. I think he thought he could hustle me right back into bed."

"You know, not all men are creeps."

"Seems most of the good ones are taken."

166

"I wish you could have met my protégé," I said. "Smart and tough. Loyal and dependable. Good-looking kid, too."

"More age-appropriate?" she said.

"Much more," I said.

"I wish I could say Brooks was the only older man I've dated," she said. "But somehow they're drawn to me and I to them. I really can't explain why."

I knew but nodded and kept my mouth shut.

"I guess that's more of a discussion for Dr. Silverman."

I nodded again. The rain fell harder and I watched a woman in a rain slicker and Red Sox cap jog past the window. She wiped the rain from her eyes and headed into more puddles ahead.

"God," she said. "What do I do?"

"Contact me the minute Welles calls you."

"And then?"

"Give me a chance to reason with him."

"Do you think any of it is real?"

"I think someone is trying to kill him," I said. "That part is real. But I doubt the reason has anything to do with government service or international intrigue."

"Oh, God," she said. "The first time we met at your office, I told you I was an idiot. I have gotten involved with a liar and probably a criminal. Why didn't I see it?"

"Sometimes we believe what we want to hear."

"Do you?"

I smiled at her. "Only the very best parts."

25

Bright and early the next morning, Lundquist called to let me know the ATF wanted to meet with me as soon as possible. I was so flattered, I finished up my training with Henry, took a nice shower, and ate breakfast before heading over to Causeway Street. The ATF kept offices on the seventh floor of a nondescript office building within spitting distance of the new Boston Garden. The special agent in charge was a young Vietnamese-American man named Bobby Nguyen.

"I've heard a lot about you, Spenser," he said.

"All of it's true."

"I heard you could be a real pain in the ass," Nguyen said. He smiled as he said it. He was of medium height and thin, his hair black and shiny and recently barbered. He had on the standard government-issue dark blue suit with a crisp white shirt and black tie.

"Perhaps," I said. "But I always win you guys over with my charm and resourcefulness."

"Some cops don't like you," he said. "They say you sometimes stir the pot too much."

I shrugged and smiled with false modesty.

"But you used to be a cop?"

"I worked for the Middlesex DA."

"Why'd you quit?"

"I was never into team sports," I said. "I guess I don't play well with others."

"Fair enough." We shook hands and he ushered me into a meeting room. Gray walls, a conference table, and eight black leather spinning chairs. The Feds were never much on interior decoration. Would a little splash of color kill them?

Two men stood from the table and nodded in my direction. One looked like Larry Bird, only with a bald head and a long beard that would've impressed Moses. He had on a backward baseball cap with sunglasses on top of its crown. The other was older, Latino, with salt-and-pepper hair and a prominent nose. He, like Nguyen, wore a dark blue suit, crisp white shirt, and black tie.

I'd gone for the whole devil-may-care style that day. Pawtucket Sox tee, Levi's, and tan desert boots. I did remove my cap before taking a seat.

Moses was Smith. Salt-and-Pepper guy was Cardillo. Just as we'd gotten to know each other, Lundquist joined us. He reached across the table for a carafe of water and filled the glass. I gave him a nod from across the table. Lundquist offered a sly grin.

"So," Nguyen said. "I guess you know we want to talk about John Gredoni."

I nodded.

"You may, or may not, know we were working a major investigation that involved Gredoni."

I didn't answer or respond in any way. I just let Nguyen talk, but I could feel Lundquist staring at me from across the table to keep my mouth shut.

"Agents Smith and Cardillo had been watching Mr. Gredoni for nearly six months," he said. "They were extremely close to arresting him and several of his cohorts."

"Cohorts?" I said.

Nguyen smiled wide. "We're trying to be professional here," he said. "Mr. Gredoni's death has wasted a ton of time in the field.

To be blunt, it's royally fucked up a major case."

"Just think how he feels," I said.

Nguyen didn't smile this time. Smith and Cardillo looked at their hands while Lundquist leaned back in his seat. He seemed to be enjoying the festivities like an impartial observer at a poker game. His clear blue eyes flicked back from Nguyen to me before holding up a hand.

"They want to know everything you know," Lundquist said. "I already told them you weren't aware of any gun deals."

"That's true."

"Or knew of any trades being worked by your con man," Lundquist said.

I smiled. "The esteemed M. Brooks Welles," I said. "Perhaps the most interesting man in the world if he switched from martinis to Dos Equis."

Again, no one smiled but Lundquist. I was thankful at least one person in the room had a sense of humor.

"I don't have to tell you anything about my case," I said. "But for the hell of it, I'll let you in on the basics. I was hired to find Welles. Welles is a known con man and, depending on who is telling the story, a business partner of the late Mr. Gredoni. I was looking into a land deal in Concord in which my client was cheated out of a sub-stantial sum of money."

The agents all nodded, following me. I did not mention Connie's name, the amount of the con, or that she had been in love with Welles. They could find that stuff out on their own.

"Before he was found feet-up in a dump-ster, Gredoni told me that he and Welles were about to strike it rich," I said. "I understood this didn't mean either hitting the Lotto or a successful trip up to Fox-woods."

"Did Gredoni mention selling guns?" Nguyen said.

"Obviously you haven't seen his billboard by Fenway," I said.

Nguyen leaned forward into the confer-ence table. He stole a quick glance at his two agents. Smith stroked his beard and Cardillo scowled. Thoughtful.

"Did Gredoni tell you anything about this major deal he was working?" Lundquist said.

"Gredoni didn't exactly confide in the man who was trying to run down his former partner."

"What else did he say?" Nguyen said.

"He mainly tried to convince me that Welles was the real deal," I said. "A real-life

Jason Bourne."

Smith continued to stroke his beard. Cardillo remained unimpressed. "But have you heard anything about Gredoni selling illegal weapons in the past?" Nguyen said.

I nodded.

"Do you mind telling us from whom?"

"Whom," I said. "Nicely done. But no. No. I can't tell you."

"Why not?" he said.

"Because that's confidential," I said. "But why does it matter now? You're telling me that Gredoni did some dirty deals. I don't think anyone is surprised."

"Three months ago," Nguyen said, "John Gredoni sold more than fifty assault rifles on the black market. One of them was used in a murder last week in Roxbury. Another in Mattapan."

"Gangs?"

Nguyen nodded.

"Yowzer," I said. "That's not good."

"No, it's not," Nguyen said. "We could have arrested him then. But we wanted to find out where he got them."

"And did you?"

Nguyen shook his head, looking again at his two agents. Neither man looked up from the table. I now saw they'd been brought along to the principal's office to work it all out. I leaned back in my chair and waited.

"We did some excellent work," Nguyen said. "This second shipment was supposed to be even bigger. Maybe a hundred assault rifles. Not to mention countless handguns and possibly a fucking grenade launcher."

"That's rocket-propelled grenades, Spenser," Lundquist said.

I nodded my appreciation. Lundquist grinned.

"We know the guns made it to Boston," Nguyen said. "And we planned to intercept the guns once a buyer, or buyers, were in place."

"But the best laid plans," I said. "And all that."

"Unfortunately," Nguyen said, "with Gredoni dead, we hoped you might help us understand exactly what the hell is going on."

"Nope," I said.

"As in you can't help?" Nguyen said. "Or won't?"

"Can't," I said. "I don't know anything. Gredoni didn't exactly trust me. But since I came when called, perhaps you can share what you know about Mr. Welles?"

Everyone but me turned and looked at Cardillo. Cardillo coughed into his hand to clear his throat. "We know who he is," Cardillo said. "But not sure how he fits into all this."

"As in, you know who he says he is?" I said. "Or you know who he really is?"

Cardillo frowned even more than I thought was possible. "We know he's been quite popular on TV," he said. "And that he was a partner of some sort with Gredoni."

"That's it?"

"He's part of this gun pipeline into Boston," Cardillo said. "But we can't seem to find out his real name or where he's getting these guns. That's ongoing."

"Just out of curiosity," I said. "Were you guys watching my place in the Navy Yard a few nights ago?"

The agents didn't answer. Lundquist finished off his glass of water and reached again for the carafe. "Oh, hell, Bobby," he said. "Just say you boys lost the guns. And haven't a goddamn clue where they've gone."

"Whoops," I said.

Nguyen looked over at his two agents. He shook his head and swallowed. "Yeah," he said. "A big fucking whoops for us."

26

It was dark and raining when I left my office late that night. After removing a ticket from the windshield and tossing it in the nearest receptacle, I drove toward the Common on Boylston. The streets were slick and gutters full as traffic inched past the Four Seasons and toward Charles. My thoughts turned to dinner as the iron lamps glowed in the Public Garden and people milled about carrying umbrellas. I was planning on picking up a loaf of good bread and a six-pack of dark beer and making chicken-salad sandwiches when I spotted the tail.

I didn't wish to be suspicious or paranoid, but I was pretty sure one of the ATF agents decided to have me followed. I couldn't imagine why a trustworthy, taxpaying citizen like myself would merit such scrutiny. Maybe it was more than just my dealings with Gredoni. Maybe they thought I was in cahoots with Welles. Or perhaps they'd found out about Connie Kelly and believed we'd done the Feathered Peacock pose in Toledo and somehow violated the Mann Act.

I followed Charles along the Public Garden and Common toward Beacon Hill. A black sedan, looking very government-issue, turned with me onto Beacon and as I threaded my way to Storrow. I thought about stopping off at The Four Seasons and inviting them in for a quick one. But if they didn't have a sense of humor, I doubted they drank on the job.

I didn't have a second thought about who was following me until the sedan clipped the rear bumper of my Land Cruiser. It jacked me forward a bit, my seat belt catching my chest, as I uttered an obscenity, pressed my accelerator, and sped forward. They sped up, too. I turned my windshield wipers on high, crossing over the river locks into East Cambridge.

I tried to recall if I'd offended any of the men I'd met earlier. Did I mumble? Slump in my seat? Did I spit on the sidewalk when leaving the office? Or perhaps they knew I'd tossed my parking ticket in the trash? The sedan nicked my bumper again. I knocked it into third, hit the gas, and threaded through two, then three more cars. The rain fell harder, pinging off my hood, making it tough to see who was following. I moved in and out of more cars, stopping for a long moment at a stoplight before breaking the law and shooting through a gap in the traffic.

I thought I'd lost them at the overpass. But traffic slowed again and soon they were back. I spotted two figures in the front seat. And now it appeared two black SUVs were joining us. They looked very much like the Yukon that tried to run down Welles in Lynn. Lovely.

I might've outmaneuvered them on the crooked streets of Charlestown, a neighborhood I knew very well. But I'd made great effort to hide my new address and few knew where I lived. I headed up onto the expressway toward the Mystic River Bridge and onward into Chelsea.

I crossed the river and took the Fourth Street exit. All three vehicles followed. I made a quick right turn onto Pearl and then shot back up onto Park and then to Central Avenue. I raced down Central, past the big cemetery, the sedan passing me in the opposing lane and sliding ahead, leaving the width of a prosciutto slice between us. One SUV took the same path in the wrong lane, scattering an oncoming car up onto the sidewalk. The second SUV moved close behind, the crew boxing me in. Storefronts, packies, and triple-deckers whizzed by my window as the SUV bumped me.

My Toyota was an older model, what some might call a classic, that had a retrofitted V8 and a new suspension. They'd have tough going on denting in the hood. I had a big grille guard and a winch out front. If I found a break in the parked cars, I could run up on the sidewalk and race ahead. But after seeing *The French Connection,* I had a weak stomach for pedestrians and baby carriages.

Their box maneuver didn't last long on the narrow streets. A delivery truck lurched forward in the opposite lane, slowing the SUV and sending it to the rear of the class.

We were headed fast and hard for the Chelsea Bridge, seeing the tall lit towers now visible far in the darkness. I slowed to put more space between me and the sedan. The SUV bumped me from behind but it was too late. I had at least twenty feet between me and the sedan. I zipped forward, clipping the sedan hard at the left taillight, sending it spinning out at the next intersection. The back end swung around three times before stopping and crashing into a parked car.

The two SUVs tightened up the chase as I zipped around the car.

I downshifted into third at a red light, the second SUV and I barely making it though. As we raced forward, the second SUV got T-boned by a white van, sending it reeling and spinning in the rearview. Unless the last SUV was equipped with a gun turret, I could lose them. We both headed over the Chelsea Bridge and into East Boston. I heard sirens but did not look back.

We were out of the narrow neighborhood streets and deep into a no-man's-land of metal warehouses and big oil tanks, gated lots locked with high chain-link fences. My plan was to keep driving and trying to evade, all the way to Canada if necessary. The driver grew more aggressive in the open space, coming up fast in my rearview mirror. The SUV nudged me again, the driver trying to duplicate my pit maneuver, but wasn't quite able to gather enough speed. I was going at least ninety along the long fence line, the SUV right behind me, our headlights stretching into the rain and darkness.

Ahead, two pickup trucks exited an access road, blocking my path and making me brake hard into a long sideways skid. It was enough for the SUV to pick me off, knocking my car up off the road and careening toward and through a chain-link fence.

My head hit the steering wheel and my ears flushed with blood. I caught my breath, unlatched the seat belt, and reached for the door handle. I ran from the Toyota across a gravel lot to behind the wide expanse of an oil tank. I heard car doors jack open and turned in time to see two men, again with ski masks and brandishing automatic rifles, exit the Yukon.

I dove Pete Rose–style into the dirt by the tank and bear-crawled twenty yards around the circular tank. They opened up with the guns, undeterred by the FLAMMABLE signs, bullets plinking off the metal holding thousands of gallons of oil. I didn't even realize I already had my .38 in my hand. I found a metal staircase to hide under and wait and pray we weren't blown all the way to Nantucket.

My breath was harsh and lousy in my ears. The rain was in my eyes. I wiped my face and found blood and sweat on my sleeve. I waited. I heard footsteps and yelling.

I found a spot to level my .38 on a metal step, waiting for the first one, who rushed forward in the blackness.

As he appeared, I fired off two shots.

I caught him high in the chest and he

tumbled backward. Four more shots from the other guy. I waited. I steadied my breath. I swallowed.

There were sirens. A lot of sirens coming from the Chelsea Bridge.

The black SUV raced forward and I aimed my gun right at the driver, squeezing off three shots. And then another. It slid to a stop and I reloaded. The driver leaped out, tossed the downed man in the GMC, and took off. I ran out, aiming for a back tire. But missed. The car fishtailed out onto the slick street and headed out of sight.

I walked back to my Toyota. My head felt like I'd just gone twelve rounds with Jake LaMotta. I wiped my face, blood coming from my nose.

My Land Cruiser sat crooked in a ditch, a long stretch of chain-link fence caught up under the back tires. The lights glowed and the windshield wipers slapped back and forth.

I spit out some blood, reached inside for my phone, and called Belson.

27

"And how long did that shit jam you up?" Hawk said.

"Only six hours," I said. "I left BPD this morning at two."

"Be me," Hawk said, "and my ass still be in the tank."

"You don't think it's my stellar and unblemished record with local law enforcement?"

"Sure," Hawk said. "That must be it. And your lily-white Irish ass."

We were sitting in a booth at the S&S at Inman Square. I'd had the Parisian French toast with a cup of black coffee. Hawk ordered the Nova Scotia omelet with a glass of champagne. It was eleven in the morning.

"You think you killed him?" Hawk said.

"I don't know," I said. "Belson is checking all the hospitals."

"Of course he is," Hawk said. "But if he's

a pro, he ain't going to no hospital."

I looked down at his plate. "What exactly is in a Nova Scotia omelet?"

"Eggs with lox and onions," he said. "Figured you'd know, as you into Jewish women."

"Just because I have sex with a Jewish woman doesn't make me kosher."

"Okay, white boy," Hawk said. "Next time it'll be the gefilte salad."

"Oy vey."

Hawk sipped his champagne. A gathering of old women in a nearby booth eyed him as if they'd just spotted a rare jaguar. He lifted his glass toward them and grinned. The women smiled back and nervously looked away. They chittered away among their little group. "You got some kind of trouble, Spenser," Hawk said.

"Do tell."

"And I ain't talking about the radiator on that old rattletrap you driving."

"It's a classic."

"Nothing but another word for old," Hawk said, taking a bite of his eggs. He grinned and sipped some champagne. "Might look into buying a tank. These boys you dealt with ain't like homegrown talent."

"Who are they?"

"Soldiers of fortune," Hawk said. "That's

what Sergeant hearing. Maybe working for Gredoni and mighty pissed when he ended up dead."

"They think I killed him?"

"Maybe," he said. "Maybe they did it. I only run across one of them in my travels. Fella named Brother Bliss."

"Bliss?"

"Former Army sniper," Hawk said. "Been around a long while. His passport look like a kids' coloring book."

"Doing what?"

"Same thing I do," Hawk said.

"Winning hearts and minds?"

"Sure," he said. "That what you want to call it. Heard Bliss took out three ISIS motherfuckers last year with a machete."

"And the others?"

"Figure he got a crew," Hawk said. "Don't know names." He motioned the waitress for another glass of champagne.

Hawk could probably drink a tanker full of the stuff and not feel it. I'd been up late. I stuck to black coffee.

"Bliss works out of North Carolina," Hawk said. "Cold-blooded. Covered in tattoos. Real good with a gun. Urban warfare. Blowing shit up. Why these folks want you dead?"

"Professional jealousy."

186

Hawk didn't laugh. He toyed with the stem of the champagne glass.

"They must have me mistaken for someone else."

"As in you working for Mr. Welles?" Hawk said. "Not against."

"Something like that."

"How about you try and explain it to them?"

"I tried," I said. "But it was hard to talk as they were running me off the road and shooting at me with assault rifles."

"Complicates things."

"You know a way of reaching out to them?" I said. "See what they want?"

"I'll talk to Sarge."

"I met with some ATF agents yesterday," I said. "They told me a big shipment of guns had gone missing. Probably what this Boy Scout troop is looking for."

Hawk nodded. He drank some champagne. One of the old women wandered up and asked if he played for the Patriots. She had a pen and paper in her hand. Her grandson apparently was a big fan.

I laughed. Hawk didn't.

He took the pen and paper, signed it with flourish, and gave it back. The woman beamed and wandered back to her table.

"What's it say?"

"Motherfucking Tom Brady."

"I could tell from your UGGs."

Hawk jutted his leg out and showed off his black crocodile cowboy boots. I picked up the bill and pulled out my wallet. Hawk looked at me.

"Only fair," I said.

"Where you think you're going?"

"Home."

"Nope."

"They don't know where I live."

"They will."

"I didn't ask you to jump into this mess."

"Too late."

I nodded. "Your standard rate?"

Hawk grinned. I paid the check and we left together.

28

"Don't you feel bad?" Susan said.

"Not at all."

"You're in bed naked with me," she said. "And Hawk is out there. Somewhere."

"Would it be better if I were punishing myself with some form of self-flagellation?"

"Maybe."

"He'd still be out there," I said. "Watching. If he's not, then he won't do any good."

"I still feel bad."

"He's Hawk," I said. "Not a puppy."

"Can I bring him some coffee?" she said.

"I'll bring him some coffee," I said. "I'd like you to be clear of all this mess until it's over."

"I'm already in it," she said. "In fact, I was in it before you."

"Have you spoken with Connie?"

Susan's head was on my chest. I was drinking a bottle of water. Pearl was out in the family room, snoring on Susan's couch.

I could hear the TV playing Animal Planet. Pearl was a big fan of Animal Planet, particularly shows about rare or endangered species.

"I don't think it violates any ethics if you confirm she's had an appointment."

Susan didn't answer. I stroked her slick hair and handed her the water bottle. She drank down most of what was left and turned on her stomach, looking up at me through a tangle of black hair. "You didn't tell me about your visit with Connie the other night."

"Not much to tell."

"She's pretty tough on herself," Susan said. "Being taken for that kind of money by a man no one seems to really know has hit her hard. Her confidence. Her self-esteem. She's pretty lost and desperate."

"Welles, or whatever his name is, is a true predator," I said. "He was looking for a woman just like her to con."

"Do you think he might hurt her?"

"Physically?" I said. "I don't think so. But I can't figure out why he'd want to see her again. He has her money, after all. I don't believe it had anything to do with calling me off."

"Ego," Susan said. "He must make her understand that what he did was right. And

190

in her best interest."

"A true con man would've been long gone," I said. "And wouldn't look back."

"Do you think he might have killed Gredoni?"

"At this point, everything is on the table," I said. "But as Gredoni continued to sing his praises, I believe these men just happened to get to him first. They were partners. Welles is next on their list."

"And you?"

"I'll try and keep a wide berth until I sort it out."

"All about guns?"

"It seems that way," I said. "The ATF believes Welles was Gredoni's supplier. A few of their guns ended up in some gang action in Boston."

"Did Connie discuss leaving this alone?"

"No," I said. "Unless you know something I don't?"

"Perhaps you need to discuss the matter with her," Susan said. "If she were to drop the case, about getting her money back, what would you do?"

"Leave it to the Feds," I said. "This isn't my job."

"Exactly."

"I know you can't say," I said. "But can you give me a hint just exactly what the hell

191

is going on? It seems I can't get a straight answer from anyone these days. Welles, Connie, the Feds, and now the woman who shares in my carnal delights?"

"Carnal delights?"

"What else would you call it?"

Susan whispered into my ear.

"True."

Susan pushed herself up off the bed. Her body was lean and impressive. When she wasn't shrinking, she took a lot of yoga classes. I turned on my back, hands behind my head, and admired her. She slipped into a silk robe and sat at the edge of the bed.

"Were you looking at my ass?" she said.

"Yes."

"I don't like to break down these barriers," Susan said. "I have my work. And you have yours. But I involved you in something that's grown to be quite dangerous. This happened one time before, and although I'm serious about my profession, I don't care to see my sweetums filled with a bunch of holes."

"Aw," I said. "You do love me."

"Madly," she said. "You big galoot."

Susan placed her hand on my knee. I had a fresh pair of jeans somewhere and some clean underwear and T-shirts. I planned on showering and then taking Susan to the basement dining room at the Russell House Tavern. They had the best deviled eggs this side of Alabama.

"She's seeing him," she said. "For whatever reason, she wants him back."

"Damn," I said. "I didn't see that one coming."

"She's still very in love with Welles."

"She told me a much different story the other night."

"She didn't want to disappoint you," Susan said. "You might have noticed she has a thing for needing approval from older men."

"I told her to find a nice man her own age."

"That won't happen."

"Would it be too trite to make it all about daddy issues?"

"Not at all," Susan said. "My job is often to uncomplicate the complicated."

"And where might I find Welles?"

Susan stared at the opposite wall. She'd hung a very long print of Monet's *Water Lilies* there. She'd bought it on her last trip to the Musée de l'Orangerie in Paris. I understood it had been painted to give a sense of peace to urban dwellers. Susan swallowed and put her hand on my knee again.

"Any higher and I might scream."

"She didn't say for sure," she said. "But she hinted he'd been in her bed."

"Now, was that that hard?"

"Yes."

"The things a gumshoe must do to get information."

Susan grinned and tightened the sash on her robe. "I'll leave the cash on the dresser, sweetheart."

29

Hawk and I spent the next two nights watching Connie Kelly's place. We ate a lot of grinders, drank a lot of coffee, and talked a lot about baseball, boxing, old movies, and jazz. I had nearly convinced him that Ella was as good, or perhaps better, than Billie Holiday. We both found common ground on Count Basie and Duke. There was discussion on Blossom Dearie and Rocky Marciano. At some point we analyzed the films of David Lean, deciding there was nothing better than *Lawrence.* We took turns going to the bathroom at a nearby 7-Eleven and on the first night drove off at daybreak.

We slept most of the next day at my condo in the Navy Yard and were back on it at nightfall. Hawk brought a couple CDs by Ali Farka Touré and we discussed his recently discovered Mali heritage. He played the melodic music in his Jag, since my

Toyota promised to be in the shop until Christmas.

On the second night, Connie left and we tailed her to the Trader Joe's on Newbury Street. Hawk followed her inside and came back with a bag full of donuts and two hot coffees.

"How good is your source on this?"

"Pretty good," I said. "I traded sex for the information."

"That's got to be worth at least a nickel."

"Shall I detail my amazing stamina?" I said.

"Nope."

"Anything changed for you in that department?"

"Only gotten better, babe."

"Of course it has."

Hawk grinned and turned up the West African music. We followed Connie back to the South End and watched her park and walk back inside her brownstone. Hawk studied her gait as Ali Farka Touré played a song called "Ruby." He explained a little bit about Mali forging the DNA for American blues.

"Maybe you should teach a class at Harvard," I said.

"And you on white ballplayers no one heard of."

"Good to know stuff."

Hawk nodded. "How much this woman really know about Welles?"

"Next to nothing," I said. "But despite him ripping her off, somehow she trusts him."

"Guess you really never know someone."

"Sure you do," I said.

"What's my real name?" Hawk said.

I shook my head. He'd used a couple different names back when we were fighters. I wasn't sure which one was correct. Neither seemed right to me.

Hawk told me. It was neither.

"No foolin'," I said.

"No shit."

Hawk leaned back into the driver's seat. The rain came down in long, driving silver sheets. It was very loud on the roof of his Jag.

"You know where I live?" Hawk said.

"Never wanted to know," I said. "In case someone asks, I can never lie."

We drank some coffee and ate a few donuts. We listened to some more music from Mali. He played a woman he'd played for me before, a woman named Oumou Sangaré. We talked a bit about when we were young fighters, opponents we'd both faced. The ones who'd gone on to fight title bouts and make something of themselves. And others who never did anything with their lives.

"You came from out West," Hawk said.

"Laramie."

"Raised by your daddy and your momma's brothers."

I nodded.

"Why'd they come to Boston?"

"Work," I said. "They were all carpenters. More stuff to build in Boston. One of my uncles was seeing a woman from Waltham."

"Any still living?"

I shook my head. "Last uncle just died," I said. "He'd gone back to Wyoming a long time ago. He became an old man. You?"

"Family?"

"Yeah."

Hawk shook his head. We didn't talk for a long while as the rain kept on coming down. I saw a light switch on in the turret of Connie's condo and her brief shadow appear. The donuts weren't bad but were a far cry from Kane's. Still, I'd met few donuts I didn't like.

"You boxing awhile when we met," Hawk said.

"My uncles," I said. "And then I met a cop who got me into a gym."

"What happened to him?"

"Someone shot him," I said. "He died."

At ten, Hawk got out with an umbrella and went to the convenience store down the street. Fifteen minutes later, he was back. I took the umbrella and walked to the store, used the facilities, and got more coffee.

"Then you got Henry to train you," he said. "And I got Bobby Nevins."

"Good men to know."

"Damn right," Hawk said.

A little past midnight, a silver BMW pulled up across the street from Connie's place. A man in dark clothing got out and walked across the street. A car passed by him and flashed light into his face.

It was Welles.

30

I knocked on the door. And Connie Kelly answered.

She didn't look pleased to see me, but I gave her my very best smile in return. It was the kind of smile that made grown women run in circles and climb walls using only their fingernails. I held the umbrella high over my head and waited on the stone steps. "Would you believe my car just ran out of gas," I said. "Can I use your phone?"

"I wish you'd called," she said. "Now isn't a good time."

"Company?"

"Yes."

"Anyone I know?"

"My private affairs are none of your concern," she said. Connie tried to shut the door. I stopped it with the flat of my hand.

"If you don't let me in," I said, "I'll start singing 'On the Street Where You Live.'"

Connie didn't seem to know what to say.

She was wearing skinny jeans and a tank top. As she clenched her jaw, she folded her arms over her chest and glowered at me. "It's late," she said.

"I have some new information."

"We can speak in the morning."

"This can't wait," I said, pushing past her into the foyer. A television was on in the living room, playing some kind of war movie. A lot of bombs were dropping and guns firing. An older man's voice called out, wanting to know who was there. It was loud and boastful, full of a lot of self-confidence and authority.

"Come on out, Welles," I said. "Someone put on some coffee. We need to talk, and this might take a while."

"This doesn't concern you," Connie said.

"Since when?" I said.

Welles walked out from the TV room. He had on khaki pants and a blue Oxford cloth shirt rolled to the elbows. He had a shiny gold watch on his left wrist and a pistol in his right hand. I walked up and snatched the gun from him and told him to go sit down. Connie looked nervous, wrapping her arms around her body and shaking her head. Welles stared at me, openmouthed.

"Cream," I said. "One sugar."

I followed Welles into the living room,

pocketing the gun and reaching for the remote to turn off the television. They'd been watching a very bad movie, a retelling of Pearl Harbor with little or no historical accuracy and abhorrent acting. The room suddenly became very still and silent.

"Your friends from the other night tried to kill me," I said. "What are they looking for?"

"Connie," Welles said, never breaking eye contact with me. "I'd like some coffee, too. I think you, me, and Spenser need to have a little discussion about the details of his employment."

He tried out a smug look. It would have been pleasurable to knock it off his face. "The details change when someone tries to shoot me," I said. "Maybe I'm the sensitive type. I take it personally."

"Like I told you," Welles said, settling back into the sofa. A man trying to look very much in charge. The nodding gray head, the folded hands. "This does not concern you. You drop out and no harm will come to you. You saw what they did to John Gredoni. I mean, my God."

"Brother Bliss killed Gredoni?" I said.

Welles attempted to look unfazed that I knew the name. He just stared at me and nodded. But I saw a little flicker in his left eye, knowing the information took him aback.

"Okay," I said. "Why?"

"John was outmatched on this," he said. "He didn't know his limits. I should have never agreed to include him."

I couldn't help myself. I started to laugh.

"You think this is funny?" Welles said. "You say you know Brother Bliss. But do you know who he really is? What he does to people? His reputation."

"I heard he's an artist with the machete," I said. "And no friend to terrorists."

"Or low-level Boston snoops."

"Don't kid yourself, Welles," I said. "I'm a very high-level snoop."

Connie brought in a tray of coffee. She set it down on a table and then stood back, as if the cups and saucers might explode at any minute. I was bold. I reached over, added one sugar and a little milk. I stirred it all very carefully in case it contained any explosives.

"Gredoni went back on his word," Welles said. "It's as simple as that. Then they wanted him dead. And me, too. I've tried to explain I have nothing to do with what happened and have absolutely no idea how this all fell apart. There was trouble with Gredoni, but they've gotten it into their heads that you and I are part of this."

"The gun deal."

Again, Welles tried to look calm. His gray hair had been combed neatly over his head.

His khakis were perfectly cuffed at the ankle. He crossed his legs, not making any moves for the coffee and not saying a word. Again, the left eye crinkled a bit as he readjusted the golden watch on his wrist.

"Lots of assault rifles," I said. "An RPG or three. A good little starter kit to take over a bank or a third-world country. Where are they now?"

Welles smiled. He nodded. "You're good," he said. "Very good. I guess you're not low-level after all."

"Thanks so much." I drank some coffee. It was warm and pleasant in the room. A small fire was going and a light, cold rain tapped against the window.

"I wish we'd had more men like you at the Agency."

"Aw, shucks."

Welles offered his palms and shrugged without modesty. He reached over and added a lot of sugar to the coffee. Connie stood frozen in the doorway. She continued to wrap herself with her arms as if very cold. Her chin quivered just a bit.

"I don't want anyone else hurt," Welles

said. "Connie wanted you to find me. Guess what? Now I'm found. I'm standing right in front of you. Mission accomplished."

"Nope," I said. "Connie wanted me to find you, turn you upside down, and shake loose the money you stole. And unless you're carrying around two hundred and sixty thousand dollars in a money belt, I'm still on the clock."

"Stop it," Connie said. "Just stop it."

She'd been so quiet that her words seemed to echo in the room. We both turned to look at her. She began to cry and wiped her face with the back of her hands.

"We're done," she said. "Brooks and I have discussed it. Everything is over. I don't need your help anymore."

"Okay," I said. "But there's the small matter of Gredoni. A friend of mine at BPD is very interested in meeting you. Can I borrow your phone?"

"No," Connie said. This time shouting it, more than just making a statement. "No, no, no. It's over, Spenser. I will pay you for your work. But I want you gone. I want you to leave me alone. I want you to leave Brooks alone. Your infringing here will only get me killed."

"Damn," I said. "I almost forgot. I have a phone in my pocket."

She and Welles exchanged a quick glance. She licked her lips and took a deep breath.

"You call the police and I'll file a complaint," she said. "You are no longer in my employ."

"A woman of a less formal education would've just told me I was fired," I said. I took another sip of my coffee. And then I stood.

I looked down at Welles and said, "Since I've met Connie I've been lied to, threatened, shot at, and had my wonderful SUV nearly destroyed. I'm out a lot of time and a lot of patience. I don't care for liars and have little stomach for con men. Especially ones who build their reputation on nonexistent military valor."

"Did you serve?" Welles said. He sounded very haughty.

"Yes," I said. "Want to see the tattoo?"

"You're a good man," Welles said, offering his hand. "You saved my life. And I owe you. But if you turn me in to the police, I'll be dead tomorrow. Brother Bliss has people everywhere. Do you really want that on your conscience?"

I shook my head, feigning sadness. "Lucky for me," I said. "I date a high-dollar shrink who can mend my psyche for a discount. But I appreciate your concern."

Welles looked to Connie. And then he looked behind her to the hallway and the front door. He removed his hands from his pockets and leveled a serious look at me. "Are you really going to stand here and make me speak with the local police?"

"You bet."

31

Late the next afternoon, Hawk and I were in the homestretch, running clockwise around the river on the Esplanade. We were nearing the Hatch Shell when the cell rang in my pocket. It was Belson. He and Glass wanted to talk. I hadn't heard a peep from them after sitting on Welles until they arrived.

"I'll get cleaned up and drive your way."

"No," Belson said. "We'll come to you."

Hawk and I barely had time to catch our breath before Belson's unmarked sedan illegally parked by the footbridge. Along the river, the sycamores and river birches had a golden glow. Willows brushed and swayed in the morning wind. It was almost pleasant until I saw the scowl on Glass's face.

Hawk kept walking toward the Shell. I moved toward the Charles River Bistro, a little open-air restaurant. Glass took a seat at a round table. I joined her.

"You sure know how to pick 'em," she said. "That Welles is slicker than goose shit."

"You're welcome."

"Like you had a choice," she said. "You lose him a second time and people would start to talk."

"What people?"

She pointed to herself and didn't smile. Captain Glass never smiled. Belson walked up to the table carrying a couple coffees and a bottle of water. He handed me the water and looked back toward the Shell.

"Hawk didn't even say hello," Belson said. "I wanted him to meet Glass."

"One hoodlum at a time," Glass said. "Tell me what Welles said last night."

"He wanted me to leave him alone," I said. "He'd convinced Connie Kelly, who, at this point, you know is my client, to say she no longer needed my services."

"Was she being coerced?" Glass said.

"In a way."

"What the hell does that mean?"

"He understands her weaknesses," I said. "She's susceptible to his targeted confidence and direction. Don't ask me how or why."

"Aren't you dating a shrink?"

"Yep."

"She didn't care for me much."

"I imagine you're an acquired taste, Glass."

"I don't have the time," Glass said. "I'm the captain of BPD Homicide. A dead person isn't a joke and I don't have time to jack around with some PI all day. I need to know what Welles told you."

"Probably the same thing he told you," I said. "That a death squad is trying to hunt him down and he fears for his life. Right?"

"Something like that," Belson said. He bit the end of a Tampa Nugget cigar and plugged it into his mouth. When he lit it, Glass looked annoyed. As did the man sitting at a nearby table. The cigar smelled of a decomposing trash heap.

"I believe some of it," I said. "I have the holes in my Land Cruiser to prove it."

"But I don't believe the why," Glass said. "Or the who. Welles blames everything on John Gredoni stiffing some gunrunners. He says these guys are blaming him, too."

"Yep, that's what he's saying."

"I think he's completely full of shit."

"He hasn't exactly gained my trust."

Belson looked across the table at Glass. Glass looked annoyed but nodded back. She reached into her purse and pulled out a thin file. She shoved it across the small table to me with a bit of distaste.

"What's this?"

"Welles's file," Glass said. "He told us his real name is Michael Wells. Without the *E*. His middle name is Bertrand. He has at least three civil suits against him in Georgia and South Carolina. He's swindled a few other women before he met Ms. Kelly. Sometimes he's a minister. Sometimes he's a financial consultant. He's been arrested three times for practicing law without a license."

"Shocking."

"Military service?" I said.

"None," Belson said.

"I couldn't find anything, either," I said. "But I was looking under the other name."

"CIA?" I said.

"Great thing about that old chestnut," Belson said, "is that the Agency can't confirm or deny. Wells is sticking by it. He says he changed his name to throw off his enemies."

"Of course."

"Harvard?"

"Ha," Glass said. "Two years at the University of Georgia in the seventies. And a couple years at Kennesaw Junior College. Animal husbandry."

"What did he say about all this?" I said.

"We had to let him go," Glass said.

"You're kidding me," I said.

"We couldn't charge him with being an asshole," Belson said.

"Or being a fraud," Glass said. "I think he has plenty of civil matters to answer for. But all I care about is finding out who killed Johnny Gredoni."

"And what did he say?"

"He gave us a couple aliases of shooters he knows," Glass said. "Not a single name that we could run. Got a couple descriptions and some slim leads. But that's about it. The funny thing about him is that even when we told him we knew his real identity, he didn't budge. He claimed to have been doing covert business in Vietnam and South America throughout the eighties. Real *Miami Vice* stuff."

"Do you like him for Gredoni's murder?" I said.

"He's a person of interest for sure," Glass said.

"But we don't have a motive?"

She shook her head. I drained half the bottle of water. I nodded my appreciation to Belson.

"What about Gredoni's body?" I said.

Belson and Glass exchanged a long look. Glass was much slower to trust any cop business with me. It would take time, but my charm would wear her down.

"A single shot with a .22," Belson said.

"Not exactly the Gunfight at the O.K. Corral," I said.

"No sign of a struggle," Glass said. "It was quick and effective."

"And cowardly and impersonal," I said.

"If Wells did it," Belson said, "we'll get him. Despite all the bullshit and bravado, he ain't that smart."

"He's going to disappear," I said.

Glass nodded. Belson didn't answer. He just puffed on the cigar and looked out at the Charles River. All three of us sat at the table for a while. The wind off the river rattled the branches of the trees. Red and yellow leaves twirled and floated down in ticker tape succession.

"I hear the water's getting so clean that they'll allow swimming next year," Belson said.

"Would you jump in?" I said.

"Hell, no," Belson said. "I know how many bodies are down there."

32

A week later, I had been paid by Connie Kelly and closed the books on her case. Although still watching my back, Hawk widened his circle a bit. I was at my office. Hawk was at the gym. I was still changing up my routine, taking different routes home, and Hawk would show up at unexpected times and places. At night, the cops rolled by the Navy Yard courtesy of Belson. I was sick and tired of M. Brooks Welles, Mike Wells, and Connie Kelly. I was sick of head games and misdirection. I was sick of the back-and-forth and attempts to pull me into the drama. I wasn't a fan of getting shot at. But more than that, I resented not being able to expose a fraud. Connie's check cleared and I was looking forward to some mundane, hopefully pedestrian, insurance work for Vince Haller.

It was early fall, but the Sox were still in the hunt. They were battling it out for first place in the division despite not being able to pull out the clutch games. I was listening to a pretty disappointing sixth inning against the Blue Jays when M. Brooks Welles — I still thought of him by that name — walked into my office.

He looked dandy in a tailored gray wool suit, a crisp white shirt with cuff links, and shiny black loafers. He had on a crimson tie adorned with the Harvard insignia. I didn't say anything. I'm sure it was a lot flashier than one from Kennesaw Junior College.

"Good afternoon," Wells said.

I nodded.

He took a seat in a client's chair without being asked. I reached over and flicked off the radio.

"Not good," he said.

"What's that?"

"The Sox," he said. "Down by two. I don't think it's their year."

"I only get nervous when they win," I said. "This streak keeps 'em hungry."

He didn't seem to understand, blandly smiling. He crossed his legs and kept the bemused smile on his face. I had half of a turkey grinder on my desk and an empty coffee cup. My .357 sat next to my table lamp, where I'd been oiling it. Happiness was a clean gun.

"I understand why you called the police the other night."

"I'm so glad," I said.

"I know you're an honorable man and have a reputation to uphold with the locals."

I didn't care for the way he'd said "locals," as in saying something was small. I nodded and let him continue. I had time. I wasn't meeting Hawk for another hour.

"I know they told you some things about me that you may, or may not, have known."

I shrugged. Chatty Cathy. Lee Van Cleef had more lines.

"But I want you to understand that my exact name or where I'm from doesn't change who I am," he said. "Or what I've done."

"Nice tie," I said.

He didn't look down. Nothing showed on his face, only a grim little smile. "I was recruited at a very early age to be in a nasty war," he said. "The sacrifices we made to stop Communism almost seem quaint today."

"Are you trying to sell me a book in the Time-Life series or do you have a point?"

"Connie is safe."

"Okay."

"And very much loved."

"As much as the two socialites suing you

in Atlanta?"

"That was a misunderstanding," he said. "Connie is very different. We have something very, very special. Those women were shallow and coarse."

"Sure."

"You don't believe me?"

"Wells, if you were to tell me we were sitting in the Berkeley Building at this very moment, I may begin to have doubts."

"That's fine," he said. "I don't need you or anyone else to believe me. I used to have a family, and my wife and children had no idea what I did on these so-called business trips. They believed I worked for Gillette and was selling razors in third-world countries. Isn't that funny? I would come home after equipping guerrillas with U.S. weapons and go to PTA meetings and baseball games. No one knew then. Few believe me now."

"Maybe you should write a book?" I said. "You could call it *American Patriot*. Catchy as hell."

"This book is going to illuminate a lot of people about what we were doing in Vietnam."

"You and Oliver Stone."

"And also won't make excuses about arming the Contras," he said. "Reagan was right. We all know that now."

"Ever see *Cattle Queen of Montana*?" I said. "Reagan and Barbara Stanwyck. Stanwyck was just terrific."

"I didn't kill Johnny Gredoni," he said. "I tried to protect him. He sold some bad guns to some bad hombres and paid the price. I liked him. He was very impressionable and very passionate. I think he would have sold his soul to do what I've done with my life."

"Be a professional liar?"

Wells laughed. It was deep and hearty, a man laughing at his own in-joke. If I hadn't been behind my desk, I would have slapped my knee.

"You can believe me or not," Wells said. "I came here to let you know you can now relax. Your life is no longer in danger. The men who killed Gredoni understand he did what he did alone. I just met with them personally. They know you were working for Connie and had no idea what was going on. They have left Boston and will never bother you again."

"Whew," I said. "That's a relief."

"Some pressure was applied," he said. "I called in favors to some old friends."

"Thank God."

"Can we just shake hands?" he said. "I think under different circumstances, we

218

might actually be friends."

"No," I said. "That would never happen."

"Connie loves me," he said. "And I love her."

"So the darkness shall be the light, and the stillness the dancing."

"Who said that?"

"I did," I said. "I just said it."

"It's real."

"Sure," I said. "Of course."

Wells stood, put on his two-dollar smile, and offered me a facsimile of the old Harvard handshake. I stood up and looked at his empty hand. "You are right about one thing."

The smile hung on his weathered face.

"If you hurt her, or steal from her again, no one will be able to call me off."

33

"Is it possible for a person to lie to themselves so constantly and deeply that at some point they believe it?" I said.

"You're kidding," Susan said. "Right?"

"No," I said. "I'm serious. Do you think at some point Mike Wells, aka M. Brooks Welles, believes he really has gone on all these adventures? That he really believes he's an American patriot?"

We strolled through the Public Garden at twilight. The reflection of the yellow and red leaves shimmered on the lagoon. Susan had on a black jumpsuit with tan clogs and a matching tan leather jacket. Her inky hair was pulled back in a bun, enormous gold earrings dangling from her ears. I was glad she was on my arm as we walked over the Lagoon Bridge. A jogger rushed past us. Two men held hands as they passed and smiled at us. They had an elderly corgi on a leash who sniffed at our legs.

"Need I remind you I have a practice dealing with people who lie to themselves every day," Susan said. "Sometimes people lie to themselves for good. Sometimes people lie to themselves to cover up guilt or deal with some kind of childhood trauma. We could probably speak indefinitely about all the ways a person can lie to themselves."

"But to believe it," I said. "To actually believe you are actually someone else."

"Like George Washington?" Susan said, pointing up at the statue. "Or even God?"

"Don't get too deep on me here, sister," I said. "I just can't figure out why Wells continues to stick by the ruse to someone who knows the facts."

"What are the facts?"

Susan linked her arm tighter in mine as we moved. The swan boats had been put up for the winter and soon the lagoon would be drained for an annual cleaning. I wondered where all the ducks had gone down south. Did they always go to the same lakes and ponds? Like all Bostonians with time shares in Florida.

"The man never finished college," I said, "but he wears a Harvard tie."

"A lot of people lie about their education."

"And he claims to be a decorated vet," I said. "About as close to Vietnam he got was

221

a bowl of pho at Dong Khanh."

"Are you asking, is he a sociopath?" Susan said.

"Yes."

"Perhaps," Susan said. "But Connie Kelly has her own issues. Maybe larger than his."

"Do they deserve each other?" I said. "When push came to shove, she sided with Wells."

"I don't know what Connie deserves," Susan said. "She's a special case. But she no longer wants my help. I can't force therapy upon her."

We stopped walking. I looked to her. A willow tree at the edge of the lagoon flitted in a brisk wind, just touching the surface of the water.

"She's leaving town," Susan said. "She's quitting her job and running off with Wells."

"Might be good to know if she, or this case, were still my problem."

"No white-knight dilemma this time?" she said. "To right the wrongs and uncover the truth."

"And avenge Johnny Two Guns?"

"Exactly."

"No, thanks," I said. "As I get older, I realize I have a limited amount of time and a limited number of cases. This is Belson's and Glass's problem now."

She squeezed my arm and leaned up to kiss me.

"What's that for?"

"An apology," Susan said. "For admitting you into the circus."

"Always knew she was nuts?"

"Like I said, she's a complex case."

"How so?"

"When it comes to people shooting at you, I'm glad to let you know," Susan said. "But opening up a patient's case history isn't something I like to do. It's bad for business."

"A good reason to be nuts?"

"I told you I can't discuss it."

"Some really dark stuff?"

Susan didn't answer, silence showing her annoyance. We kept walking. We were headed to the old apartment on Marlborough to see how the renovation was going. I had no illusions about getting my place back, but we were both curious. After that, we had reservations at our table upstairs at Grill 23. I had my mind set on the scallops for an appetizer and a small filet for dinner.

"She had been routinely and consistently abused," Susan said. "That makes a person susceptible to putting their immediate trust in a person of power."

"Even if the power is fake?"

"Confidence is a draw for many."

"And why didn't she throw herself at me?"

"You were off the market," she said. "Taken by another key authority figure."

"Ah," I said. "Did I tell you Wells has at least three other lawsuits against him? All women. All former lovers who he conned."

"I imagine it will be lovely until the cash runs out."

"Some people aren't happy unless they get back to what they know."

"Abuse."

"Abuse by those in power."

"And for children," I said, "that would be a parent. A father. Or an uncle?"

Susan pulled me in tighter and said, "You're pretty smart for a guy with an eighteen-inch neck," she said. "But let's change the subject. It's making me feel uncomfortable."

"Scallops?"

"Yes."

"And a gimlet?" I said.

"Of course," Susan said. "Fresh lime juice and Ketel One."

"Stick to what you know."

"As a comely Jewish woman," Susan said, "I expect nothing less."

"It's nice to have the best."

"You bet your ass."

34

Ten days before Christmas, I drove Henry Cimoli to Logan. He was spending a week with Zebulon Sixkill out in LaLa Land.

"You'll like it," I said. "Everyone is short out there. Alan Ladd was only four feet tall."

"Five-six."

"I stand corrected."

"Veronica Lake was wasn't even five feet," Henry said. "Now, that was a broad."

"I figured you were more a Mary Pickford man," I said. "When did you see your first talkie?"

"Christ," Henry said. "Why'd I ask you for a ride? I should have taken a cab. At least a cab would've had heat."

"They fixed the back end," I said. "The heater works on its own time."

"Only you would go out and buy a dinosaur," Henry said. "I'm freezing my nuts off here."

"Maybe why Z moved back out West?"

"It'll be good to see the kid," Henry said. "Thank God he got away from you and Hawk. Pretty soon he would've been sitting around and drinking a fucking pinot noir and talking about fucking luxury cheese."

"We did our best."

"I'll let him know," Henry said.

I drove up to ticketing, popped the back hatch, and walked around to the rear of the Toyota. The body shop had done nice work. I couldn't tell where the damage had been. And the paint had much improved on the original. I lifted out Henry's suitcase, pulled out the telescopic handle, and pushed it toward him.

"You and Susan really headed to Maine?" he said.

"We plan to celebrate the holidays in front of a roaring fire at the cabin," I said. "Very Robert Frost."

"How's that sit with Susan?"

"I told her if things went south, we were within miles of a Ritz-Carlton," I said.

"Good luck with that," Henry said. He offered his hand and disappeared past the automatic doors and into the terminal. Behind the glass, large artificial trees blinked with red and white lights.

I planned on driving back to the Navy Yard to grab my duffel bag and two boxes stuffed with holiday food. Susan had her last appointment at five. That meant it would take her at least two more hours to prepare. With any luck, we'd be at the cabin sometime past ten o'clock. No cable, no electricity, enough split wood to keep us warm until April. And if all else fails, I would implore Susan to help keep me warm with her body heat.

I took the Sumner Tunnel back to the Charlestown Bridge and onward to Chelsea Street. This was one of the times I was glad not to be at my old address. As Christmas approached, Newbury Street would be impossible. Not to mention parking close to the Common, with everyone wanting to skate on the Frog Pond and see the ice sculptures. Escaping town with some good food, a portable turntable, and a few Johnny Mathis records was fine by me. I had said nothing to Henry about all the good cheese and red wine I'd packed for the trip.

My cell rang when I hit the Charlestown Bridge. It was Belson. I picked up.

"Connie Kelly is dead."

I didn't say anything.

"They found her body in some bumfuck town outside Atlanta," he said. "I thought you'd want to know."

"How?"

227

"Shot," Belson said. "Looks like a suicide. I don't know details. Not my problem."

"It's my problem."

"How's that?"

"When your client dies," I said, "you tend to want to do something about it."

"Don't get stupid and honorable, Spenser," Belson said. "You're too old for that."

"It's bad business," I said.

"Maybe," he said. "But you know as much about Atlanta as I do Taipei."

"That's where you're wrong."

"How's that, hotshot?"

"I worked a case there," I said. "Ten years ago. Someone was shooting at horses. And then someone killed the owner of the stables."

"Good for you," Belson said. "Do what you want."

"What's the town?"

"Conyers," Belson said. "Case is being worked by the Rockdale County Sheriff's Office."

"Bad Day at Black Rock?"

"Sure," Belson said. "Why the fuck not?"

Belson hung up. I drove on into the Navy Yard, parked my SUV, and headed upstairs to my condo. Pearl was waiting for me at the front door. I took her outside and called Susan as we walked. I left a message.

I called the Rockdale Sheriff's Office and left a message for the detective working the case. I called up my travel agent and asked for the first flight to Atlanta and a comfortable spot to hang my hat for a few days.

I walked back inside with Pearl. I poured her a fresh bowl of water. I poured myself a fresh glass of bourbon. Christmas lights had been strewn across the masts of the ships in the harbor. Even Old Ironsides had taken on a festive glow. I turned WBUR on the kitchen radio and began to pack.

A few minutes later Susan returned my call.

"I can't go to Maine," I said.

"Oh, thank God," she said.

"You didn't want to return to the days of yore?"

"They are days of yore for a reason," Susan said. "I prefer at least four-star service. A few Michelin stars would be nice."

"I have to go to Atlanta," I said. "Connie Kelly's dead."

"Oh, no."

"I'm trying to get a flight now," I said. "I'll bring Pearl back to you."

"I knew this," Susan said. "Somehow I knew."

"We both did."

35

I flew out at nine, rented a car at the Atlanta Airport, and drove to the edge of the Perimeter, where I stayed for the night. I got up the next morning, ate a quick breakfast, and journeyed out to the Rockdale County Sheriff's Office. A few minutes later, I met Detective Sergeant Ray Hambrick, a trim black man in his mid-thirties. He invited me into his small office and offered me water or coffee. I still had half a cup from the hotel that tasted slightly better than motor oil.

"Are you kin to Ms. Kelly?"

"No," I said. "I'm a private investigator from Boston."

"Her body was just released this morning," he said. "Her family is having a service somewhere up there for her."

"Framingham," I said. "She grew up in Framingham."

"I knew she wasn't from around here,"

Hambrick said, speaking in a cool good-ol'-boy voice. "But most folks aren't from around here anymore. Used to be just Atlanta. Now Atlanta is pretty much half the state."

"May I ask who claimed the body?"

"May I ask why you're down here?" Hambrick said. He had on a black fleece zip-up jacket with a silver star pinned on the chest.

"Sure," I said, shrugging. "She was my client."

"And what did she hire you to do?"

"And here I thought I flew all the way from Boston to ask you a few questions."

"I got a dead woman," he said. "Woman didn't seem to have a job. Or any friends. You damn right I'm going to ask a few questions."

"You don't think it was suicide."

"I didn't say that."

"You didn't have to."

Hambrick opened a side drawer of his desk and removed a tin of Copenhagen snuff. He pinched off a bit and placed it between his teeth and gum just like they say in the commercial. He reached for an empty paper cup on his desk to spit. I'd seen ballplayers and cops dip snuff, but I'd never had the smallest desire. I took it the snuff was meant to imply he was serious.

231

"Wait," I said. "No one local identified the body?"

"Nope," he said. "Neighbors in the apartment complex said she lived alone. No one seemed to know her. Or a damn thing about her."

"Where was she found?"

"Under some electric transformers outside city limits," he said. "A few miles from where she lived."

"City limits being Conyers?" I said.

He nodded and spit again. I was happy to be sipping on the bad coffee.

"Ever hear the name Michael Wells, or perhaps M. Brooks Welles?"

"No," Hambrick said. "Funny name. Should I?"

"He was her boyfriend," I said. "I'd originally been hired to find him. He'd conned nearly three hundred thousand from Miss Kelly. And then they reconciled for some reason."

"Damn."

"And he's originally from these parts."

"Double damn."

"See," I said. "Pays to be nice to wandering snoops."

"Yes, sir." He stretched and yawned, spitting a bit more into the cup. Behind him hung several framed photos of Hambrick in football gear. I nodded up over his left shoulder to the wall.

"Where'd you play?" I said.

"Georgia Southern," he said. "You? You look like a linebacker."

"Strong safety," I said. "I put on a little weight since then. Played a couple years at Holy Cross."

Hambrick nodded. His phone rang and he took the call, saying "Yes, ma'am" a half-dozen times before hanging up. He looked up and smiled back at me. "Wells?" he said. "Right? Mike?"

He wrote down both names. I also gave him a date of birth and details about the lawsuits filed in Gwinnett and DeKalb counties.

"Appreciate it, Spenser," he said.

"You mind telling me how she was killed?"

"Blunt-force trauma to the upper body."

I smiled. "I'm not a newspaperman," I said. "And as you might have noticed, I'm good at sharing."

"Shot behind the left ear," he said, ".32 cal."

I felt a bright bit of cold spreading along my back. I took a long, deep breath. "Many people shoot themselves behind the ear?"

"In my experience?" he said. "Not really."

"Find anything else?"

"Nope," he said. "Just the gun. She'd been there maybe two, three days. Some kids skipping school found her. Messed them up real good."

"Any other trauma?"

"Like, was she beaten or raped?"

I nodded.

"Not anything our coroner saw," he said. "Body was sent to state examiner in Atlanta and then released this morning. Should get more tests back at the first of the year."

"Holidays are a bad time for murder."

"State's always slow," he said. "And we don't exactly break murder records out here in Rockdale."

"Who else did you speak to besides the neighbors?" I said.

"Her mother," Hambrick said. "Local cops knocked on her door. I called up after. She told me that Miss Kelly had moved down from Boston for her work. Said Miss Kelly had been going through a lot of stress lately because of her new job."

"She didn't move down here for work."

"I know," Hambrick said. "She quit her job up in Boston back in September. I spoke to her boss. Some woman, I can't remember her name, at some charity? The woman said Miss Kelly just walked out."

"To be with Wells."

Hambrick nodded. "I'll definitely pass it on."

"Wait," I said. "Isn't this your case?"

"Not anymore," Hambrick said. "Couple boys from the ATF stopped by yesterday. They said they are taking it over."

"They tell you why?"

"Nope," he said. "But I figured with ATF it could only be three things."

"I can tell you it's not about alcohol or tobacco."

Hambrick had been spinning the tin top of his Copenhagen on his desk. He stopped and lifted his eyes at me. "You shitting me?" he said. "This lady connected to guns?"

"I'd like to talk to the agents," I said. "Mind passing on their names?"

He reached into a desk and tossed me a card. It was Bobby Nguyen from the Boston Field Office. "Y'all must be old friends," he said.

"Nope," I said. "But he'll be thrilled to see me just the same. Where exactly is the Atlanta office located? I'd like to surprise them."

"Right near the Varsity," Hambrick said. "Best hamburgers in the city. My daddy used to work there as a carhop. You know it?"

36

Bobby Nguyen met me at the Varsity. At first, I thought he wanted to treat me to lunch. And then I learned he didn't want me setting foot in the Atlanta branch office. I had shaved, put on a clean button-down, and wore my best pair of Asics, all for nothing.

"You could've just called," Nguyen said. "Instead of hopping on a plane and showing up here. We do have work to do."

"I didn't just show up," I said. "First, I flew. And then I drove down to Rockdale County. Lovely county. Did you know they have the best equestrian center in the Southeast? They had the Olympics there and everything."

"I know you're upset," he said. "I know you want to find out what happened to your client. But it's the best thing for everyone involved if you just pack up, head back to Boston, and have a merry Christmas."

"Doesn't work that way," I said.

"Why's that?"

"Connie Kelly hired me to help her," I said. "Now she's dead. I'd say I owe her."

"Maybe," Nguyen said. "But what happened to her is now our business. Not yours."

"Was she killed?" I said.

"Yes," he said. "And we're pretty sure we know who killed her."

"Okay." I said. "Who killed her?"

Nguyen looked at me as if I were a dim-witted student. He only shook his head and said, "Nope."

We sat on a riser up from the endless counter of the world's largest drive-in. I'd ordered four hot dogs, which I learned meant they came dressed with chili and mustard, whether you liked it or not. Lucky for me, I liked it. I also asked for an order of onion rings and a Coke. Beyond the plate-glass window and along the interstate, the Olympic torch still burned. I watched it for a moment, ate some onion rings, and then said, "Then where's Wells? I'll ask him."

"Damn, Spenser," said Nguyen. "Come on. You start nosing around, bothering people, asking questions, and you're going to implode months and months of investigation."

"As in I might make you guys lose a truckload of automatic weapons?"

"Exactly," Nguyen said, pointing at my chest. "Yes. Exactly like that."

I took a bite of hot dog and chewed. The bun had been steamed, the chili perfectly seasoned, and the dog itself everything a hot dog should be. I approved and nodded to myself.

"Your chin," Nguyen said.

Nguyen passed me a napkin. I wiped my chin.

He wasn't eating, only sipped coffee from a foam cup. Most of the top deck of the Varsity was vacant. A checkered linoleum floor stretched out wide like a giant chessboard. I'd heard that during game weekends for Georgia Tech, they served half the city.

"It's no secret that Wells is down here," Nguyen said. "And I don't think you'll be surprised that he's a major part of what we're looking into."

"You think he killed Connie?"

Again, the thousand-yard stare. And then a disapproving look.

"He told me he didn't have anything to do with Gredoni's murder," I said. "He said it was some gunrunners that were double-crossed."

"Wells may be an absolute fraud," Nguyen said. "But he's also greedy and stupid."

"And you're not down south for the good food and hospitality," I said. "What's the connection? Besides Connie Kelly being dead."

"I was down here long before that," Nguyen said.

"Why?"

As I waited for him to decide whether he was going to answer, I ate the rest of my hot dog. I sampled a couple more onion rings. Sizzling-hot and crunchy. Henry was wrong about me. I wasn't a food snob. I just happened to like all food, as long as it was good and honest.

"If I tell you what's going on," Nguyen said, "will you leave?"

"Probably not."

"Fair enough," he said.

"But I promise to share what I learn."

"Do you remember what I told you when we first met?" Nguyen said.

I nodded. "You'd heard that I was a real pain in the ass."

"Which turned out to be true."

"I'm sticking around," I said.

"For how long?"

I shrugged. "My girlfriend is Jewish," I

said. "Christmas is just another day to go to the movies."

Nguyen took a long breath, shook his head, and reached for his coffee. He took a long sip and looked around at the empty tables. He then closed his mouth and smiled at me across the table.

"If you're down here," I said, "then guns are coming from here. This is the source of all your problems. The Georgia/Boston pipeline. Not me."

Nguyen stayed silent. I started in on the second hot dog. He didn't speak as I ate. Not surprisingly, the second was every bit as good as the first. I thought as I chewed.

"But who's the seller?" I said. "Only Wells?"

"I'm asking you to leave," Nguyen said. "And I said please."

"I would imagine that getting guns down in old Dixie is a hell of a lot easier than up in Mass," I said. "Probably worth a hell of a lot more up north, too."

"If you really want to find out who killed your client, you'll back off."

"Some of those pros who made a run at me would be involved," I said. "Maybe they're the ones bringing the weaponry up to Boston?"

"Jesus Christ."

" 'Tis the season," I said.

Nguyen shook his head, got up, pitched the rest of his coffee in the trash, and walked out without another word.

37

I doubled back to Rockdale County, where Connie Kelly had spent her last few months in an apartment complex called Magnolia Village. The apartments weren't likely contenders for *Architectural Digest*. A grid of white three-story buildings were dressed up with green spindled balconies and high shingled gables, supposedly with the vague sense of the antebellum South. Each building had different names, like Tara, Twelve Oaks, and Aunt Pittypat's. They would've looked equally at home outside Cincinnati or Detroit.

According to Sergeant Hambrick, Connie had lived in a central building on the far side of a third floor. I followed the staircase up and around. At the top of the landing, a curtain moved a bit. Nosy neighbor. *God bless us, every one.* I made a mental note and continued.

After knocking and waiting a minute or

two, I picked the lock and walked inside. Connie's apartment reeked of stale food and hot air. Two uneaten baguettes sat on a counter along with unopened bags of peanut-butter cookies and tortillas. Other than food, there was little to tell this unit from a demo model. Corporate furniture with cheap prints of flowers, dissected into scientific parts and species. The couch was yellow cloth, with modern, weirdly shaped blue chairs nearby. A large flat-screen TV hung over the fake fireplace.

I wasn't sure if the cops, or Connie's family, had removed everything of importance. There was a master bedroom, an open kitchen, a living room, and a dining room that had been turned into an office. The most notable thing about the apartment was the lack of clutter, except for the food out in the kitchen. It looked oddly clean and staged.

I checked out the bedroom first. Connie's clothes still hung in the closet. Dozens of fancy dresses and enough shoes to impress Imelda Marcos. I checked for clues in the usual spots, under the bed, between the mattresses, and in all the drawers. I had an icky feeling going through a dead woman's clothes. The smell of her perfume was still strong in the room and on her things.

After about twenty minutes, I moved on to the converted office. I found several receipts for dinners and movies, department stores, a hairstylist, and a nail salon. I placed anything of remote importance inside an empty shoebox. There were credit card bills, electric bills, and a few letters and birthday cards. None of them said much. Two of them from her mother in Mass, others from college friends. I kept on searching.

The stale air and the smell of Connie's perfume started to get to me, and I cracked a kitchen window. I moved on to the kitchen drawers and under the couch cushions and in every nook and cranny. I reached into heating and cooling ducts and came out with a handful of lint. I checked inside the toilet housings and under vanities. Connie may have made poor decisions in her love life, but no one could accuse her of being a slob.

The heat inside was tremendous. I splashed some cold water on my face and checked her refrigerator. Inside, I found a six-pack of Blue Moon ale. I took one, knowing she wouldn't mind.

I cracked the top of the beer and drank it, wandering from room to room, double-checking and looking for anything I might have missed. This time I went into her jackets and pants, searching for any shred of a clue. Sometime after five, I'd finished the beer, stuffed the shoebox full, and decided to get back to my hotel.

As I headed back to the landing, I'd nearly forgotten the nosy neighbor. Sloppy. On the list of crime-busting techniques, talking to the nosy neighbor was always in the top five. I knocked. No one answered. I knocked once more. Again, I spotted the slight flutter in a side window. I knocked again. This time, the door opened.

Nosy Neighbor was a sturdy-looking woman in her sixties. She had on a baby-blue jogging suit and wore a canary-yellow hat that read *Destin Beach.* She was very wrinkled, the makeup caking around her eyes. Her lips had been painted an unnatural hue of red, her hair bleached the color of hay.

"My name's Spenser," I said. I quickly flashed my identification that might have said Georgia Bureau of Investigation or Buck Rogers Kid Cadet. Either way, she didn't blanch.

"Miss Kelly," she said. "How very awful."

"Did you know her?"

Nosy Neighbor, who'd yet to give me her name, shook her head. "Not very well," she said. "Oh, I mean, we said hello on the stairs

245

or if we saw each other at the grocery store. Most people here don't know each other. I keep on trying to get them to have more functions at the clubhouse. Like a book club. Or something. Maybe some karaoke?"

I smiled. Mr. Wonderful. Mr. Understanding. Karaoke, what a grand idea.

"She seemed perfectly happy to me," she said. "I never would have believed it."

"The police aren't really sure," I said. "She might've been killed."

She looked confused and cocked her head like a dog hearing a high-pitched noise.

"Was Miss Kelly friendly with anyone in the complex?" I said. "Or did you notice anything strange?"

Nosy Neighbor shrugged. At the edges of her ears, her unpainted skin was lily white and paper thin. In the falling afternoon light, her face had taken on the strange look of a kabuki mask. The roots of her strawlike hair were a shocking white.

"I probably shouldn't be saying this."

I placed my hand at the top of her door frame. I gave her enough space not to feel pressure, but close enough to get her to trust me.

"This is awful," she said. "So very, very awful."

I nodded.

"I don't think Miss Kelly was a very nice woman," she said, placing her fingers to her mouth. "Now, I know she was a churchgoer. She was a Christian. I will say that."

"Church?" I said. "Where?"

"The big one," she said. "The great big one off the interstate. Greater Faith Ministries. Nobody can miss it. They have a cross up by the roadside that you can see clear on up to Atlanta."

"Why don't you think she was a good person?"

"I think she ran around with men."

"Goodness gracious."

"Yes," she said. "I saw men coming and going at all hours of the night. She didn't hold a job, I know. One man in particular was here most evenings."

I pulled out my phone from my pocket and scrolled over to a picture of Wells. I showed it to her. She narrowed her eyes but shook her head. "I don't know," she said. "I don't think so. This fella had a lot of dark hair. He looked a lot younger than that man. He got over here most nights at one in the morning."

"Nice to have a neighborhood watch."

"I'm not some kind of Peeping Tom, if that's what you're saying," she said. "I like to be careful. The world has changed."

247

I continued to smile.

"I just don't like the way things are headed these days," she said. "Our country is going to hell in a handbasket. Morals aren't morals like they used to be. Men marrying men. Blacks burning up the streets. Where does it all end?"

If I stayed here any longer, I was worried I might find myself in the middle of a Klan rally.

"Do you mind if I ask if you work?"

"I'm retired," she said. "I taught school for thirty years."

"And you don't think Miss Kelly worked?"

"She was here during the days," she said. "She'd go to the Kroger. And then to church. Did I tell you about her and that big church?"

38

I spoke with the apartment manager, who knew even less than the Nosy Neighbor. I knocked on a few more doors and got pretty much the same, but far less judgmental, answer on Connie Kelly. No one really knew her. But those who spotted her saw her in the company of a dark-haired gentleman late at night. He dressed well. Seemed polite. Sometimes she was seen carrying groceries up to the third floor. She went to Kroger. She did not join the Fantastic Friday Mixer at the clubhouse or start conversations with her neighbors. In fact, few people I found even knew Connie Kelly had lived and died at Magnolia Village at all.

It was dark by the time I drove back to Atlanta on Interstate 20. I had dinner downtown at Gladys Knight's Chicken and Waffles. I ordered the signature dish along with a side of fried green tomatoes and braised oxtails. I planned on heading back to Rockdale in the morning and checking out the church. I'd spotted it as I turned onto the interstate. The Greater Faith Life Center looked large enough to house an NFL practice facility. The cross facing the highway was massive, too. About fifty feet into the air, with spotlights illuminating the grandeur.

I ordered a second beer and a side order of collard greens. Always thinking healthy. The restaurant was narrow and neat. Framed pictures and gold records of the famous owner hung on the walls.

About nine, I valeted my rental and strolled into the Ritz-Carlton lobby. It was cold, colder than I imagined Georgia to be, and I walked with hands deep in the pockets of my jacket. I figured I might continue my night by combing through the second-half of M. Wells in the Greater Atlanta phone book when I spotted Hawk at the lobby bar.

Hawk was sitting with an attractive woman in a sparkling blue dress. She was laughing at something he had said.

"Is this man bothering you?" I said.

Hawk beamed. "You know it, babe."

He introduced me to the young woman. Her name was Madison. She was tall and brown-skinned, with legs like Cyd Charisse.

She smiled, stood, and crushed a cocktail napkin into Hawk's hand before walking off. Hawk and I both watched her walk.

"She leave you a list of her favorite books?"

Hawk studied the cocktail napkin.

"Sure," he said. "Look like she a fan of the Kama Sutra."

Hawk had an open bottle of champagne chilling in a silver bucket and a single glass. "Join me?"

"You just in the neighborhood?"

"Can't let you have all the fun down south, white boy."

A waitress walked up and I ordered a Blanton's neat with the water back. I removed my jacket and settled into the deep leather chair. The hotel gardens sprawled out wide and far in the darkness beyond. Small white lights had been strewn over the bare trees as they did back home on Newbury Street. The lobby was brass, leather, and oil paintings, just in case you wondered if they rented rooms by the hour.

"Connie was definitely killed."

"Talk to the cops?"

"Feds took it over," I said. "The Boston field agent is down here now. Guy named Bobby Nguyen."

"He must've been thrilled to see you."

251

"His enthusiasm was palpable."

"Learn anything?"

I shrugged.

"Besides nothing," Hawk said. "What else you got?"

"Looks like Connie Kelly found God in the Bible Belt."

"Just in time."

"Yeah," I said. "She's a member of a mega church down in Rockdale County."

"Rockdale," Hawk said. "Mill River. Shit, man. The stuff you get me into."

"Connie asked me to help her and I couldn't do it."

"Hard to do when she asked you to butt out."

"I should have kept pressing on Wells," I said. "Find out who he really is. And what he really does."

"You do that for free?"

"I'm doing this for free."

The waitress returned with my bourbon. Hawk and I clinked glasses. I took a warming sip.

"Brother Bliss got work down here."

"Of course he does."

"And I know some folks who ain't fans of Brother Bliss."

"Will they meet with me?"

"They will meet with us," Hawk said, taking a big sip. He pulled out the bottle and refilled the glass. Iron Horse Wedding Cuvée.

"When?"

"When you want?"

"Sooner the better," I said. "I'd planned to spend the holidays with Susan at the cabin I built with my own two hands."

"Shit," Hawk said. "Susan said to keep you down here long as it takes."

"You tell her I was at the Ritz?"

Hawk stared at me, sipping the champagne. He just smiled.

"And who exactly are we going to meet?"

"Some boys who worked for Bliss," he said. "Got to one through Sarge. Sarge say they been screwed out of some money they owed. Might take a little money to get them to open up."

"Ho, ho, ho."

"You drunk?"

"No," I said. "But I'm not against the idea."

I drank some whiskey and looked around the lobby. There was a medium-size tree with white lights and small candles lit upon tables around the bar. Simple and tasteful. Quiet and relaxed.

"Don't you have somewhere better to be during Christmas?" I said.

"Nope."

"If you're here," I said, "these dudes must be pretty bad."

"The baddest," Hawk said.

"Terrific."

"My specialty."

We clinked glasses again and made plans for the morning.

39

We agreed to meet with Hawk's contact the next morning at a Cuban restaurant on Buford Highway. Buford Highway was pretty much the Route 1 of Atlanta. Plenty of fast-food franchises, run-down strip malls, and car dealerships. Many of the businesses along the highway advertised in Spanish. I pondered this momentarily while ordering a café con leche and an egg sandwich. Hawk drank a shot of Cuban coffee and studied the door. Hawk always sat facing the door.

"I haven't had Cuban food since we went down to Florida."

"Good times," Hawk said.

"Jackie DeMarco's crew."

"Jackie ain't done with your ass yet."

"Nope," I said. "He's stupid. But not forgetful."

Hawk stretched in a black turtleneck and a black leather jacket cut so tight it looked like second skin. I'd been wearing my A-2 since we landed. But I'd switched up the Braves cap for the Sox road cap, showing diversity and loyalty.

"How do you know this guy?" I said.

"We on the same team a few times."

"You trust him?"

"Much as I trust anyone."

"Much as you trust me?"

"Haw." He sipped on the small cup of oil-black coffee. A few minutes later, a beefy man with a buzz cut and a mustache walked in the front door. He had on a blue cop uniform and a walk and build similar to Ferdinand the Bull. I was disappointed to see he didn't carry a flower in his teeth.

Hawk introduced him as Drew Frye. He was a former Marine and a current patrol officer for Atlanta PD. He had small, mean eyes and a crooked, busted nose. His nose was only slightly better than my own. Frye clasped Hawk's hand warmly and smiled, saying it had been too damn long. Hawk introduced me. I shook his hand.

"Don't tell me y'all want to work for EDGE?" he said. His voice sounded as if he gargled with gravel.

I looked at Hawk. He didn't answer, nothing registered in his eyes.

"Well, if you do," Frye said, "good luck

getting paid. Folks leaving that operation like rats off a leaky ship."

"How much they owe you?" Hawk said.

"Five grand," Frye said. The radio on his hip squawked for a moment before he switched it off. There were six other people in the restaurant, most of them getting to-go orders at the register. Coffee in foam cups and food in white paper sacks. Morning in motion.

"Who runs things?" Hawk said.

"Brother Bliss," he said. "Remember him?"

Hawk nodded. "Mmm."

"That thing in Burma."

"Yeah."

"Some real shit," Frye said.

"Yes, indeed."

I leaned back and ate my sandwich. It was nice having someone to take the lead in the investigation. I had more time to enjoy breakfast and check out the comely young commuters grabbing their morning coffee. I smiled at a nice woman in skinny jeans and a parka with a fur-lined hood.

"Since when is Bliss down this way?" Hawk said. "Last I heard, he was somewhere in North Carolina."

Frye craned his neck behind him, and then glanced around the restaurant. His mustache twitched a bit. "Came down two years ago," he said. "He set up a training school and a gun range for macho dipshits from the city. I helped at first. But then the paychecks stopped coming. I don't have time for that crap."

"Ever heard of a man named Wells?" I said. "Says he's a former CIA officer?"

Frye looked at me and shrugged. "Nope," he said. "But I wasn't out there long. Taught a few classes. Mainly worked the range."

"Where they train?" Hawk said.

"Rockdale," Frye said. "It's about —"

I held up my hand. "I know it," I said. "Where, exactly?"

Frye said the range was fifteen miles from Conyers on a back road deep within Rockdale County. I was sure a couple city slickers like me and Hawk would fit right in. Frye adjusted his meaty elbows on the table and smoothed down his mustache.

"I can hook y'all up," he said. "A friend still works for Bliss. God help him. He doesn't like or trust him one damn bit."

"Love to meet him," I said.

"So," Frye said, leaning back and crossing his arms over his barrel-size chest. He stared at me, and then switched back to Hawk. "What's y'all's deal in this?"

"No deal," Hawk said. "Just getting the

lay of the land."

"Sounds like you going after Bliss," Frye said.

"I don't give a good goddamn about Bliss."

"Sure," Frye said. "But if you do, my friend will watch your back. He's a cop, too. Just looking for a little side action."

"Why's he still with Bliss?" I said. "If he doesn't like or trust him."

"Sticking around until he gets what's due," he said. "Hard head. Keeps believing he'll finally be paid out."

Hawk nodded.

"Man, it's good to see you, Hawk," Frye said. "I tried to find you after we got airlifted out. But you're a hard man to track down."

"Found you right quick, Frye," Hawk said.

"Shit." Frye shrugged. "I got nothing to hide."

Hawk smiled.

"Just what went on in Burma?" I said. "Handing out condoms to the poor?"

"Do you really want me to tell you?" Hawk said.

"Might it implicate me in some international shenanigans?" I said.

"Just business," Hawk said.

Frye grinned. He readjusted the shield on

his chest and grinned. "Long time ago, man," he said. "Now I got a wife, two kids, and one big-ass mortgage."

"Anything get you out of retirement?" Hawk said.

"And back in the life?"

Hawk nodded.

"Oh, hell, no," Frye said. "After the last one we did, I burned my damn passport."

40

"What do you think?" I said.

"No reason to doubt Frye," Hawk said. "But better be locked and loaded."

"Then what?"

"I'm just making this shit up as I go along, babe," he said. "How 'bout you?"

"I'd switch up my style," I said. "But so far, so good."

We were headed east on Interstate 20 in my rental. I was driving and Hawk was staring straight ahead behind his dark sunglasses. He was humming "Rainy Night in Georgia." The sun was beginning to set, a deep chill settling in down south.

"Ambush?" I said.

"I know Frye," he said. "Not this other motherfucker."

"Sure," I said. "What could go wrong?"

"That's why we called a meet in a public place," Hawk said. "Ain't no black man likes to spend time with gun-toting honkies in the piney woods."

"People still say honky?"

"Yeah."

"Good to know."

"You still in touch with that gay caballero down here?"

"Tedy Sapp."

"Yeah, Tedy."

"He used to send me a Christmas card every year," I said. "And a mix tape of dance music that he knows I don't like."

"Still doing security work?"

"Far as I know."

"Might be good to have an extra hand," Hawk said. "Just in case."

I nodded. Hawk began to hum again. This time it was "Delta Dawn" with a slight little vocal bit, *"What's that flower you got on."*

"Just how does a black man get into country music?"

"Outlaw country, man," Hawk said. "Outlaw country."

"You, Willie, and Waylon."

Hawk didn't answer, just kept humming. Not far past the Rockdale County line, I spotted the exit where we'd agreed to the meet. I edged off the highway, driving through a thicket of trees and around the back of a large brick building perched atop a hill. There were bathrooms, Wi-Fi, travel information, and picnic tables for visiting gunmen for hire. Hawk exited the car and disappeared. I wandered into the rest stop and looked through brochures to Six Flags over Georgia and a laser light display to Confederate heroes shone upon Stone Mountain. I learned you could still pan for gold in the mines of Dahlonega.

Thirty minutes later, dusk turning to night, a black SUV wheeled into the lot and two men got out of the front seat. I spotted Frye with another white man who wore military-style khaki pants and an Army-green shirt. Frye had changed out of his Atlanta PD uniform into jeans and a dark blue jacket. He held a big flashlight loose in his hand. I walked the perimeter of the inside of the rest stop, checking out the entry road and the exit. I watched the tree line. I watched the front lot. I watched the back.

I knew Hawk was doing the same. Maybe a dozen or so families milled about the open space. Some walked dogs. Others let children play in heavy winter coats and wool hats. A fat woman in a pink coat held the hand of a young girl in a parka, walking back to their car. Frye and the other man headed over to a picnic table and sat down on the top. I wasn't sure of the law in

Georgia, but both men wore guns on their hips. If they wanted to start trouble, there would be a lot of witnesses. And they wouldn't make it far down the interstate from the Highway Patrol.

Hawk emerged from somewhere in the woods a minute later and approached them. I walked past a man and a woman and their two young boys. The children were complaining about really needing to pee. I dismissed the family as clever assassins.

I walked back into the cold, down a concrete walkway to where Hawk stood with Frye and his pal. They looked my way but did not stand, or offer to shake hands. The lack of southern hospitality was disconcerting.

"This here's Mr. Miller," Hawk said.

I nodded but didn't introduce myself. Frye nodded in my general direction.

"Who's this?" Miller said, jacking his fat little thumb in my general direction.

I shrugged. "Package deal. Like salt and pepper."

Miller scowled. Frye smiled.

"Heard y'all on the outs with EDGE," Hawk said.

"Hard to respect an outfit that won't pay what you're owed," Miller said. "That whole

shit show is unraveling by the fucking minute."

"Bliss still running the show?" Hawk said.

Miller looked to Frye. Frye nodded. It was
very cold and our breath clouded the air.
The trees were tall, leafless, running for
miles into the deep woods. Cars came and
went. A large RV wheeled into the lot, and
a group of Asian men and women crawled
out, exhausted.

"Ever heard of a guy named M. Brooks
Welles?" I said.

Miller nodded. "Hell, yeah. Of course. I
know Pastor Wells."

"Pastor?" I said. I couldn't help but grin.

"Sure," Miller said. "He started the whole
operation for Greater Faith. Shit, I thought
you knew all about these guys."

I tried not to look surprised. Pastor Wells.
Greater Faith. Guns, guts, and glory. Sure,
I know the whole damn thing. I was just
down here whistling Dixie.

"Before he claims he found Christ, he
worked for the Agency," Miller said. "He
runs security for the church and the training compound. After I retired from the
Army, I started to work out at the range.
Are you trying to bring down the church
and Wells? Because if you are, I'm so fucking
in."

"What do you think of Wells?" I said.

"I think he's as phony as a three-dollar bill," Miller said.

"That's pretty phony," I said.

"I don't think he was ever with the Agency," Miller said. "Or did all those things he claims he's done in his sermons. Arming the Contras. Fighting the Vietcong. All this Navy SEAL bullshit. Did you know he's on television? He told us that Michael Bay was going to be making a big movie about his life."

"Amazing," I said.

"Miller can get you inside, Hawk," Frye said. "If that's what you want? Bliss knows who you are and what you do."

This time Hawk and I exchanged looks. Although Hawk didn't show a thing on his face or behind the glasses. He simply nodded, taking it under consideration. They seemed friendly and eager to help. If they could get Hawk on the inside, he might be able to find out Wells's mission. Which I didn't believe involved helping the meek inherit the earth.

"Have you heard the name Connie Kelly?" I said.

Miller shook his head.

"She was killed last week," I said. "She was Wells's girlfriend."

"Girlfriend?" Miller said. "Ha. That sounds about right. Most of the time he's preaching about being a big family man. Great husband who lives for his wife and kids."

"Wells ever talk about his time in Boston?" I said.

"Listen, man," Miller said. "You can stop all the secrecy. I know who you are. And why you're here."

"You do?"

"Wells paid me and another guy to attack him in that alley in Boston," he said. "And then he was supposed to pay us for taking you out."

"Glad that didn't work out."

"That's when we knew it'd gone too far," Miller said. "You fucking shot me."

"You're looking pretty good now."

"I was wearing a vest," he said. "When I got back, Wells stiffed us. We could've gotten arrested."

"Did you guys kills Gredoni?"

"No way."

I studied his face. He stared back. His eye didn't twitch, nor did he stutter. Sometimes even a veteran crime buster like myself had a hard time spotting liars.

"What about running guns?"

"Oh, no," Miller said. "That deal was

between Brother Bliss and Pastor Wells."

"Where's Wells now?"

Miller looked at his watch and then back at me. "Where else?" he said. "Church. I heard he's even preaching tonight."

"Praise the Lord," I said.

Hawk grinned. Just a bit. Frye shined the flashlight down the path to the parking lot. "This is far as I can take you," he said. "Good luck."

Frye shook our hands and left with Miller. We watched them drive off and head back onto the interstate.

"Trust is a slippery slope."

"Trust?" Hawk said. "Joining up with this crew more about faith."

41

I wasn't really sure how to dress for the Wednesday-night service of Greater Faith, as I hadn't been in church since the Carter administration. I wore a navy jacket with gold buttons over a white button-down and khaki pants. As soon as I entered the sanctuary, I knew I'd overdressed. Many people wore jeans and T-shirts. Some had on sweatshirts and baseball caps. If I'd worn a ball cap inside a restaurant or church, my father would have made me eat it.

Hawk decided to skip the show, running down other business. The crowd was black and white. Many Latinos.

By the time I found a place to sit, the service had started. It wasn't hard, as there were hundreds of empty seats. The seats were fanned out in theater style with a Jumbotron set high above the pulpit. A rock band and a gospel choir played together on a brightly lit stage. The music was a bit like

Andrew Lloyd Webber meets Three Dog Night. By the third song, I had yet to year "O Come, All Ye Faithful" or "Silent Night."

The congregation stood and swayed with the music, hands raised high. I would have raised my hands but feared my .38 might drop into the aisle.

I spotted Wells enter the stage and stand by several of the performers. He'd dyed his silver fox look to a dark brown and wore a conservative navy suit. After a song finished, he took to the pulpit.

"It's a wonderful privilege to be able to worship freely," Pastor Wells said. "But as many of you who follow my sermons and newsletters know, that's not the same for our brothers and sisters in the Middle East. Christians continue to be persecuted and killed for their faith in Iraq, Lebanon, Libya, and Syria. In Syria, Christians face a mass genocide we haven't seen since the Second World War."

I didn't doubt the message. But I waited for him to get to the money.

"As we celebrate a season born in this region, we are now faced with putting our faith to work," Wells said. "Christianity has become the most persecuted religion in the modern world. We face no less than genocide in these countries run by Muslim extremists. We must be vigilant. We must be active."

And then it started. Wells just happened to know how to get money into the hands of freedom fighters. The group was called OCS, Onward Christian Soldiers. And for pennies a day, you could make sure the terrorists didn't win.

I didn't refute the message. Only the messenger.

After he finished, Wells took a seat near the pulpit as a large black man helped a frail old white man to the podium. The old man had a hump back and great shock of white hair. His suit was blue with a wide-collared white dress shirt and wide yellow tie. His face and body were skeletal, with sunken-in eyes and saggy jowls. When he cleared his throat, a hush fell over the sanctuary. His face appeared big on the screen with the words *Dr. Josiah Ridgeway*. I might've been watching a scene from *Poltergeist*.

"Jesus Christ is alive and well," Ridgeway said in a strong but shaky voice. "Praise God. He is the King of Kings, the Lord of Lords. He is the head of the body of Christ. The strongest and most powerful thing that's ever been on the planet is the church. Father, we praise You! Love is in this house. He is in me. He is in you."

I checked my watch. Another half-hour to go.

"Whatsoever you should ask the Father in My name," Ridgeway said. "He will give it to you. He will."

Ridgeway read a passage from the Bible, complimented the choir and band, and then ran down some events on the social calendar. A Spanish service on Saturday. More volunteers were needed for a live Nativity scene. The food pantry had run low. I kept on waiting for more assault-weapon donations.

The choir and the band continued for a few more numbers. People yelled "Amen." Some cried. Lots of hands raised high and swaying. A very large woman next to me pulled me close and hugged me. After about an hour, it was over and the congregation made it toward the exits. Some walked toward the pulpit. There was a lot of talk about love. There was a lot more hugging.

I made a beeline for Pastor Wells.

He stood near a twenty-foot-tall Christmas tree wrapped in bright colored lights and big metallic-looking balls. A sign read *Merry CHRISTmas*. Wells saw me over the shoulders of a group he was greeting. His big, toothy smile disappeared and he met my eye.

I nodded in his direction. Men and women wandered up to him, shaking his hand, hugging him close. They handed him envelopes and folded checks. He patted them on the back. Double-shook their hands. I noted the small American flag pin on his lapel.

I was patient. I waited my turn.

He stood at the top of six wide carpet-covered steps. The creepy preacher, Ridgeway, sat on the opposite end, greeting others. If we waited any longer, I feared he might disintegrate into dust.

"Wow," I said. "You really have reformed."

"This is what I do," Wells said. "This is who I am."

"You washed that gray right out of your hair and dropped the *E* in your name," I said. "A complete transformation."

"This is a special place for me."

"And for Connie," I said. "Until she was killed."

"Not here," he said. He looked furtively around the sanctuary.

"Connie was my client," I said. "She was your lover. Someone killed her. Let's talk."

"Not now."

"When?" I said. "Ever hear of a come-to-Jesus moment?"

"It's not safe," he said. "She knew that. She came with me anyway. She wanted to be part of my mission. My work. I should've never put her in danger."

"Who killed her?"

I took a few steps up toward the pulpit. He continued to search the aisles with the congregation heading toward the exits. Something caught his eye and I turned to see a middle-aged woman in a bright red dress walk down the aisle with three girls. She gave him a big smile and waved. The woman held the hand of a girl in each hand. An older girl, early teens, trailed behind, looking at her cell phone.

"Mrs. Wells?" I said. "Without the *E.*"

"Please," he said. "I promise I'll tell you everything."

"I'll be waiting on pins and needles."

"My position," he said. "My position here in the church is very important. It's everything to me. It's who I really am."

"Not the international man of mystery."

"That's the old me," he said. "But this is my life. My work and passion."

The woman and the three children joined Wells up on the stage. The woman wore a curious, but bemused, expression. She had on a great deal of eye makeup and lipstick. Her brownish hair had been teased and sprayed to an exact stiffness. One of the younger girls hugged Wells's leg. The other stayed at her mother's side and stared up at me. I winked at her.

The teenage girl didn't know I was there. Or her family. She was texting someone.

"When?"

"Tomorrow."

"Mike?" the woman said. "Aren't you going to introduce us?"

He made a clunky intro to me and said something about me being an old and special friend. He clasped my hand with both of his and pumped it up and down. He leaned in and said, "Be careful. They're out there. Watching everywhere."

I tried my damnedest not to shudder.

42

"How was church?" Hawk said.

"Not as enlightening as I'd hoped."

"Ain't got that ol'-time religion?"

"They don't sing the old hymns anymore," I said. "The new songs give me a toothache."

"You see Wells?"

"Yep," I said. "I even shook his hand, against my better judgment."

"What'd he say about his old lady?"

"His old lady isn't his old lady," I said. "His real old lady was at the church. Along with his three children. He seemed to find it gauche to discuss his dead mistress in church."

"Damn," Hawk said. "Spy, TV personality, preacher, family man. Just how does he do it?"

"Hard work and integrity."

"Sure," he said. "He say anything about Miss Kelly?"

"He begged for me not to make a scene," I said. "And promises to talk tomorrow. Says we were being watched."

"Were you?"

"I doubt it," I said. "But then I'm predisposed not to believe a thing he says."

We'd switched hotels to a clean, efficient Holiday Inn just on the edge of the Perimeter. The room had two full beds. Hawk was lying on one with his hands behind his head, resting. The TV was on mute, playing *Shane*. I was at a small writing desk, counting out the ammo I'd brought. The desk had a couple postcards from the motel, a pen, and a large unopened Gideon Bible. It was late. The curtains were drawn.

"I met with Bliss," Hawk said.

"How'd that go?"

"He offered me some work," he said. "Bygones be bygones and all that."

"Won't he suspect me and you showing up at the same time?"

"Don't take me for a fool, babe," Hawk said. "He know me with contact made through Sarge. Now I got Frye and Miller vouching for me. Man knows my rep and don't know where I hang my hat. Or what kind of riffraff I associate with."

"You calling me riffraff?"

Hawk didn't answer. He pushed himself

up off the bed and walked to the bathroom, where he'd placed a bottle of Moët & Chandon in an ice-filled sink. He felt the bottle, nodded, and poured a healthy portion into a hotel glass. I'd bought a six-pack of Blue Moon and two turkey sub sandwiches. We'd both eaten but hadn't finished our libations.

"What's the job?"

"Instruction," Hawk said.

"Dance or tap?"

"Tap, tap, tap," he said. "Gun work. Busting heads."

"Might need to split up for a while."

"Bliss offer me room and board out on the range," he said. "Says he got a new crew of folks needed breaking in. That's what they do out there. They make a lot of dough training city folks for the impending end of America. I don't know how the gunrunning figures into it. Working on it."

On TV, Shane rode up to the old homestead. Jean Arthur looked worried.

"You don't have to do this."

"I didn't ask you," Hawk said. "This woman Connie a friend of yours. A friend of Susan."

"*Friend* may be too strong a word," I said. "She was our client."

"All the same."

"You find out Bliss's deal with Wells?"

"Not yet," Hawk said.

"From everything I see, the church is run by this preacher," I said. "Josiah Ridgeway. He and Wells are in cahoots. They tell the church they're raising funds for Christian freedom fighters in the Middle East."

"Instead they raising money to buy guns and flip 'em up north," Hawk said. "Josiah. Bless his old heart."

"Looks like the Crypt-Keeper mated with Lionel Barrymore."

"Lovely."

"Lots of music," I said. "Lots of hugging."

"Any black folk?"

"Plenty," I said. "You know, your people sure can sing."

"Swing low," Hawk said, singing in a decent Paul Robeson. *"Sweet chariot."*

"I'll pull some corporate records tomorrow," I said. "See how Wells, the church, and the gunrunning to Boston all shakes out."

"And talk to your boy Tedy?"

"The number I have isn't good," I said. "Might have to drive up his way and track him down."

"Figure if Wells wants you gone, he'll employ Bliss," Hawk said. "He put Bliss in motion, I'll be there to stop him."

"You really do like me."

"I ain't telling Susan that I'm bringing your ass home in a carry-on."

"I'll find Tedy," I said. "Wells will want me gone fast."

"Folks around here know his real story?"

"I'm sure he's conned plenty of locals, too."

"Guess the small shit don't matter," Hawk said. "Only if he killed Miss Kelly."

"If he didn't, he'll know who," I said. "And he'll definitely be part of the why."

"You got all the shit figured out."

"How's the champagne?"

"Mother's milk."

I drank some beer. The television flickered images from *Shane* across the spare hotel room. It was nearly the part where Shane and Van Heflin get into a big scrap. Soon horses would be spooked, water troughs overturned, and fences busted. The kid would watch with wide eyes as he finally saw some spunk from his old man.

"I'm not sure I like this plan," I said. "Lots of ways to blindside us."

"You got something better?"

"Nope."

Hawk didn't say anything. He sipped on the champagne, grinning when Shane socked Van Heflin in the jaw. At midnight, I walked over and turned off the TV. Hawk had fallen asleep with the glass in his hand.

As I reached for it, his hand shot out and snatched me by the wrist. A big .44 Magnum pulled from under a pillow. For a moment, I wasn't sure if he recognized me.

"Only me, friend," I said. "Only me."

I took the glass, washed it in the sink, and returned to bed. When I returned, Hawk lay facing the door. The trucks and cars zipped along the cold interstate outside the window.

43

I was shocked Wells wasn't at the church office the next morning. So I told a secretary
I would wait.

Not long after, two large men came into
the room and asked me to leave. These were
not the men I'd met before. They were new
and not at all friendly. They had freakish
large muscles bulging from identical blue
polo shirts with a Greater Faith logo and
cross on the breast. The secretary offered to
call the local cops. The men just stood there
and tried out tough-guy looks.

"Pastor Wells asked me to meet him this
morning," I said. "He's going to try and
work me into Sunday's show. I'm a juggler."

No one smiled.

"Juggling for Christ," I said. "Pastor Wells
knows a thing or two about keeping his balls
in the air."

I walked back to my rental and searched
for records on his wife, Patrice Wells. My

exhaustive Google search yielded an address in less than five seconds. I routed my car in that direction and set the phone on the dash. Sleuthing with Google just didn't seem fair.

Wells and his family lived in an upscale McMansion community about ten miles from the church. The tract homes had been built around a golf course and large recreational facility. Nearly all the homes looked the same. A light stone façade, tall pitched roof, and bay windows. Many of the homes had three- or four-car garages. I spotted several walkers, a few joggers, and some couples zipping around on golf carts. The neighborhood seemed very golf cart–friendly.

I parked outside the Wellses' house and rang the doorbell. Wells must've seen me from a window. He opened the door before my finger had left the buzzer.

"Good morning, Pastor."

"Just what the hell do you think you're doing," he said. "This isn't the time or place."

"Not at the church," I said. "Not at your home. Not last night. Not this morning. I'm beginning to think you don't want to talk with me."

"Not now."

"Not in a boat," I said. "Not with a goat."

"My wife is here," he said. "And my young daughters. This is my private residence."

I looked at him. "It's the middle of the day," I said. "Do I need to inform the local truant officer?"

"My children are homeschooled."

"You had two men waiting to brace me at the church," I said. "This is as good a time as any to talk. Tell your wife we're going to sit outside and have a Bible study. We're going to talk redemption the hard way."

"Are you mocking what I do?"

"You?" I said. "Yes. Very much."

"I can't speak about Connie," he said. "Under advisement of my attorney."

"I bet I can change your mind."

Wells turned his back to me and walked into the house. But left the door wide open. I followed. The giant room was cavernous, with snow-white carpeting but oddly bare of furniture or decoration. A bluish couch, a TV hung over a fireplace, some dolls with slack jaws lying on the floor. An open space near the kitchen stood wide open, no dining room table or chairs. Nothing on the walls. There were many dirty plates and glasses in and around the sink. I heard kids yelling upstairs.

He offered me a coffee. I accepted and

followed, cup in hand, to the backyard patio looking out onto the edge of a pine forest. Even with his new inky hair, Wells seemed too old to have such young children.

"You must understand my position," he said. "My work, my life elsewhere, is very separate from my home and family here."

"And you must understand mine," I said. "Your lover and my client was found dead. I'm down here to find out why. And get her money back."

"She fired you," he said. "And her money is hardly an issue anymore. Not after she killed herself. What does it matter?"

"Three hundred grand," I said. "Not a penny more. Not a penny less."

"You're joking," he said. "She's gone. She took her own life. There are much greater concerns than money."

"Nope," I said. "To be paid to the charity where Connie worked for three years. Jump-start. In your case, I'd prefer a cashier's check."

"She invested two hundred and sixty thousand in the Concord project," he said. "When it crashed, we all lost our money. I am not responsible. If you'd like to see a contract, I will speak to my attorney."

"Extra is for interest," I said. "And you're going to tell me what happened."

"She was very depressed," he said. "She'd been drinking and making threats. I didn't even know she owned a gun. Why would you think I'm responsible?"

"Wells," I said. "The only thing I think of you is not much. You are a B-movie flimflam man. You've made a living telling people you were a SEAL and a spy. And now a man of God. None of it's true."

"You're wrong," he said. "You don't know a damn thing about me. Or my faith."

"I don't care if you were Vietnam's Audie Murphy," I said. "Or the evil spawn of the Moral Majority. What happened to Connie Kelly? Who killed her and why?"

Wells placed both hands over where his heart would have been. He had on a gray cardigan over a plain button-down. He'd recently shaved and his newly brown hair had been parted neatly to the side. He had on tortoiseshell glasses in an attempt to appear studious.

"I was no longer with her."

"So she moved South for the fresh air and fine country living?"

He looked to a sliding glass door. His wife, Patrice, stared back behind the glass. She had on black pants and a long black sweater that stretched to her knees. Her arms were crossed over her chest. Wells held up a hand to her and turned back to me. "You knew her," he said. "She could be quite emotional and prone to making rash decisions. I told her I no longer in good conscience could be with her."

"God bless you, Pastor."

"She came down on her own," he said. "By the time she found me, she'd already quit her job and rented an apartment. I told her there was no way I was leaving my wife. She told me that it didn't matter. She said she'd have me any way she could get me."

"True love."

"She was too young for me," he said. "I know that. I was overstressed trying to make the business in Boston work. The Concord project was falling apart. John Gredoni had turned on me. What I did was wrong. I am not a perfect man. I know that. But now it's between me and my God. I have asked for forgiveness."

"And what did He say?"

"Someone like you can't understand," he said. "My faith is very important to me, Spenser. You can mock me and mock my church. But you're crossing the line when you talk about my very true and close personal relationship with Jesus Christ."

"I haven't met Jesus yet," I said, "but I'm pretty sure he'd think you were a creep."

Wells took off his glasses and rubbed his eyes. Slipping them back on, he looked as if he were seeing me for the first time. "When I learned Connie was dead, I hadn't seen her for weeks," he said. "We never had anything going down here. I never touched her. Our physical relationship was in the past. I give you my word."

"You never visited her apartment?"

"No," he said. "Of course not. I don't even know where she lived."

"Yeah. You did."

"Why would you think someone killed her?" he said. "The police said it was a suicide."

"Because she was about to out you and your frauds," I said. "Not only to your wife, but to your church down here and the good ol' Reverend Josiah."

"Reverend Ridgeway?" he said. "Do you think I haven't confided in my own pastor about my failures? He knows everything. Connie tried to poison my relationship with the church. She called him incessantly. Go ahead, tell him. He knows far worse things about me than you do."

It was bright and sunny and cold that morning. The flagstone patio was nearly covered in scattered leaves. Plastic toys and rusted bicycles lay haphazardly in the back lawn. A small pink plastic playhouse stood with an open door to the empty forest behind it. I drank some coffee and waited for more of the growing list of lies from Wells.

"You do realize a military record is easy to check?"

"Not mine."

"Really?"

"In 1968, I was recruited into a very special, very secret program right out of the University of Georgia. It was another time. Things were chaotic."

"And here I thought you were a Harvard man."

"I went to Harvard some years later, for graduate studies."

"Harvard has no record of you."

"Much of my life has been about disappearing," Wells said, trying his best to pass on an understanding smile. "I have eliminated much of my life before I met my wife. She and my children are top priority for me. What I have to do is all for them. I am first and foremost a husband and a father. My work as a pastor is a calling."

"Jesus."

Wells rubbed his face with frustration. "How can I explain this to some liberal

Yankee who has no idea about what I stand for?"

His face had grown red. I leaned in very close to Wells, maybe a foot from his nose. "I know about your business with Brother Bliss," I said. "I know about the gun deals with John Gredoni."

"Bliss isn't connected with the church."

"Nope."

"My work with him is separate," he said. "OCS is a special group, doing very special things. I help raise money for them. But it's not affiliated with the church."

"Why Connie?"

"I loved her," he said. "I loved her, Spenser."

"That's not what I asked."

"You won't leave this alone," he said. "Will you?"

"You're just now getting that?"

"Connie was crazy. She could not let me go. When she couldn't have me, she —"

"She what?"

Wells swallowed. I looked inside the house and pretended to wave to his wife.

"Goddamn it."

"Goodness gracious," I said.

"Who you see here is me," he said. "Simple old Mike Wells from Conyers, Georgia. Please give me a chance to be with my family. Give me a chance to make up for horrible things I did when I was with the Agency. I'm so sorry for what happened to Connie. But I had to walk away. I had to make things right."

At any moment, I expected Rod Serling to step into the picture and announce, *"Beyond this door is another dimension."*

"This is more than a waste of time," I said. "It's performance art. I'm not even sure if you know the difference between fantasy and reality."

"Connie killed herself," he said. "Sometimes things are just exactly as they seem."

"How can you see through the smoke and mirrors?"

Wells didn't answer. He just stared out beyond the pink playhouse and deep into the pine forest, hand over his mouth, with thoughts perhaps even God didn't know.

44

"Mike Wells?" the big woman said. "Of course I know him. I've lived here most of my life and have run this paper for the last ten years."

We were in the office of Mrs. Betty Mc-Cullough, editor and publisher of *The Rockdale Citizen.* When all else fails, contact the local muckrakers for the skinny. I found the office in a little yellow house on Main Street where I presented my card. McCullough seemed to be halfway impressed to meet with a big-city snoop like myself. She sized me up like a hungry dog following a Christmas ham.

"What's he into now?" McCullough said.

"I was hoping you might tell me."

McCullough was a stout woman in her early sixties with stylishly cut red hair and clear blue eyes. She had on a black blouse with designs of birds, numerous bracelets on both wrists, and a large wedding ring.

The office smelled like perfume and cigarettes.

"Are you asking about all this spy nonsense?" she said. "He's been telling that story since he came here ten years ago. He was selling used cars over at the Ford dealership. People around here ate up the story. He was a frequent speaker for the Kiwanis. Wanted me to do a story on him, but he could never prove what he said."

"And a veteran?"

"He marches in all the parades," she said. "Goes to the VFW and talks Vietnam. Some people believe him. Idiots. I think it's absolutely shameful. My father was in Korea. I know what that man went through. You in the service?"

I nodded.

"When?"

I told her. It had been a while. But not as long as some might believe.

"Then you know what I mean."

"When did he get on with the church?" I said.

"Oh, he's been with the church since Ridgeway rolled his traveling medicine show into town," she said. "Have you met Josiah Ridgeway?"

"I heard him preach last night," I said. "I guess I need to make room for more love in my heart."

"Ha," she said, reaching across her desk for a pack of cigarettes and a BIC lighter. She lit one up, stood, and opened a side window. The cold air rushed into the room, fluttering the many papers on her desk. "And a bigger wallet. He's a piece of work, too. But if I were to write a column about what I really think about Ridgeway, they'd run me out of town on a rail. Publicly, he welcomes minorities. Privately, he's a racist bastard."

"Popular?"

"And powerful," she said. "Why are you down here anyway?"

"The woman who was found dead last week," I said. "She was my client."

"Sure," she said. "Of course. Connie Kelly. Lived in some apartments outside town. I tried to do a little bit more on that story. But no one seemed to know her. She didn't have a job or any connections to Conyers. The police wouldn't give me any information on her family up north. You think she's tied in with Greater Faith?"

"She's tied in with Wells," I said. "And the church. But I don't understand what a big church like Greater Faith has to do with some military training facility and private hired guns."

McCullough smiled and dabbed the hot end of her cigarette toward my chest. "Good question," she said. "Been trying to find out that for myself. I know Ridgeway is part of the deal. He's very vocal about us preparing for the government failing us. I never have been able to wrap my head around why Christians need guns. But I'm sure Ridgeway and Wells have tried to make an argument for us."

"Ever heard of a man named Bliss?"

She shook her head and waved the smoke from her face.

"Does he work out at the compound?"

I nodded. "Big, ugly, and lots of tattoos."

"Press isn't exactly welcome out there," she said. "And if you haven't noticed, we're not equipped for any major project stories. We do local news. Friendly news. My board of directors says they want stories that grandparents can be proud to post on their refrigerator."

"You're kidding."

"I got laid off at the *AJC*," she said. "I covered courts for ten years in Cobb County. I'm not rocking the boat down here. Besides, if I did, no one would really give a crap."

"So Wells and Ridgeway showed up here about the same time," I said. "From where?"

"Ridgeway is from Kansas," she said. "Maybe Wichita? I'm not sure. Wells is from Georgia, but didn't grow up around here. They took over a storefront downtown, and before we knew it, they had started an executive committee to build that monstrosity by the interstate. I always figured it was some kind of tax dodge. And I know they made a hell of a lot more money fundraising for that big-ass cross than they spent on it."

"I like how you talk, ma'am."

"Nice to have some straight shooters in town," she said. "You do know Wells is on his third wife?"

"Lucky her."

"Really nasty divorce with wife number two."

"Any idea on where to find wife number two?"

"No," she said. "I'm pretty sure she left town. But if you're looking for people who lost money to Wells, I have quite a list."

"I don't doubt it," I said. "But I'm more interested in the training compound. And anyone who might have known my client."

McCullough shook her head, crushed out her cigarette in a coffee cup, and looked at me. She gave me a big smile. "Sure would be good to have some real action in this town," she said. "Please let me know if you decide to take down the Greater Liars."

"Excuse me?"

"A private joke in town about Greater Faith."

"Anything else I should know about Ridgeway and Wells?"

"I know Ridgeway was in prison," she said. "I ran a story about it and got my ass chewed out by the board and the owner of the paper."

"What for?" I said.

"Embezzlement. Writing bad checks. That kind of thing. He did five years at Leavenworth."

"What did his congregation think?"

McCullough let out a long, tired breath. "Only made them love him more," she said. "He took it into his personal narrative as a story of faith and redemption. A real lovable loser. Folks are suckers for that crap."

"Of course."

"I'm a southerner," she said. "And I go to church every Sunday. God and me are okay with each other. But damn, how I hate these guys. They make us all look bad, Boston."

"You have my card."

We shook hands. I headed back to the motel to find Hawk.

45

Hawk was gone. He'd moved out of the Holiday Inn and hadn't left a note. I knew he'd call when it was safe.

I lay down on the bed, curtains open to show a breathtaking view of a Waffle House, a Chevrolet dealership, and the interstate, and called Susan. She would have just finished her last session.

"What are you wearing?" I said.

"No hello?" she said. "No 'How was your day?' You just want me to gratify your sick fantasies."

"You know me so well."

"I could describe everything in great detail," she said. "But as you are thousands of miles away, that kind of discussion might only lead to frustration."

"Way past that," I said.

"Absence is good for the heart," she said. "Bad for the libido."

"Damn," I said. "You sure talk fancy,

Yankee. Let me grab a dictionary."

"Picking up a southern drawl already?"

"What can I say, I blend into all environments," I said. "My skill set as a professional sleuth, ma'am."

"And how's the sleuthing?"

"Slow going," I said. "Perhaps even terrible."

"Are you any closer to finding out what happened to Connie?"

"You mean with actual witnesses and evidence I could turn over to a district attorney?"

"Yes," Susan said. "That type of thing."

"Not really," I said. "But I do have a better idea of Wells and his life down here. Did I tell you he's an ordained minister?"

"I never had any doubts."

"And he has a wife, three lovely daughters, and a McMansion," I said. "According to Wells, Connie followed him down here against his will. And that he broke things off immediately. His conscience wouldn't allow philandering."

"A true gentleman," Susan said. "How's your bullshit detector?"

"Obliterated," I said. "I know he was seen several times at Connie's apartment. He's also being untruthful about his hair color. His hair is now darker than mine."

"We all have our secrets."

"Really?"

Susan didn't answer. I stretched on the bed. The traffic was stalled out on the interstate ramp.

"She was killed," I said. "I think so. The local cops and Feds think so. What does her shrink say?"

"Connie was impressionable and needy," Susan said. "But I never thought of her being emotionally impulsive."

"And I find it hard to believe anyone could shoot themselves in the back of the head."

"Wells?"

"He's at the top of my list," I said. "And had the most to lose."

We were quiet for a while. The motel's wall heater rumbled to life. Traffic along the interstate moved as quickly as maple syrup.

"Where are you now?"

I described the motel down to the nearby Chevy dealership and the Waffle House. However, it took some time to explain the concept of a Waffle House to Susan.

"Don't you have any other dining options?" Susan said.

"My dining options tonight seem to be a Panera or Chipotle," I said. "Take your pick."

"No Pano's and Paul's?"

"Alone?" I said. "Besides, I hear it's no longer in business."

"That's a shame," she said. "Where's Hawk?"

"Hawk's indisposed."

"Doing what?"

"He's joined up with the bad guys," I said. "In an effort to help the good guys find out exactly what's going on."

"Are you worried?"

"Would it matter?" I said. "Hawk does what he wants."

"Just who are these people, anyway?"

"Some kind of outcropping from a big church down here," I said. "The preacher is a seasoned con man from Wichita turned respected member of the Rockdale County community. He's as handsome as Gollum."

"And Wells?"

"Wells has kept the same Navy SEAL, CIA persona but with more emphasis on preacher and family man," I said. "Did you know that Jesus Christ was a big proponent of fully automatic weapons?"

"Are you getting any help down there?"

"From cops?"

"From anyone."

"ATF Boston field agent is down here," I said. "He's working the same thing we're working. But I don't think he's a fan."

"Making friends as you go."

"I tried to reach out to Tedy Sapp, but he's a tough man to find."

"Did you call that place he worked?" she said.

"Bath House Bar and Grill," I said. "Yep. Line's been disconnected. Might ride up there tomorrow."

"Be careful."

"Yes, ma'am."

"Hawk, too."

"Yep."

"And don't get your Jingle Bells shot off."

"I'll do my dead-level best."

"Love," Susan said.

"Love," I said. And hung up.

46

I took Susan's advice and drove thirty minutes for a good meal. At the OK Café in Buckhead, I ate a blue-plate special of meatloaf topped with creole sauce washed down with two bottles of SweetWater 420. I was feeling so homesick I didn't feel guilty about the hot pecan pie and coffee for dessert.

Afterward, I headed back to the Holiday Inn, calling Rachel Wallace on the way. She wasn't in and I left her at least two minutes of rambling questions. I hoped she might shed a little light on the larger picture of the Greater Faith Church's outreach and philanthropic mission. I would run down corporate filings tomorrow. And try to make a connection to the gun range and EDGE. But I asked Rachel to find out about EDGE's work internationally through some of her friends in the State Department.

I checked my messages at home. And

through my answering service at my office. No word from Hawk. When he had something, he'd find me.

I parked and trudged up to the second floor, now growing used to the concrete landscape of Atlanta's Perimeter. Cars and trucks zipped up on the interstate. Eighteen-wheelers coming and going from the truck stop next door. I reached into my jacket for my hotel key when I realized my unit's door was cracked open.

I stepped back to the outdoor landing and heard car doors slam. I saw two men rounding the corner of the second floor and moved fast down the concrete steps. Two men met me at the landing. The parking lot was nearly empty, a half-dozen cars gleaming in the artificial glow of the streetlamps. I was twenty yards away from my rental and forty yards from the hotel lobby.

I grabbed my car keys, pressed the unlock button, the horn chirping and lights blinking. The men closed in on me, yelling for me to stop. I reached the driver's-side door and nearly got inside before two more men approached me from the street. In all, six men had come to roust me at the hotel.

The two men from the second floor closed in. The men behind me showed me their guns. Very impressive. A pair of bright chrome Taurus nine-millimeters. One tried to hit me. I dodged the punch and his hand struck a nasty dent in the top of the rental. The other grabbed the leather sleeve of my jacket and pulled me toward him. I countered with an overhead right and reeled him back several steps.

Someone yelled to stop. It was a voice of authority.

A bald man walked toward me. He was built like a Mack truck and had the dark outline of a beard of the same length as his shaved head. He had on jeans and a dark green Henley shirt. He carried a sawed-off shotgun as it were a loaf of bread. His eyes flicked up and down on me, leaning into the fella who'd braced me on the stairs. "Toss him in the trunk," he said. "Take the car. This fella is checking out."

Before he got the last bit out, I kicked at the knees of the closest man, finding purchase in the cartilage and bone and sending him to the asphalt. I tried to run but two of them were on me; the bald man was standing close with the shotgun in my face. "Up," he said. "Easy. Up."

"You must be Brother Bliss," I said.

"And you must be fucked."

"Onward, Christian Soldier."

One of the men started my rental and

popped the trunk. Despite my protests, three of them got me into the trunk. I had no doubts Bliss would have used the shotgun in the lonely parking lot. The men were of varying sizes and ages. The only thing I knew for sure was that Hawk wasn't one of them.

The trunk closed over me with a solid *thunk.* Even in the glow of the taillights, I couldn't find anything like a release. Despite the swerving and braking rolling me back and forth, I did get into the well for the spare and pulled out a lug nut wrench. I tried to use the wrench to pry open the trunk. When that didn't work, I cracked out the back taillights with hope some passing motorist might report the car.

They had me in the car for more than a half-hour. After the ride, the car stopped and the engine turned off. I heard men's voices but could not make out what they were saying. I was pretty sure they weren't praising my demeanor or saying I was a really swell guy. Finally, the trunk opened and I saw Brother Bliss's face staring down at me. He was not a handsome man. He had scar tissue under his eyes and part of his ear was missing.

"Get out," Bliss said.

I was stiff but crawled out, trying to be

aware of my surroundings. It was only three men this time. Bliss and two others. Each of his men carried an assault rifle. Bliss stuck to the tried and true, the sawed-off shotgun.

"With me," he said. "Move."

We were in the woods somewhere. It was very dark and very quiet. I could see a blanket of stars overhead and smell wood smoke down a winding trail. I did not like being led into the woods in the dark. I especially did not like being led that way by three men with guns.

I started to whistle. "O Come, All Ye Faithful."

"Shut the fuck up," Bliss said.

I stopped whistling.

Bliss jacked the twelve-gauge into my back and I tumbled forward. We were now into a clearing and moving up to a bright white trailer. The good Reverend Josiah Ridgeway awaited me with a big smile, slabs of big white teeth, and open arms.

"Hallelujah."

47

The trailer was tight, cramped, and airless. It had been gutted to fashion a classroom of sorts, complete with small plastic chairs, a big whiteboard filled with handwritten Bible verses, and a world map with hand-drawn swooping arrows emanating from the Middle East. I didn't know what they were doing but was pretty sure they weren't working for ways to distribute their UNI-CEF donations.

Two men dressed in dull green fatigues and ball caps stood by the front door. They each held AR-15s. Bliss leaned against the wall near the board while creepy-old-man Ridgeway stepped in close. He had very large white teeth and the permanent grin of a huckster or someone who'd long ago lost touch with reality. He wore an out-of-style gray suit, a bright blue shirt, and no tie. Even with a thorough dosing of cologne, he still gave off a musty old-man smell.

"Are you a praying man, Mr. Spenser?" Ridgeway said. His teeth were a bright, artificial white.

I didn't answer him. Bliss pulled a Glock from his waistband and made a "get on with it" motion with the barrel.

"I prayed for the Sox to make the play-offs," I said. "And for mercy on Tom Brady. Does that count?"

"You mock people like us," he said. "You Godless liberals who will break America right in two."

"Maybe I walked into the wrong class-room?" I said. "I was looking for underwater basket weaving. This must be Crazy 101."

"You're not a part of this, sir," Ridgeway said, shaking his head sadly. "Nor were you invited. We're doing God's work. Your presence down here only interferes. Christian people will die if you make trouble for us. Many good folks. Are you following me?"

I shook my head. "To be honest, your accent is pretty thick."

"Why are you here?" Bliss said.

"A woman named Connie Kelly died," I said. "I worked for her. And I believe your people here killed her."

"That's an outrageous lie," Ridgeway said, still grinning. "Miss Kelly was an honored member of our church. I baptized her myself in front of nearly two thousand people. I was sad to hear she'd taken her own life. For some hotshot private eye from up north, you sure don't know shit from Shinola, sir."

"Got me there, Rev," I said.

"When a member of my church is called home, we all suffer," he said. "Why on this earth would you accuse me of such a horrible thing?"

"Maybe not you," I said, jacking my thumb at Bliss. "You don't have the stomach for it. Probably Sergeant Rock."

I looked at Bliss and smiled. Bliss didn't react. He stuck the Glock back into his belt and placed his hands on his hips. I stared at him and he stared back. If we did this any longer, we might get engaged.

"Get the hell out of here," Bliss said. "Out of Rockdale County and the state of Georgia. And we won't kill you."

"Is there a second option?" I said.

"Some things are just bigger than you, son," Ridgeway said. "Times change. What our Christian community is facing these days ain't unlike the olden times. *If a thief is found breaking in and is struck so that he dies, there shall be no bloodguilt for him.*"

"Lovely sentiment," I said. "But I'm not a thief."

"You have come down here to accuse us and take money from our church," Ridgeway said. "From our ministry. Surely that is theft, sir."

"I came for the two hundred and sixty grand Pastor Wells took from her."

Ridgeway nodded to Bliss. Bliss stepped up and took a swing at my kidneys. I blocked him with my forearm and hit him in the throat. Bliss staggered back a few steps and then tried to punch me in the face. I ducked it. He shook his head and pulled a gun.

The door opened. Hawk walked in.

Bliss kept the gun beside his leg. He nodded at Hawk. "You got the vehicle ready?"

"Yes, sir."

Hawk said something to the two men by the door. They headed outside. Hawk leaned against the wall. He wore the same dull green uniform as the other men. I had to admit he still looked sharp in the costume, although green wasn't really his color.

"Pack your bags, son," Ridgeway said. "And get gone."

"Why'd you kill her?" I said. "As a favor to Wells?"

"You got sand in your ears?" Ridgeway said. "The woman kilt herself."

Bliss snatched the gun out and hammered

311

a blow against my left shoulder. It didn't leave a pleasant sensation, but I kept my feet. I didn't look at Hawk. I didn't want anything to pass between us. If Bliss tried to kill me, he'd be stopped.

"Sir," Ridgeway said. "You wouldn't be so smug if you knew what Christians face today. A man like Mr. Wells, with his contacts and experience, is our only hope. He is a warrior of faith who does what needs to be done."

"Selling guns to crooks?" I said. "I'm no biblical scholar. I'm missing your message."

"Perhaps the good brother can clear it up for you, sir."

Ridgeway kept on grinning and patted me on the shoulder on the way out. After he was gone, Bliss cocked his pistol with his thumb and reached for my upper arm. He nodded to Hawk and Hawk stepped forward, getting my other arm. I didn't fight it, as a Glock was aimed at the back of my skull. I tend to notice details like that.

Hawk opened the door and Bliss kicked my legs out from underneath me. I tumbled down the rickety steps and into the dirt. Four of the guards stood around an oil-drum fire, warming their hands. Ridgeway's car disappeared down a dirt road.

I got to my feet and the men formed a

little circle around me. Bliss tossed one of the men his gun and made a running leap, taking out my legs. I rolled to my feet and hands and caught his slick bald head in a headlock, twisting it like a prize steer. He groaned and fought, pummeling my ribs with his sizable fists. His head was hairless and oily and loosened from my hands. He snatched a bit of my hair and drove a right into my jaw. There was a bit of a flash behind my eyes, but nothing I hadn't felt before. We circled each other in the firelight, Bliss feinting into me and then darting back. His nose was bleeding down into his lips and across his bright smile. The other men cheered for him and someone tossed him a big piece of wood.

I slowed my breathing, watching his hands lower from his head. A crooked nail embedded in the two-by-four glinted in the firelight. Out of the corner of my eye, I saw Hawk standing there, arms crossed over his chest, right hand brushing against the pistol on his hip. Bliss stepped into me with the piece of wood and connected with a lot of force, the nail stabbing into my upper arm. The men hooted.

Bliss held the wood high and swung for the cheap seats, the nail missing my face by less than an inch. I caught the wood in my hands and twisted it away from him. I tossed it far into the woods, wiped the blood from my face, and moved in toward him. I punched him one, two, three times in the solar plexus and face. It felt very much like punching an oak tree. He spit blood and moved in, missing a shot and then landing a solid thump in my kidney. More bright light. More yelling from the acolytes.

I tried to keep the other men in view, but someone hit me with something hard and solid from behind. The blow was so hard it knocked me to my knees. Bliss kicked me in the stomach and reached for my hair, pulling me into the dirt. I felt blood coming from the back of my head. I could taste blood in my mouth. I didn't like the feeling one bit.

"Shoot him," someone yelled. "Kill him, Brother. Kill him."

Bliss was tired, sucking in air hard, wavering on his feet. Hawk pushed himself off the truck and walked forward, his hand still touching the gun.

I held up a hand in his general direction. Hawk stayed put. My eyes connected with his for a brief moment. I made the briefest shake of my head. Save for the firelight, it was dark. Bliss was too tired to take notice. He wiped the blood from his face and spit on the ground.

Two men came for me, clasping my arms.

"Send him back to where you found him," Hawk said.

Hawk led them back to the rental car, and they shoved me inside. The trunk closed with a solid slam. I heard the sound of my own breathing and muffled talk outside.

Soon the car started and rattled down the dirt road.

We did not stop for a long while until they left me inside by the interstate. The trunk had been popped and the keys were still in the ignition.

48

I drove myself to the closest emergency room, waited nearly two hours, and then got stitched up by the intern on the night shift. He was a lanky Indian man who didn't say much as he worked. As I was slipping back into my semblance of a shirt, he turned to me and said, "You slipped and fell on a bar of soap?"

"The soap was very slick."

"And sharp," he said.

"Would you believe I cut myself shaving?"

"In cases like this, I'm supposed to call the police."

I nodded.

"You will be very sore for a few days," he said. "Some of the bruises and cuts are very deep. You need to take it easy. Rest. Drink water."

"Thanks for putting the stuffing back in, Doc."

He nodded and shook my hand, and I

drove to the closest liquor store for a bottle of Wild Turkey. I then drove back to the Holiday Inn and took a long and painful shower. I wrapped myself in a towel and examined my chest, back, and arms in the mirror. It wasn't pretty, but it wasn't that horrible, either. I poured some whiskey into a short glass, turned on the television, and sat at the edge of the bed to view *How The Grinch Stole Christmas.*

I thought about calling Susan. But I could not lie to her.

I hoped Hawk would call to let me know he was safe. If he'd done anything to interfere, they would have killed us both.

After a large second whiskey, the Grinch had just had a terrible, awful idea on what to do with all those Whos down in Whoville. I wondered if he wanted to beat them all with a nail-studded stick. I drank more of the whiskey. I checked the lock on the door, placed a chair under the knob, and lay down in bed. I felt like I'd gone twelve rounds with a sharp-toothed Mike Tyson. On TV, the Grinch had finished his robbing and had rethought what he'd done. He rode the sleigh with his trusty dog Max down into the village to dine on roast beast and sing carols.

The whiskey was working. I sang with them.

I fixed another drink. I sang some more. Being loopy had a nice, calming effect.

I thought of home and of Susan. I thought about Pearl snoring at the edge of my bed.

Sometime in the middle of the night, I walked to the bathroom and drank a gallon of water. I was watching the cars pass on the Georgia interstate when the phone rang.

"How you doin', slugger?"

"Dandy."

"Take more than that."

"Yep."

Hawk hung up. I lay back down and tried my best to sleep.

49

It was still dark when I got up, dressed, and drove two hours to Lamarr, Georgia, to find Tedy Sapp. It wasn't easy. The Bath House Bar and Grill was now a florist and the local cop I'd known had moved away. I used an online database to run down Sapp's latest phone number and address. It didn't take long before I found him sitting at the edge of the bar at a place called the Paddock Tavern. He was drinking coffee, reading glasses down on his nose, and going through receipts. After he wrapped me in a big bear hug, I learned he'd been promoted from security to manager.

"The owner thinks all gays can cook," Tedy said. "And decorate."

"Can't you?"

"I'm much better at shooting people," Tedy said. "But I know everyone in town. And I'm good at running the local talent."

"Still dating the ophthalmologist?" I said.

"No."

"Sorry to hear that."

"Actually, we're married," he said. "As of last year. Small wedding. Two groom's cakes. Honeymooned at Disney World."

"Weren't you Eighty-second Airborne?"

He nodded. "We just can't help it," Tedy said. "It's the happiest place on earth."

Tedy looked pretty much the same as I'd seen him last. He and some other friends had joined me to help clean up a town called Potshot in Arizona. He was just as big and muscled now, his arms nearly splitting the tight black T-shirt he wore, with very blond, almost white, hair. He looked like the Hulked-out version of Guy Fieri.

"What's the job?"

"Why would you say that?" I said. "Maybe I was just driving through Georgia and thought I'd stop off at dear old Lamarr."

Tedy looked skeptical. He took a sip of coffee, walked behind the bar, and poured me a cold beer in a frosty mug. The paddle fans overhead twirled away like those in a turn-of-the-century hotel.

"Since when do you travel without Susan?" he said. "Or that dog?"

"Hawk is with me."

"Wow," Tedy said. "Things must be bad."

I made a so-so gesture with the flat of my

hand. "We may have run into a few issues south of Atlanta."

"Yeah?" he said. "It's written all over your face."

"I cut myself shaving."

"You shaving with a weed whacker?" Tedy said. He grinned and drank some more coffee. A waitress walked up to him and asked if he had time to talk to their sales rep about a delivery. "I'll call him back," he said. Tedy rested his forearms on the bar and turned to me.

"You're a busy man," I said. "Married, settled down, a respectable job. Maybe this isn't for you."

"Excuse my French," he said. "But how the fuck do you know what is or isn't for me?"

"Hawk isn't on our side."

"And how does that work?"

"He's on our side," I said. "But he can't admit he's with us."

"I wouldn't admit I was with you, either."

I smiled. "Just how do you get your hair that damn white?"

"I shampoo with Clorox," he said. "What's the job?"

"A woman who hired me in Boston was killed down in Rockdale County," I said. "People said it was a suicide. But she had a complicated relationship with a local con man who's running guns for a big church down there."

"Oh, that old story," Tedy said. "Hard to keep up with all the crooked preachers down south."

"Don't you know you gays are ruining our American values?"

"I did three tours with the Eighty-second," he said. "I'm married. I go to church. I pay taxes. I'm damn fine with my American values."

"The locals are made up of a bunch of hired guns," I said. "Some of them very good. Some of them are just local talent. Hawk joined up to find out more about the operation and what happened to my client."

"Hold on," Tedy said. "Why would a church need a bunch of mercenaries and weapons?"

"They claim to be helping Christians overseas."

"You don't buy it?"

"What do I know?" I said. "I'm just a liberal Yankee interloper."

"Lord help us."

"I could use a little backup," I said. "While I sleuth."

"To be your white Hawk?" he said.

"No," I said. "To be my gay, white Hawk.

With cooler hair."

"Hawk doesn't have hair."

"True," I said. "Just don't tell him."

I drank the rest of the beer and reached for my wallet. Tedy shook me off. He sipped his hot coffee and studied his reflection over the booze bottles behind the bar. Little bright lights twinkled through the racks of booze. After a few moments of introspection, he nodded.

"You're in?" I said.

"Let me talk to the hubby," he said. "And grab my guns."

"There you go again," I said. "Quoting John Wayne."

50

I thought it best to change hotels. Not that the Holiday Inn's service wasn't excellent. I just took exception to the EDGE people knowing where I stayed and trying to poke a few more holes in me during my stay. I paid the bill, packed my bags, and walked down the steps to where Tedy had parked next to my rental. He drove a brand-new Ford F-250 painted a bright blue with both a rainbow flag and deer-hunting bumper sticker.

As I crossed the lot, I saw he was speaking to two men in suits. One of them was Bobby Nguyen. He looked fine and dandy in his dark blue suit, with his slicked-down hair and government-issue sunglasses. The other was Agent Cardillo, whom I'd also met at the Boston Field Office.

"Spenser?" Nguyen said. "We need to talk."

"I tried to talk to you at the Varsity," I

said. "I even offered to buy you onion rings."

"Can we please cut the crap?" he said. "What exactly went on last night?"

Nguyen nodded to Tedy and Cardillo as he walked toward the motel office. I joined him. The air was brisk and cold late that afternoon. It wasn't yet five, but the sky had already started to turn dark. I pulled my ball cap down lower for fear it might blow away.

"You know we have Greater Faith and the EDGE camp on surveillance," he said. "How'd the meeting go with Dr. Ridgeway and Brother Bliss?"

"Lovely," I said. "They've asked me to testify on Sunday. They heard I might lay hands on some parishioners."

"Looks like they laid some hands on you."

"Couple guys," I said. "And one big stick."

"This isn't good," Nguyen said. "Or funny. Do you know what my grandmother used to say about situations like this?"

"Actually, I have no idea," I said. "I never met your grandmother."

"She said adversity brings wisdom," he said. "She was Vietnamese. We talk like that. I'm hoping you may have a different perspective after last night. And that you'll be leaving town and let us handle this ginormous shit show."

"My ancestors were Irish," I said. "They taught me to never like a beating."

"What happened to your other friend?" he said. "The big black guy?"

"I don't describe my friends that way," I said. "You're just a pushy ATF agent. Not a pushy Asian guy."

Nguyen made a sour face. He shook his head and just stood there, right hand deep in his suit pocket. The wind fluttered his tie and he snatched it, placing it inside his coat. "Just what did Ridgeway and Bliss say to you?"

"They swore my client Connie Kelly was a dear friend to the church," I said. "Ridgeway said he knew for a fact she shot herself."

"Of course he did."

"We both know these guys are running guns up to Boston," I said. "I don't care where they get them or why they ship them north. I only want to know what happened to Connie and get her money back."

"All that will shake out," he said. "We just need to catch them in the act."

"Mind sharing a few details?"

"Did Reverend Ridgeway explain why they were doing all that training?"

"He said it was some kind of Christian call to arms," I said. "I tried to ask more, but it was tough to talk after I'd been designated a human piñata."

Tedy stood in the dark, talking to Cardillo. Something Tedy said made Cardillo laugh. He pointed out the sticker on Tedy's truck and Tedy said something else. They both were laughing a lot now. The spirit of cooperation.

"We don't know what Ridgeway told you," Nguyen said. "But I'm sure it was something like 'Get the fuck out of town or we'll kill you.' "

I shrugged. "Crudely paraphrased."

"These guys aren't kidding," Nguyen said. "Ridgeway is a certifiable nutjob with priors. He spent most of his life in a federal pen. But Bliss? Oh, man. He's another story. What concerns us is another fucking Waco situation. If you haven't been watching the news, separatists and militias are back in vogue."

"Been a while since Oklahoma City," I said.

"Some of these people don't even remember it," Nguyen said. "I knew it. I had two good friends die. This movement, these people, are pretty much preaching the same message."

"I think it's a different message," I said.

"What's that?"

"Old-fashioned greed."

"You willing to put a wager on that?"

"Sure," I said. "Why not?"

"You must be the most stubborn son of a bitch I ever met."

"Shucks," I said.

"These people killed your client and John Gredoni," Nguyen said. "Just what do you think they'll do to an asshole like you?"

"I'm not going anywhere."

"We could have you arrested."

"You could," I said. "But you won't."

He stared at me for a good thirty seconds before he waved to Cardillo to bring the car around. They left fast and wordlessly.

"How'd it go?" Tedy said.

"Lovely."

51

We rented a suite down the interstate, just off Powers Ferry Road. The new hotel offered two large beds with a sitting room, a slight bump up from the Holiday Inn. Tedy set out a couple plates and silverware and napkins he'd borrowed from housekeeping. We'd stopped off at a Fresh Market and bought two roasted chickens with sides of macaroni and cheese, coleslaw, and a six-pack of ale from the Atlanta Brewing Company. I figured the ale would go well with the little cornbread loaves that came with the chicken.

"Last night I got drunk and watched *How The Grinch Stole Christmas.*"

"I would expect nothing less," Tedy said.

"How'd you spend your night?"

"If I told you, it would only stereotype me."

"As a gay man or a pistoleer?"

"Both."

Tedy didn't drink, which was good, as it left all the beer for me. As we ate, I helped myself to a second bottle and walked to the window. I watched a long row of traffic along Interstate 275. We were about a forty-minute drive from Rockdale County. If we were needed, we could be there faster. I held out a little hope from Nguyen that the Feds might come through in a pinch.

"You're worried about Hawk," Tedy said.

"It's a strange position to be in," I said. "One doesn't often worry about Hawk."

"But you feel guilty for bringing him down here."

"I didn't bring him," I said. "He showed up of his own volition."

"Because that woman got killed?"

"Because the woman was killed, because I'd gotten in over my head with some bad people he knew, and because some kids down in Roxbury had been shot up with weapons from this crew."

"That's a lot of reasons," he said. "Hawk is a grown-ass man. He does what he wants."

"That," I said. "And then some."

Tedy started to unpack, placing his blue jeans on hangers and his sweatshirts and T-shirts in the drawers. He'd already placed his biker jacket neatly on the back of a chair.

Everything was very precise. Even the gun and ammo at his bedside.

"You really are gay," I said.

"Would you like to see me dance?"

"Not really."

"So we sit around and wait for Hawk?" Tedy said.

"For now."

"Why not drive out to Rockdale," Tedy said, "and rattle the preacher's cage?"

"Already pretty well rattled," I said. "We wait for Hawk."

I sat down and kicked my legs up onto the bed. I was very sore; my jaw hurt a great deal. I'd changed the dressing and repacked my wounds twice already. I stretched my right leg out and retracted it in. A few years ago, I'd had some knee work. The new knee wasn't built for what it had been used for lately.

"I grew up in a church like that," Tedy said.

I turned to watch him in the low lamplight.

"No kid should have to deal with that crap," Tedy said.

"My family was Catholic," I said. "My father worshipped at the house of Jack Daniel's. We didn't go to church much."

"It's not easy," Tedy said. "I was raised to

believe how I am and what I am is against God. I went through hell trying to be someone else. That's why I had to be the best hunter, the best high school football player, the best soldier."

"All while being gay."

Tedy put his finger to his lips and made a shushing noise.

"When did you know?" I said.

"When did you know you were straight?"

"When I caught three girls from down the street swimming naked," I said. "I had a very tough time walking home."

"For me, it was a Baptist youth camp."

"See, you did learn something from that religious upbringing."

"And when we were caught kissing, the pastor wanted to see us."

I didn't say anything. The darkness and the cold outside seemed to go on forever. Some office building lights, illuminated in green and red, formed the apex of a Christmas tree. I drank some beer and listened.

"He made us pay," he said. "He had a large hickory stick."

"What's with you southerners and your sticks?" I adjusted in the chair, a soreness throbbing in my lower back.

"People hate things that they fear most," Tedy said. "I think many people are driven out of self-hatred."

"There are also a lot of stupid, racist homophobes in this world," I said.

"Yeah," Tedy said. "That, too."

"You good with all this?"

"More than you'll ever know."

52

The next morning, Rachel Wallace called me at six a.m. I was already up and into my second cup of coffee. Tedy had gone for a workout at the hotel gym while I continued to move about slowly.

"This guy Dr. Josiah Ridgeway is a true and authentic prick," Rachel said.

"And I found him to be so very charming."

"Yuck."

"Did I mention he smelled of gingerbread and mothballs?"

"As his public views seem to reflect nineteenth-century intolerance, I'm not surprised."

Tedy walked in the door and left me a new cup of coffee and a blueberry muffin on the bedside table. He was wearing his workout gear and covered in sweat. I took the coffee and walked to the chair by the window.

"His real name is John Kenton Ridge

Junior of Wichita, Kansas," Rachel said. "I found his real name connected to the EDGE Corporation, whatever the hell that is. Before having his religious conversion, he passed himself off as a financial guru. Back in the nineties, he held get-rich-quick seminars at airport hotels and promised wannabe investors to put their stagnant money to work."

"Multifaceted."

"Oh, yes," Rachel said. "He took a hundred thousand from a woman going through chemotherapy and nearly a half-million from some country music producer. When he was sentenced, he refused to admit what he'd done was wrong. He said he'd been a pawn like everyone else and blamed his business partner."

"What happened to the business partner?"

"Oh, he committed suicide," Rachel said. "Family said he'd been killed. But no one was ever charged."

"What an amazing coincidence."

"After Ridge was paroled, he tried to loop investors into a plan to produce biodiesel in Ghana," Rachel said. "He made nearly two million before he was caught and sent back to prison. When he got out, he tried the same scheme, this time pimping Chile. No difference."

"At what point did he become the good reverend we know and love today?" I said.

"About the time he was selling luxury vehicles," she said. "He'd offer Ferraris and Lamborghinis below market prices, they'd wire money, and then he'd distribute to different accounts set up by other parties. The cars would never arrive and he'd disappear."

"Hold on," I said. "Are you saying that Dr. Josiah Ridgeway isn't an honest man?"

"He's so crooked he has to screw himself into a pair of pants to get dressed every morning."

"Nicely done."

"Thank you," Rachel said. "Basically, he's a piece of human garbage. He's such a naked ridiculous crook that I found some of what he did was quite amusing. Ten years ago, he had a call-in prayer show in Tampa, Florida, where you could leave a credit card number and he'd lay hands on the camera. That's when he came in contact with a Florida televangelist who got him into the diamond business."

"And how exactly did that work?"

"This televangelist owned several diamond mines in South Africa," Rachel said. "You can imagine the working conditions. Pretty much slavery. Very dangerous. Ridge, who by now was our Dr. Josiah Ridgeway, was the broker between America and Johannesburg. It appears he used the funds to start Greater Faith. EDGE Corp and the supposed overseas missions happened later."

"With Wells."

"Exactly."

"Thank you," I said. "How can I repay you?"

"By not getting killed," she said. "And buying me a case of bourbon. Not just a single bottle. Unless that bottle is Pappy Van Winkle and old enough to vote."

"Done."

"These are bad people," Rachel said. "They are criminals who incite uneducated masses. They use bigotry and hypocrisy to line their pockets."

"Perhaps they should be stopped?"

"Even better than the booze," Rachel said.

53

We spent most of the day laying low at the hotel and waiting for Hawk to call. I tested my pain threshold by doing push-ups and sit-ups with Tedy. By last count, we'd hit more than three hundred of both. It felt like hell. My joints ached. My back was still sore. Tedy found a lot of humor in my plight.

"This is almost like *Midnight Express,*" he said.

"Except for one major detail."

"Being caned by Turkish prison guards?"

"There's always hope."

At six, Hawk called. He told me to meet him at a barbecue restaurant off Interstate 20 in thirty minutes. Tedy and I drove that way. It was rainy and cold, slow moving on the highway. It took us forty minutes.

The restaurant, a rustic-looking one-story building called The Hickory House, wasn't far off the highway in Tucker. It had old horseshoes and washboards tacked on the walls. A few wagon wheels had been fashioned into chandeliers. It was folksier than the Country Bear Jamboree. Silver tinsel on a miniature tree by the cash register. Gene Autry on the jukebox.

Tedy and I ordered coffee. Five minutes later, Hawk strolled in and offered Tedy his hand. Tedy stood up, smiled big, and gripped Hawk in his infamous big bear hug. The only person I'd ever seen greet Hawk that way was Susan. He patted Tedy on the back and slid into the booth.

"Bees buzzing 'round the hive, babe," Hawk said. "They know you still in town."

"Did they think I'd flee Atlanta with my tail between my legs?"

"They coming for you," Hawk said. "And this time, I don't know if I'll be there to stop them."

"What's it to them?" Tedy said. "If you stay or go."

"Spenser pissed off the two head honchos," Hawk said. "He drawing some serious attention to their operation."

"The gunrunning?" Tedy said.

"Gunrunning, charitable donations, laser light show, patriotic hoopty-doo," he said. "All that shit, man."

"And Connie."

"Oh, they killed her," Hawk said. "Bliss

bragged about it. Put one behind the ear and threw down that .32. She was making trouble for Wells. Wanted him to leave his family or else she'd run to the cops."

"Shit."

"Whole bunch of it."

"And what's up next for our good folks with EDGE and Onward Christian Soldiers?" I said.

"Pretty much what we thought," Hawk said. "Brother Bliss and Wells trying to fill up a big ol' tractor-trailer with a mess of guns and ammo. A little fund-raising trip up to Boston. Seem like they short of cash. Problem is, they halfway there. More trouble you make, the more it spoil their big Christmas surprise."

"Let me guess, it's a big drive for the troops fighting the battle overseas."

"Mmm," Hawk said. "Toys for Tots. Just some good ol' Christ-loving white boys. Far as I can tell they ain't never left the States. Bliss got his own work. Doesn't have a damn thing to do with Christian soldiers."

"What do they do at that training camp?" Tedy said.

"Make a bunch of privileged white assholes from the city drill," Hawk said. "They got ropes to climb, walls to scale, wire to crawl under. EDGE have them bunk in some ratty old trailers. Ruck in the morning, shoot in the afternoon, and talk Jesus at night. The End Days are coming. Don't say it while I'm around, but there's talk of a race war."

"You people planning something?" I said.

"You know it," Hawk said. "Don't you watch the news?"

"My people, too," Tedy said. "We're going to try to make straight men dress better."

"And what happened to you?" Hawk said.

Tedy had on an Epcot '81 sweatshirt cut off at the elbows, threadbare jeans, and unlaced running shoes.

"Work in progress."

Hawk nodded. He rolled the sleeves of his green uniform to the elbows. The insignia on the pocket read EDGE.

"Tell Bliss you can help with guns," I said. "And all the ammo they can handle."

"And how do I do that?" Hawk said. "Go down to the Walmart and fill my buggy?"

"Maybe," I said. "Or maybe I can arrange for some samples."

Hawk smiled and nodded. Tedy looked at me. He looked doubtful.

"Good," Hawk said. " 'Cause I'm getting damn tired of eating grits for breakfast."

"I like grits," Tedy said.

I nodded in agreement. "Especially with

bacon crumbled up in them."

"And a lady up in Boston been missing my company."

"Just one?" I said.

Hawk shrugged. He attempted to look modest. But like me, he had a hard time pulling it off. The waitress came over and brought us all some Brunswick stew and a basket filled with hot corn muffins. She refilled coffee for me and Tedy. Hawk drank some water.

"If I were to make this work," I said. "And that's a big if. Just exactly what merchandise would garner their attention?"

Hawk dipped a corn muffin in the stew and ate, thinking. He reached into his front breast pocket and pulled out a folded piece of paper.

"Thought you'd never ask," Hawk said. "This here what I call the naughty list."

"Lot of guns," I said.

"Sho' nuff."

54

"You've got to be shitting me," Bobby Nguyen said.

"I shit you not."

"Don't you recall the wise words of my grandmother?"

"Sure," I said. "She said when opportunity knocks, open the door."

"She never said that."

"How do you know?" I said. "She very well might have."

We were driving down Peachtree Street in Midtown Atlanta. It was sometime between breakfast and lunch and the traffic wasn't completely horrible. Nguyen picked me up near the ATF offices in his unmarked unit. He said if I came inside, I'd only embarrass him.

"Boston needs to look out for Boston."

"I was born and raised in Biloxi, Mississippi."

"But you're a Boston guy now," I said.

"And Wells came to your town to run his cons and his gun pipeline. That's why you're down here three days before Christmas."

Nguyen had no answer. He deftly moved in and out of traffic, driving at a decent rate to nowhere in particular.

"I can't just set up a sting operation overnight," he said. "That takes planning. Besides, I'm down here to work with the Atlanta office. I don't run the Atlanta office. Those guys would truly run you out of town. Or put you in jail."

"A deal is already in the works," I said. "I only need some guns."

"That's crazy," he said. "If I were to even propose something like that."

"What if you just happened to be in the right place?" I said. "At the right time?"

"And then make the arrest?"

"Exactly."

"I could be accused of entrapment," he said. "And pretty much lose my job."

"You know who Ridgeway is," I said. "And what he does?"

"You know I am a veteran federal agent?" he said. "I have conducted one or two investigations in my time. We know he's a snake-oil salesman from way back. And a true sociopath."

"How did you know about my run-in with

344

him and Bliss the other night?" I said. "I didn't exactly arrive announced. Or even in the front seat."

"I told you," Nguyen said. "We have the church and the compound under surveillance."

"But you didn't see what happened to me," I said.

Nguyen didn't answer, zipping down Peachtree Street, and then slowing as he approached a red light. We sat there in silence, waiting for it to turn. He tapped his fingers on the wheel.

"You have a man inside," I said.

Again, nothing.

"If you're down here," I said. "Maybe your man is down here, too. And if it's connected to Boston, that would mean it's Wells."

"You think you're pretty smart?"

"Yes," I said. "I do."

"But it isn't Wells."

"He got Connie Kelly killed," I said. "She was going to go to the cops if he didn't leave his wife. That guy Bliss did it."

"And how the hell do you know that?"

"A little bird told me."

Nguyen took a deep breath and then slammed the flat of his hand against the steering wheel. "Wells is a fucking moron," Nguyen said. "He's the front guy. The

Walmart greeter for Ridgeway and the whole Christian soldier thing. He takes donations, shakes hands. The whole land deal in Boston blew up because that was Wells trying to be clever and going out on his own with Gredoni."

"Who killed Gredoni?"

"Who do you think, hotshot?" he said. "Bliss."

"Again, to protect Wells and his dealings."

"Gredoni knew a lot about this Georgia pipeline," Nguyen said. "He could've made a lot of trouble for them. He wasn't going to be left with a flaming pile of shit for that land deal. Wells left him hanging, with a lot of investors calling for his head."

The light turned green. Traffic started to move as fast as it could ever really move along Peachtree Street. Nguyen didn't glance over at me, finding a parking lot in a strip mall to make a U-turn and head back to downtown.

"That's it?" I said. "Ridgeway's acolytes kill two people, run another truckload of guns to God knows where, and you're going to just play wait-and-see?"

"We have some considerations."

"Your person inside?"

"It's not Wells," he said. "You believe a guy like Wells would stand up and do the right thing?"

"Good point."

Nguyen took a long breath, staring straight ahead at a ribbon of blacktop curving up a small hill. "Son of a bitch."

"If we had the guns," I said, "it's one-stop shopping. Wells, Ridgeway, Bliss. I can make it happen."

"I don't think so."

"How can you be sure?"

"Your friend," he said. "The guy they call Hawk? We spotted him out there with Bliss. He's a well-known figure at the Boston office. He's the one putting this all in motion. Right?"

I didn't answer this time. I waited.

"They know who he is," Nguyen said. "And why he's here."

"Shit."

"Yeah," Nguyen said. "A gun dealer in Roxbury, guy named Sarge, is in direct contact with Bliss. You need to get his ass the hell out of Rockdale County. He's not going to last long."

55

"What do we do now?" Tedy said.

It was night and raining down in Rockdale, Georgia. He'd just run into the sanctuary of Greater Faith to find Hawk with no luck. We'd tried calling and texting. I'd worked out a type of SOS code with him before he joined the ranks of Brother Bliss that didn't seem to be working. On the interstate, the big white cross blazed tall with white light. A living Nativity scene was in full swing on the megachurch lawn. Three obese wise men stood at the ready with their frankincense and myrrh.

"What exactly is that stuff?" I said.

"Exotic herbs," Tedy said. "They smell nice."

"Ah."

"Maybe we should ride out to their compound," Tedy said. "I can tell them their prayers are answered. A big tough gay dude to join their ranks."

"I hate to tell you this, Tedy," I said. "But the hair is a dead giveaway."

"What exactly did this Nguyen guy say?" Tedy said.

"He says they know who Hawk is," I said. "And will probably try and kill him."

"*Try* being the operative word," he said. "Hawk is fine. He's just fine."

I nodded. We drove away from the mammoth white church and into downtown Conyers and beyond. The windshield wipers slapping away the rain, the colorful holiday lights a blur through the wet windows. Bright lights and storefront displays. Tedy turned the radio to an all-Christmas station to get our mind off Hawk. Nat King Cole, "Little Drummer Boy."

"I'm good," Tedy said. "Let's head straight in."

"They have at least a dozen men."

"We've dealt with more."

"True."

"But these are better than those guys in Potshot?"

"Much better."

"Let's call it a challenge," Tedy said.

"Are you always so damn positive?"

"The attitude goes with the hair," Tedy said. "We can't count on anyone else to help us."

"Nope."

The EDGE compound was about ten miles outside Conyers, a good mile of the property line marked with a long chain-link fence and lots of *No Trespassing* signs. The main entrance didn't have a gate or a guard, just a wide opening that I had spotted the other night heading down a long drive. The cold rain had picked up and made it difficult to see as we turned down the gravel road. There were no lights and little to see beyond the five feet of headlights. The Christmas hits kept on coming. Now it was "A Holly Jolly Christmas."

"I always identified with Hermey the elf," Tedy said. He had his .45 Colt auto in his lap. He was loading a second and third magazine like a monkey playing with a peanut.

"The dentist?" I said.

"He wasn't talking about fixing teeth."

I kept on driving down the road, the ruts and potholes in the road kicking us up and down. I saw some light at the far end of the road, a bright white blur where they'd taken me the other night. I felt a sickness in my stomach and another unpleasant sensation of wanting to see Bliss again.

"And who were you in *Rudolph*?"

"Yukon Cornelius."

"Of course," Tedy said. "Perfect."

He placed two of the magazines in his jacket pocket and pulled down the bill on his ball cap. The cold and rain were a holiday blessing. We could get up near the trailers and bunk houses without being spotted. Whoever the crew had left behind, we could snatch up and reason with them. I wanted to find Hawk fast and get out just as fast.

"How far do we take this?" Tedy said.

"Far as it takes."

"Works for me."

"You sure?"

"Are you trying to insult me?" Tedy said. "You ride with a man and you stick with him. Or you're no better than some kind of animal."

"We're in a rental car," I said. "Not on a palomino."

"Does it matter?"

A truck veered into the road behind us, shining its headlights high and bright into the rear window. I drove a little faster, car bucking up over more holes, windshield wipers on double time. I reached down to turn down the volume of Burl Ives.

"If you can U-turn fast," Tedy said, "I can shoot out their tires. Or I can shoot the driver."

"Can you see in this mess?"

"Well enough."

"We need to catch them alive."

"I'll see what I can do."

The bright light in the distance grew until we hit a stretch of telephone poles with lamps attached and the double-wide trailer where Bliss tried, and failed, to teach me a lesson. I yanked the steering wheel hard to the left, spinning out the back wheels into gravel and racing us forward toward the other vehicle. Tedy had the window down now, Colt extended and firing off shots as I drove fast. He knocked out one of the headlights and looked to have hit the windshield of the SUV running toward us. If they drove like the guys in Boston, they'd be headed straight for us and look to knock us into a ditch. Instead, the SUV slammed on its brakes and stopped hard and fast. The gravel road was narrow, with brush and timber lining each side. There was no place to pass and I had to slow the car. No one returned fire.

The hazard lights flicked on the SUV, orange lights pulsing in the dark and rain.

A car opened and a large figure appeared. Hands up and walking toward us.

In the headlights, I spotted the familiar smooth black head. Hawk.

He got to my window and tapped on the glass.

"License and registration," he said.

"Who's with you?"

"The boy you met at the rest stop," he said. "Miller. He got no love for Bliss. And knows what's going down."

"They're on to you," I said. "That's why we're here."

"You heard wrong," Hawk said. "Brother Bliss just gave me a promotion. 401(k), benefits, all that shit. Calls me his second-in-command."

"Sarge turned you in," I said. "They're gonna kill you."

"No, sir," Hawk said. "Sarge is a cutthroat motherfucker, but he doesn't want no truck with me. He turned in one of Bliss's other people. A man he knew to be working for the ATF."

"Shit."

"Reason I got the promotion."

"They killed a federal informant?"

"That and then some, babe," Hawk said. "When we gonna go ahead and start this gun and ammo hoopty-doo?"

"ATF doesn't want any part."

The rain beaded off his head and sluiced down his face. Another man sat at the wheel of the SUV, watching us behind the spiderwebbed glass.

"New developments might change their opinion," he said. "If it do, this is the where and when."

Hawk rolled out a plan of where they expected the guns to be delivered and how they wanted them to arrive.

"I don't like it."

"Never do."

"Why now?"

"Reverend Josiah's ass and Bliss ready to settle up and mosey on down the road," Hawk said. "Lots of cash on the barrelhead for one big deal. And then they gonna disappear."

"I'll talk to my contact," I said.

"Yeah," Hawk said. "You do that. Fast. Or you ain't never gonna see these boys again."

56

On the night before Christmas Eve, I sat on a bench inside Lenox Square Mall, waiting for Bobby Nguyen to show. Tedy Sapp waited with me, drinking our second cup of coffee of the night and watching the shoppers in line to see Santa Claus. We didn't talk. I watched the women pass. Tedy watched some of the men. We had checked out of the motel and slept part of the day in the rental car outside the mall where Hawk had arranged the meet.

We didn't know the time until an hour ago. The mall was very festive. Shiny baubles, bright lights, a big tree.

Nguyen wasn't thankful or pleased. But he didn't say no.

He showed up thirty minutes late, dressed down from the government suit. He had on a black windbreaker and a black ball cap without a logo. I wondered if the taxpayers bought his underwear, too.

"I didn't know the man they killed," Nguyen said. "But the folks in the local office are upset."

"As they should be."

"They don't like your plan," Nguyen said. "But if it happens, they don't want you anywhere fucking near us."

"Merry Christmas," I said.

"If I so much as see you walk within five hundred feet of my people, I'll have your asses arrested."

"And a happy New Year," Tedy said.

I introduced Nguyen to Tedy. Nguyen nodded and shook his hand without interest.

"Hawk wants Tedy with him," I said. "Tedy was a cop. And was a decorated soldier in the Eighty-second Airborne."

"I don't give a shit if he's Audie fucking Murphy," Nguyen said. "He's a civilian. We have everything covered."

"Hawk can't go in alone," Tedy said.

"He has one guy who's flipped on Bliss," I said. "But I'm not sure he can be trusted. He can trust Tedy."

"No way."

"Then there's no way to ensure Hawk's safety," I said.

"I ensure his safety," Nguyen said. "We have eight agents here. And four officers from Atlanta PD."

"Where are the guns?" I said.

"They're here."

"All of them?" I said. "Because they'll walk if we're short."

"You said forty guns," Nguyen said. "We got you twenty-five M4s and fifteen AR-15s. They'll love them. Some of them have grenade launchers, scopes, and lights. Don't worry. They'll be impressed. They'll be dazzled."

Tedy looked bemused. His muscular arms crossed over his chest. "But they don't work."

"What do you mean they don't work?" Nguyen said.

"After that clusterfuck a few years ago in Arizona," Tedy said. "When you guys let all those guns walk and they ended up with the cartel in Mexico. The ATF doesn't set a trap with working bait anymore."

Nguyen gave Tedy a nasty look. He pulled at the brim of his hat like a pitcher and bent at the waist. His hands clasped before him. "They won't know," he said.

"Bullshit," Tedy said.

"You think these guys are going to whip out an M4 and dismantle it right in the mall parking lot?"

"Yeah," I said. "We do. This guy Bliss isn't

some yokel. He's a card-carrying gun freak."

"It's a moot point," Nguyen said. "You needed guns as bait. I have guns. You needed agents to make an arrest and here we are. I don't have time to quibble about my business."

"I need to be there," Tedy said.

"No way."

"Then it's off," I said. "We've delivered you a nicely wrapped package. All you have to do is scoop up these guys, get the glory and the news at eleven, and we can all fly back home."

"And what if it goes badly?" Nguyen said. "What if your man shoots and kills someone? Or worse, he gets killed himself."

"Hawk won't go if he's not there."

"Are you still with law enforcement?" Nguyen said.

"Does former head of security of the Bath House Bar and Grill count?"

"What the hell is that?"

"Best gay bar in all of Lamarr, Georgia."

"Christ, Spenser," Nguyen said. "I mean, really."

"Only two men as good as Tedy," I said. "And that's me and Hawk."

Nguyen didn't look up from the ground. I drank a little coffee and enjoyed the holidays on parade. The line to see Santa ran from

Macy's all the way down to Bloomingdale's.

"Will Wells be there?" he said.

"Don't know," I said. "But that's why it has to be Tedy. Wells and Bliss know me."

"You stay out of it," he said.

I put down the coffee and showed him the palms of my hands. I gave him a solid, friendly smile and picked up the coffee again. We sat close enough to the exit doors by Macy's that every so often a hard wind would blow into the mall and rattle the fake snow by Santa's wonderland.

"You know there are about six ways from Sunday this could all go to hell."

"And a better chance it will work," Tedy said. "How many officers are here?"

"Like I said," Nguyen said. "Twelve. Eight of our agents. Four local cops."

"And me," Tedy said. "Now, that just doesn't even seem fair."

"But we don't know who will show," Nguyen said. "Bliss is a walking freak show. Not to mention these creeps you say will accompany him."

"How far did you say to stay away?"

"Five hundred feet," Nguyen said. "Or how about make that yards."

I nodded. "I'll wait right here in Santa's lap."

"Forgive me if I don't believe you,"

Nguyen said. "You're sticking with my agents while Blondie over here rides shotgun with Hawk. I'm not letting you walk until it's done."

"Trust," I said. "Such a slippery slope."

"Blondie?" Tedy said, touching his stiff blond hair. "I like it."

57

Susan would've liked the chosen location for the exchange. The meet with Bliss and his people was called for the top floor of a parking deck outside Neiman Marcus. I felt relaxed and assured in the front seat with Nguyen and Cardillo. Meeting up with some mercenaries was only slightly more dangerous than Susan and her AmEx card.

At the appropriate time, Hawk and Tedy would roll up in a pickup truck loaded down with the wares supplied by the ATF. Bliss and his people would arrive a short time later. There was a chosen word to be spoken into a mic at the appropriate time and the bad guys would be scooped up before you could say Jackie Robinson.

"What if they don't show?" I said.

"Then we pack up and wait," Nguyen said.

"Waiting is the tough part."

"Will you go home?" Nguyen said.

"Nope."

"You mean you'll stick around until this thing is done?"

"I'm a bit obsessive," I said. "I like to see things through."

"Nothing ends neatly," Nguyen said. "You've been around long enough to know that. Bad guys get off. Money disappears. New shit happens every day."

"Job security," I said.

Nguyen smiled. The agent in back leaned forward between the sedan's front seats and said, "Here we go."

Nguyen turned up the radio in his lap. From where we'd parked, I spotted a large maroon pickup truck wind its way out from the ramp. The truck had dark tinted windows and a locking hatch cover over the bed.

"Nice ride," I said.

"Our agents took it off some cartel boys a few months ago," Nguyen said. "Local guys figured it might come in handy."

The truck pulled into an empty space at the far end of the lot. No one got out of the truck. I heard a voice over the radio let us know two cars were headed up the ramp. The entire parking lot was packed, the hoods and cabs of cars gleaming under parking lot lamps. Shoppers coming and going from the lot. Traffic, action. A good place to pull out and get lost with forty assault rifles. And an awful place to start shooting.

Twenty minutes late, a black SUV wheeled off the ramp and headed right for the pickup truck.

"That's them," Nguyen said.

"How do you know?"

"We tailed them out of Rockdale County," Nguyen said. "Like I said, I've done this a few times before."

"How many?"

"Three."

"Bliss?"

"Don't know," he said. "Stay tuned. We're about to find out."

The car pulled directly behind the truck, blocking its exit. Hawk got out from behind the wheel and Tedy from the passenger side. Two men in dark clothing and ball caps emerged from the SUV. One of them opened the back door and out crawled Reverend Josiah Ridgeway.

"Shit," I said.

"No Bliss."

"No Wells."

"Shit," Nguyen said.

I started to say something, but Cardillo turned up the radio. I could hear Hawk's voice and some small talk between him and the good reverend. For a moment, they moved out of view. I assumed to check out the Christmas packages lining the truck bed.

"Maybe it's good Bliss isn't here," I said. "He might've spotted the fakes."

"Should have known he'd be too smart to show."

"No one could say that about the reverend," I said. "He must have wanted to pray over the bounty."

"As long as he brought payment."

"What's the magic word?"

Nguyen smiled. "Snow."

"Clever."

"What can I say," Nguyen said. "I've been watching these assholes for a long while. All they do is lie."

Something caught my eye two rows across from where we'd parked. A man slammed the door of a car and walked with a lot of purpose to the entrance of Neiman Marcus. It was tough to see until he stepped directly below the lamps. A man with stylishly cut dark hair and a long gray overcoat. It was Wells.

At some point, Hawk uttered the go word and Nguyen and Cardillo rocketed out of the car. I was told not to follow them. I didn't. I moved in the opposite direction after Wells. He had a good head start, moving into the department store as I jogged across the lot. Pretty soon I was in menswear, with people shuffling along through massive piles of shirts, pants, and ties, and caught Wells as he turned toward the perfume and makeup section and, beyond that, the large entrance into the mall.

A clerk offered me assistance in dress shirts. Another wanted to show me a perfume sample for a special someone. Wells moved with his head down and more speed than I thought he possessed.

We were through Neiman Marcus and out into the mall, passing the storefronts for the Tesla dealer, the Polo shop, and Ferragamo shoes. He turned away from Macy's and toward Bloomingdale's. The mall was packed. Shoppers in heavy coats, loaded down with heavy sacks, blocked the way forward. Wells was tough to follow in the dark coat moving in and out of people, pushing past the shoppers and making his way to the escalators. I nearly body-checked an elderly man carrying a large box. Wells disappeared down the escalator. A sign with a down arrow said *Shops and Food Court.* I took the steps, turning round and round, until I came out on a small floor with more shops. California Pizza Kitchen. Urban Outfitters.

I saw Wells's new dye job sliding down

another escalator to the food court. I pushed past two women who called me a few choice names and then slid past a woman in a bright red coat. I was closing in. And then Wells turned. He hit the ground floor at a dead sprint and turned toward the food court. Chinese food, Mediterranean Market, Chick-fil-A. But no Wells. I ran toward the exit to the ground-floor parking lot.

A car slammed on its brakes and honked its horn. As I stood in the middle of the street, I saw Wells jump into the passenger side of a blue sedan and burn rubber into traffic and then out toward Peachtree Street.

I couldn't see who was driving, but I was pretty sure it was Bliss. I was out of breath. And they were long gone.

I walked the long way around the shopping mall to the deck where hopefully they'd caught the reverend with a lot of dough and a solid sermon on tape. On the upper parking deck, I found Nguyen talking with a large group of Atlanta cops. Patrol cars blocked the exits. Lights spun.

"Wells is gone."

"We'll find him," he said.

"Sure," I said. "If only we knew who he'll be next."

58

"You don't think Wells will go home?" Susan said.

"He did leave a wife and three daughters in Rockdale County."

"But he's not really what you'd call a family man."

"Nope," I said. "Or a true Christian soldier. But at some level he believes the lies he tells. It's intertwined with his ego. His ego will make him try and reclaim some semblance of the lie."

"The reason he couldn't fully change his name," Susan said. "Or break from his identity in Georgia. Starting over might be inconceivable to someone like him."

"I think he loves the accolades and the respect more than a con."

"It's a form of a con," she said. "Only the mark is themselves."

"He'll be back," I said. "Separating himself from the church and proclaiming his innocence."

We sat on my long sofa facing the boats in the Navy Yard. Most of the lights were off, my canvas travel bag dumped by the front door. I had a bourbon with ice in hand and my feet up on the coffee table. Pearl snored in my lap. A small, sad rosemary bush cut in the shape of a Christmas tree sat on the kitchen counter.

"And Hawk?"

"We flew back together."

"Tedy?"

"Home with his ophthalmologist."

"So the preacher gets arrested," she said. "But most of the bad guys go free. Including the two most responsible for Connie's death."

"Looks like it."

"Are you all right with that?"

"Nope," I said. "But stay tuned for my next thrilling episode."

"You look like hell."

"It matches the way I feel."

Susan leaned into me, head resting on my shoulder, and we watched the colorful lights twinkle on the ships. The water stretched out choppy, gray, and forever. It seemed as if I'd been gone for a year, although it had only been a couple of days. Susan smelled of lavender and good soap as I kissed her on top of her head. I could feel some warmth spreading through my chest.

"When do you leave?" Susan said.

"Bright and early Christmas morning."

"Maybe I don't like it."

"I don't like it, either."

Pearl snuffled a bit and flipped full on her back, legs stretched straight in the air. I rubbed her ears with one hand and lifted my other for the bourbon.

"Perhaps you should rest a few more days?"

"If I sit down any longer, I might not get back up."

"I guess you are too sore to . . ."

"I'm willing to risk it."

"And where exactly does it hurt?"

"Almost everywhere, doc," I said. "Almost."

I finished the bourbon and held out my hand. "Help me to bed," I said. "And I promise not to yell too much."

"We shall see."

59

Late Christmas day, I cooked two dry-aged T-bones from the Public Market on my potbellied stove at the cabin in Maine. A kale salad with pears and goat cheese and scalloped potatoes waited on a sideboard while Hawk loaded shells into his twelve-gauge Mossberg and whistled "White Christmas."

"You heard from Paul?" Hawk said.

"Sure," I said. "He sent me a bottle of hooch."

"He never sends me hooch."

"You never made him build a cabin."

"I call that free labor."

"It was character-building for a young man."

"If you say so, babe."

I seared one side of the steaks in fresh salted butter and turned the other side to get it just right. Hawk said he liked his steak bloody as hell.

He set the shotgun by the front door and walked to the window. He had on a pair of Levi's cuffed above some tall hiking boots, a tight-fitting flannel shirt rolled to the elbows, and his .44 Magnum stuck into a hand-tooled leather belt.

I slid his steak off the stove and onto a bright blue Fiesta plate. I'd already cooked the potatoes and set them on the small table that only sat two. The kale salad was in a wooden bowl waiting to be dressed. Hawk let go of the curtain and walked back to the table and uncorked a bottle of red.

"Almost romantic."

"Almost."

"Susan mind you gone?"

"No," I said. "How about Nicole?"

"Oh, yes."

"How sure are you they're going to come?"

"As sure as God made little green apples."

"You talk to Sarge?"

He nodded and sat down at the table. He took a little slice of the potatoes and waited for me to dress the salad with some olive oil, vinegar, and fresh lemon. He watched me with hands tented over his plate.

"Ain't no way Bliss gone let this go."

"Lucky for him that he didn't show for the guns."

"Lucky?" Hawk said. "That ain't the right word."

I cut into the T-bone. It was bloody, but not as bloody as Hawk's. I forked a little potato with the meat and ate. Hawk reached over and filled my wineglass. Hawk sang, *"I wish every day could be like Christmas."*

"Reverend Ridgeway is looking at a ten-year stretch."

"Too bad," Hawk said. "So sad."

"ATF raided the church yesterday," I said. "Guns weren't the only shit he was into. Bobby Nguyen said he had a pretty impressive pyramid scheme in the works."

"Greater Faith," Hawk said.

"No word on Wells," I said. "He never returned home."

"And now we get to wait for that shit to roll downhill."

"Clumsy as hell tail job."

"Almost disrespectful."

I got up and poked at the apple wood in the stone chimney and returned to my chair. The only thing bad about the cabin was that it only had one room and one bed. I took the chair. For the rest of the night, Hawk lay in bed by a kerosene lantern reading the collected essays of James Baldwin.

I rocked in an old chair made by my uncle Cash, a quilt over my legs and a .45 lever-action Winchester in my lap. It might've been Christmas a hundred years ago. The only sound was the crackling and popping of the wood and the bright electric silence out in the forest.

Sometime before midnight, I heard a car engine and doors shut.

Hawk snapped the book closed, doused the light, and moved close to the window with the shotgun.

"I figured Bliss for a more subtle approach."

"Ain't nothing that man ever do is subtle."

Hawk peered through a side window and then crouched down to the floor.

"How many?"

"I see two," he said. "That means four."

"Like we planned?"

"It's time for Operation Surprise, motherfuckers."

He opened a back door and slipped into the woods. I slid open the window a notch and rested the Winchester on the ledge and peered through the scope.

60

Bliss and another man moved down the crooked gravel road, carrying shotguns in their hands. Through the scope, I had a clear shot at both. Hawk figured Bliss would make a direct approach to talk while two of his men snuck around back.

A shotgun blasted twice in succession. And then there was silence. Bliss and friend scattered to the woods. So much for the best laid plans.

Hawk and I had worked out for him to get halfway down the road to a large oak where he'd get some cover. I watched the tree line through the scope, a .45 in the chamber and finger on the trigger. It had snowed earlier in the day, our tire tracks clearly visible up to the cabin. The tree branches drooped heavy with the bright white snow. Up the hill, a car waited. Headlines on, shining into the night.

I breathed in the cold fresh air and steadied my breath. *He will not see me stopping here to watch his woods fill up with snow.*

"Hawk," Bliss said. "We came to talk."

Hawk, being Hawk, didn't answer.

"We don't want trouble," Bliss said.

I could not see Bliss but figured him for about twenty to thirty yards away. I scanned the woods. The white snow almost bluish in a nearly full moon.

Snow fell heavy off a branch. I shot at it and jacked another round into the Winchester using one hand. John Wayne.

Hawk would be directly opposite of them now. Bliss and his man would have separated, fanning out in the snowy woods.

I heard the creak of the steps behind the kitchen. I got to my stomach and crawled with the gun the way I'd been taught in basic training. I moved on elbows and knees until I saw a face in the glass. I fired off a quick shot and heard a loud grunt. And then a fall.

The apple wood blazed a bright red in the fireplace, popping and crackling. I duckwalked to the back door, opened it, and found the man splayed in the fresh white snow. He didn't move. Blood poured from his chest. A sucking sound came from his mouth.

I spotted Hawk's tracks leading away from

the cabin. And I spotted the man's tracks moving into the opposite tree line. I picked up his assault rifle and followed his and moved into the woods. Every step seemed to make a crushing, crunching sound. I made use of the trees, walked low, tried to make myself small.

A shotgun blasted. Hawk.

I figured we could pinch Bliss in from each side. *I have promises to keep, and miles to go before I sleep.*

"Hawk," Bliss said, calling out.

"Show yourself," Hawk said. "Let's do it right."

I spotted Bliss's bald head behind a fallen tree. He had a rifle propped on it, aiming directly into the woods. I could hear the car's motor still running. The headlights were shining brightly into the snow lightly falling on a fine Christmas night.

I dropped the assault rifle and took aim through the scope of the Winchester. Hawk fired off a shot, spooking Bliss and sending him rolling and disappearing into the woods. I trotted to the fallen tree and called to Hawk. He ran across the road, snow covering the tire tracks.

We dropped to a knee in the woods and listened.

"Somebody's waiting in the car," I said.

"You take care of the driver," Hawk said. "I'll flush out Bliss."

"How are you planning that?"

"Shit," Hawk said. "I was born and raised in the briar patch."

"You said you were born and raised in the ghetto."

"Just a walk in the woods, babe," he said.

I followed the tree line, creeping low, sticking to the cover, and away from the moonlight shining upon mounds of snow. The snow covered my boots, halfway up my calves. It was tough going, but I made it to the road.

A young guy waited outside the car. He stood openmouthed and quivering. I walked toward him with the gun. He looked at me, shaking his head slowly, and then turned and ran. I walked to the car, reached inside, and turned off the ignition.

Everything was quiet now. Electric and still. The bluish light fell on jagged outcroppings of rocks and trees. I heard a crack of a branch in the woods. I watched as Bliss, and then Hawk, stepped onto the snow-covered path. They stood ten feet apart. Headlights still shining toward the cabin.

Bliss threw down his gun. And then Hawk. They moved in closer and then started to circle each other. I watched Hawk hold up his right hand before it turned into a fist. Bliss leveled a double overhand right at Hawk, Hawk ducking both. They circled and kept moving.

Bliss ran toward him, tackling Hawk to the ground, wrapping up his body and driving him deep into the snow.

I moved in closer, keeping the .40-caliber close but knowing Hawk wanted to finish it.

Hawk twisted and scissored his legs around Bliss and flipped the man hard onto his back. On top, Hawk punched a right and left with such speed it appeared as a blur.

They fell and tumbled. More fists and kicking legs until they were on their feet. Bliss had blood on his face. Hawk moved in a slow circle, keeping his breath.

Bliss spit blood onto the snow. He feinted a lunge at Hawk. Hawk darted away. Bliss moved right, and then left, and then took a run at Hawk. Hawk popped an uppercut so fast and so hard that Bliss's head jacked up like a PEZ dispenser. Bliss turned in a semicircle and crumpled to his knees.

Hawk looked to me. And nodded.

I walked toward them down the road. Hawk placed his hands on top of his head and took in a breath.

If the headlights had not been shining, I might have missed it. Bliss rolled up onto his knees and reached behind his back. He pulled out a pistol and aimed right for Hawk.

I emptied my .40-caliber into Bliss and he fell with a heavy thud. Snow scattered and twirled around us. Hawk walked up to me and nodded. I placed the warm gun back into my pocket. The air smelled like cordite and wood smoke.

"Man didn't have a code," he said.

"No rules."

"No compass," Hawk said. "No direction."

"You owe me."

"Shit," Hawk said. "You want to keep score?"

We walked back up to the cabin, where we called the local police. Hawk finished his bottle of champagne and stared long and hard at the crackling fire.

61

"And that's it?" Rachel Wallace said. "This asshole Wells disappears and nobody does a damn thing?"

"I'd do a damn thing," I said. "If I could find him."

"Aren't you some hotshot PI?" Rachel said.

"That's the rumor."

It was six weeks after the little party we'd thrown for Brother Bliss at my Maine cabin. Rachel and I were having afternoon cocktails at the Campbell Apartment in Grand Central Terminal. The cavernous room was dark and cozy, with Art Deco furnishings like a Depression-era movie house. I felt like I was trapped inside an Edward Hopper painting.

"At least you made good on your promise," she said. She raised her bourbon on the rocks in my general direction.

"Was there any doubt?"

Rachel smiled a bit. And shrugged. She hadn't changed much in the years after her publisher had hired me for protection. She'd developed a few small wrinkles around her eyes and had a long streak of gray hair that ran through her blunt-cut bob. Her clothes were gray and tailored, a no-nonsense pantsuit with a silk shirt. The shirt collar had been splayed neatly over the lapel. She didn't wear lipstick or nail polish. Doing so would be very anti–Rachel Wallace.

"If I remember correctly," I said, "you didn't like me when we first met."

"I thought you were a horse's ass," she said. "And a meathead antifeminist."

"In the end, I was simply a meathead."

"To the contrary," Rachel said. "You are a warm and thoughtful man. Some might even deem you an intellectual, heaven forbid. And even though you're good at rescuing women, you are a feminist at heart."

"Don't tell the boys at the gym."

"Don't you think they already know?"

I put a finger to my lips and lifted my draft beer. We had a comfortable corner table, our winter coats resting on the backs of chairs. The booze bottles behind the bar gleamed in the darkness. It was a fine place to share a drink as the world bustled around us.

"I'm sorry I couldn't do more," Rachel said. "Even my friend at the publisher didn't know. She said Wells pulled out of a national book tour. He says he's being hunted by ISIS and other assorted international assassins."

"Of course he is," I said. "And the Feds."

"Is that official?"

"He hasn't been named in the indictment against Reverend Ridgeway, EDGE Corp, and church officials," I said. "They're waiting for him to slip up."

"And so far?"

"Not a peep," I said. "ATF believes he may be in Orlando."

"My friend at the publisher said everything is cloak-and-dagger," she said. "He calls using a scrambled phone. He says his life is in danger."

"How has he been paid?"

"He was paid a partial advance," Rachel said. "But he'll expect another payment when the book is published."

"And where will that go?"

"Apparently, he has an attorney in Atlanta," Rachel said. "Details are in the notes I gave you."

"I'm a slow reader."

"But a fast drinker."

I looked down at my empty glass and hers only filled with ice. For some reason I seemed to consume all liquid at the same speed. Whether water or whiskey. I raised my eyebrows and nodded to the bartender. We watched him deftly pour my beer and then reach for a bottle of Blanton's.

"What would draw him out?" Rachel said. "Is there anyone who might make contact?"

"The wife and family are still in Georgia," I said. "The ATF is all over that."

"And what else?"

"Money."

"Aha."

"That's usually my line."

"Could he have money stashed somewhere?"

"Not that I know about," I said. "The church's assets have been frozen. We have no idea where he might have gone. Or who he might've become."

"How much did he take from your client again?"

"Almost three hundred grand."

"Was she wealthy?"

"No," I said. "Although Wells didn't know that."

"Could she have had more?"

I shook my head. I drank some more beer.

I tilted my head and looked at Rachel. She and I smiled at exactly the same moment.

"Perhaps she might've left him something?" she said.

"In her will."

"Precisely."

"I don't know if she even had a will."

"Do you know someone who might concoct one?"

"I only fraternize with highly ethical attorneys."

"But as a favor?"

"I don't know," I said. "That's a big favor. That might get them disbarred."

"Wells would have to fly to Boston," she said. "For the reading."

"And he'd insist on money on the spot."

"A wire transfer," Rachel said, tilting her head in the low light. "Do you think he'd fall for it?"

"I think he's full of more bravado than common sense."

"Mmm," she said. "I'll find out more on the Atlanta attorney."

"And I'll twist the arm of one of my lawyer pals."

"Lovely."

We clinked glasses and drank. She downed her bourbon in an impressive manner.

"I'd walk through a snowstorm for you,

Rachel Wallace."

"And did."

I winked at her. I could have sworn Rachel blushed.

62

Vince Haller hated the idea. And said he took great umbrage that I would even suggest involving him in such a scam.

I promised him two weeks of pro bono sleuthing and free tickets at Fenway at his leisure. He passed. I promised him a month of my services. Again, he passed.

"All I need is a formal letter and a will."

"No way."

"Do you know everything Wells has done?"

"I'm a lawyer," he said. "Not a prosecutor."

"This man stole more than a quarter of a million dollars from my client," I said. "She forgave him. When that got messy, he had her killed."

Vince was silent. I told him more about what I'd learned down south.

"The wheels of justice grind slowly," I said.

"Unless you cheat."

"It's not cheating," I said. "It's facilitating."

"Can you get her family to agree?" he said. "If her estate is involved in the bait, I'm less likely to be run out of Boston on a rail."

"In other words, the money would be offered from her estate?"

"Yes."

"Once Wells signs the documents, they could be turned over to the family's financial advisers."

"That, of course, would be up to the family," he said. "I'd be a simple emissary for the estate. I wouldn't handle the money."

"Ah."

"You know some good financial advisers?"

"I know a few guys who hang out down at the Tennessee Tavern," I said. "They know creative ways to keep books."

"Won't he suspect something?"

"As far as Wells knows, he walked away scot-free," I said. "Can you make it imperative he claims the money in person?"

"I can certainly try," he said. "And Spenser?"

I waited.

"Please keep all other details to yourself," he said. "I really don't want to know."

Haller hung up. Four days later, he told

me Wells's Atlanta attorney had called. The meeting had been set. Wells would claim his reward.

It was a bright and cold February afternoon, sidewalks scraped clean of snow and ice. As I drove up Boylston, steam rose from under sewer grates and manholes. I wasn't sure if Wells would show. But the promise of nearly half a million from Connie's estate might get him over his stage fright. After I parked under Post Office Square, I waited on a park bench watching the lobby of Vince's office. If Wells got close, even to make sure all was clear, I'd be there.

Shadows stretched through the park and over snow mounds as an early darkness fell. Wells didn't show. Thirty minutes passed. And then an hour. It was cold, even colder because I couldn't move. I began to fantasize about a hot pizza and a cold beer with Susan.

As I was about to leave, I saw a man of Wells's size and build walk down Franklin Street. The man wore a blue wool coat and an Irish walking cap. Two minutes later, Haller called me to let me know Wells had arrived.

A half-hour passed. No Wells. No call from Haller.

I stood to stamp my feet in the cold. My Red Wing boots were crusted with snow. I leaned against the park bench and stretched my legs. I tucked my hands into my jacket and attempted to get warm. Haller called. All had gone according to Hoyle. Wells had signed documents and confirmed accounts for a wire transfer.

Within a few minutes, Wells walked from the old New England Telephone & Telegraph building and crossed Franklin Street. He moved within twenty feet of me without taking notice. I watched while he headed toward the parking garage entrance. I noted a big smile on his face.

He disappeared into the glass box leading down deep into the garage built beneath the park. I followed him out of the cold and into the depths below Post Office Square. I moved steadily down the steps, turning and turning down the underground stairs.

He walked into the garage whistling an unrecognizable tune. When he reached into his pocket and I heard a car alarm chirp, I was within ten yards. He idly looked over his shoulder as I got closer and stopped cold.

"Spenser," he said.

"Pastor Wells."

He grinned some more. Somewhat

amused by the whole thing. Two old pals running into each other.

"You've been following me."

"It was either me or ISIS," I said. "I figured you'd be happier to see me."

His eyes looked over me and then around the parking deck. Red neon lights by the elevators glowed an ominous red. Wells just stood there in the middle of the garage, hands in his pockets looking to all the world like a prosperous businessman. Navy wool coat. Irish cap. Hair once again going gray at the temples.

"You should have never come back."

"She was a waste," Wells said. "She wasn't worth your time."

"But you had her killed?"

"She was going to destroy my family," he said. "The church and our mission. Bliss made the call. I didn't kill her. I swear to Christ."

I didn't say anything.

"They used me," Wells said. "Ridgeway. Bliss. They brought me in because of my work with the Agency. But I knew it was wrong. I was putting together evidence to stop them."

"Did you kill Gredoni?"

"That was Bliss," Wells said. "He killed him, Connie, and that man working for the

390

Feds. I've given my life to the United States government. I am a patriot who's had to work in some very dark places. Listen to me. Listen to me, goddamn it."

I didn't speak. I observed him.

After a moment, Wells said, "What now?"

"You're coming with me."

"Oh," Wells said. "I don't think so."

"Some people want to ask you some questions."

"Then let them find me."

He began to turn. I pulled my .38 from my hip and shook my head. Wells's hands had not left his pockets. I watched him look me over and swallow. All our movements and voices echoed on the concrete, five stories down into the earth.

"Connie's money?"

I shook my head.

"Her estate?"

I shook my head again. He chuckled and shook his head.

"My attorney will fight this," he said. "I will sue you. I will sue the federal agents who continue to try and harass my family. I will sue everyone."

I nodded. "Hand me your keys," I said. "Slowly."

His eyes flicked over mine. Both hands in his pockets. We were still alone in the garage, only the intermittent squeal and turn of tires on the exit ramp.

"Slow," I said.

His eyes leveled at mine. Serious. He swallowed again. His left hand emerged holding the keys. He dangled them before me. I stepped forward slowly. His right elbow lifted a bit.

"Nope," I said. "Really a terrible idea, preacher."

His eyes dropped. He nodded. His right hand came out empty. I snatched up the keys and reached into his coat pocket to find a Taurus G2. Lightweight and slight, but effective with .40-caliber ammo.

I popped the trunk to a nearby BMW sedan. I motioned him toward the opening.

"You can't be serious?"

"I'm in a sentimental mood."

"I have friends," he said. "People who owe me favors in Washington. I'll be out by morning. I had been working against Bliss for years. He and Ridgeway had fooled a lot of people. Including you and your hoodlum friends."

I helped him into the trunk. His Irish walking cap fell onto the pavement. I picked it up and tossed it inside before I slammed the trunk closed. He was still talking as it shut.

I started the car and drove toward the nearby ATF offices. I left the keys in the car and headed toward the Charlestown Bridge. Halfway over the bridge, I called Nguyen and told him I'd left him a late Christmas present.

It was very cold and silent over the Charles River, frozen and unmoving below me. As I walked home, the lights along the old Navy Yard glowed warm and welcoming in the distance.

63

"I thought you hated these things," Susan said.

"This is a special occasion," I said.

"Not to mention, it's an open bar," Susan said.

"Oh," I said. "I hadn't noticed."

I handed her a vodka gimlet. I had a bottle of Harpoon ale, a wet napkin wrapped around the cold bottle. We stood at the edge of the banquet room of the Boston Harbor Hotel. The sun was setting and the guests of the Jumpstart event were making the most of the bar before the speeches. Susan wore a knee-length sequined black dress that doubled my heart rate. The windows filled with an ethereal orange light.

"Did you ever doubt Wells would give the right account?"

I shrugged. "I only wanted to catch him," I said. "The fact he had siphoned off some of the church's funds was a bonus."

"Which worked out very well for Jump-start."

"I told Connie I'd get her money back."

"That," Susan said. "And then some."

I nodded and drank some beer. A friend of mine named Bill Barke walked over. We shook hands and talked for a while about hunting dogs and bourbon. Not to mention Connie's posthumous gift of half a million dollars. Soon, the sunlight started to fade and guests were called into the event. Overhead lights flickered. Men in tuxedos and women in glimmering gowns headed into the great room.

I watched the harbor go from orange to a dark black. Choppy waves and the twinkling of bright lights of the airport. A coldness spread across my chest and my lungs started to tighten.

"Are you okay?" Susan said.

"Ah, what pleasant visions haunt me."

Susan nodded. "It's done."

I nodded. She walked up to me and placed her arms around my back. I took her in close, smelling the good soap and shampoo. Lilac. The cold was gone. It was warmth and heat and now I could breathe.

"You promised to get me drunk," she said.

"And then let you take advantage of me?"

"How hard can that be?"

"I'm an easy mark."

"Will you tell me lies?"

"Never."

"We're all susceptible to little ones."

"We don't need them."

"No," she said. "We don't. And never have."

"Don't you feel sorry for all the other saps?"

"Honestly, my dear," Susan said, "I don't really give a shit."

I grabbed her hand and we strolled back to the empty cash bar. I ordered another round to make good on my promise.

ABOUT THE AUTHOR

Ace Atkins is the author of twenty books, including six Quinn Colson novels, the first two of which, *The Ranger* and *The Lost Ones*, were nominated for the Edgar Award for Best Novel (he also has a third Edgar nomination for his short story "Last Fair Deal Gone Down"). In addition, he is the author of five *New York Times*–bestselling novels in the continuation of Robert B. Parker's Spenser series. Before turning to fiction, Atkins was a correspondent for *The St. Petersburg Times*, a crime reporter for *The Tampa Tribune*, and, in college, played defensive end for the undefeated Auburn University football team (for which he was featured on the cover of *Sports Illustrated*). He lives in Oxford, Mississippi.

The employees of Thorndike Press hope you have enjoyed this Large Print book. All our Thorndike, Wheeler, and Kennebec Large Print titles are designed for easy reading, and all our books are made to last. Other Thorndike Press Large Print books are available at your library, through selected bookstores, or directly from us.

For information about titles, please call:
  (800) 223-1244

or visit our website at:
  gale.com/thorndike

To share your comments, please write:
  Publisher
  Thorndike Press
  10 Water St., Suite 310
  Waterville, ME 04901